The 15th Juror
A Novel

Steve Jackowski

This book is a work of fiction. Names, characters, place, and incidents are either products of the author's imagination or are used fictitiously. Any resemblance to actual events or locales or person, living or dead, is entirely coincidental.

Cover Art by Heidi K. Rojek

ISBN: 978-0-9899729-6-3 (print edition)
ISBN: 978-0-9899729-7-0 (ebook)

DEDICATION

To Jo Minola

ACKNOWLEDGMENTS

First and foremost I want to thank my wife, Karen Noël who not only put up with me and the associated strain on our relationship through the trial, but who helped me move past the horrors of it. I'd also like to thank Jo Minola, to whom I've dedicated this book as well as Erin Crosby, first readers of the somewhat unformed manuscript. Jo encouraged me to publish it when I was about to give up.

Deanna Pfaff, who was the primary court reporter on the case not only provided me with the majority of the transcripts from the trial, she also introduced me to the other court reporters including Retta Parsons, Heather Roseman, and Heidi Bloemker. And, she helped me understand the complexities of Court Transcripts.

Other Novels by Steve Jackowski

L'Ombre de Dieu (2017)
The Shadow of God (2014)
The Silicon Lathe (2013)

PREFACE

This is a novel based on an actual jury trial. I've fictionalized the key players, some of the locations, and the jurors and their backgrounds. Most of the case is real, though I've changed the order and types of testimony. Much went on between the attorneys and the judge behind the scenes, and while I now have some insight into that after spending time with the attorneys on the case, I've decided to tell this story from the jurors' perspectives.

I have included actual transcripts from the trial for the attorneys' opening and closing statements. For readability, particularly for eReaders, in the longer sections, I've removed the transcript line and page numbers and I've cleaned up the language, removing ums, ahs, and stutters. And obviously, I've changed the names of all the interested parties in the transcripts to match my characters. These transcripts should give you some idea what the attorneys were like; what the jurors saw every day.

I've also included the transcript of the Judge's instructions to the jury. This is very detailed in its definitions of the counts and how they're to be judged, so you might want to just skim or skip them altogether. I note that the prosecutor does a pretty good job of reiterating the charges in his closing statement.

Since there were originally sixteen jurors (the expected twelve plus four alternates), and because that's a lot of characters to keep track of, here's an introduction (for later reference) as to who they are. I've also included a list of the names of most of the witnesses, the family members, the court staff, and the attorneys.

Jurors:
16th Juror – Mark Mentor, early 60s, retired ex-Silicon Valley startup CEO.
15th Juror – Mathias Wright, Silicon Valley engineer, mid-thirties with 2 children under 5. Wife is Joan.
14th Juror – Jonathan Comstock, retired early 70s, ex-engineer.
13th Juror – Amy Friar, late 60s, retired Child Protective Services (CPS)social worker.
12th Juror – Steve Dietz, engineer in Santa Cruz startup, early-thirties, no kids. Father is a well-known prosecutor.
11th Juror – Brian Hamilton, early 50s, insurance broker, 2 kids in college – leaves mid-trial.
10th Juror – Maria Fugetti, retired physician's assistant, late 60s, 3

grown children.
9th Juror – Erica Hesse, early 40s, CEO of a rapidly growing high-tech company. Single, no children.
8th Juror – Ben Singleton, mid-30s, state park ranger, 2 kids under 10.
7th Juror – Sue Markovsky, late 40s, unmarried, no children, recent arrival to the area. Political activist.
6th Juror – Andy Harrigan, early 50s, Supervisor, California EPA. One daughter about to graduate from high school, another daughter away at college. Wife is Amy.
5th Juror – Melissa Duplisse, early 70s, retired nurse.
4th Juror – Evan Garcia, mid-40s, Hispanic, film fanatic. Unmarried, no children.
3rd Juror – Linda Lancaster, early 40s, personnel manager in a larger corporation, married, no kids.
2nd Juror – Barbara Hatch, mid-40s, ER nurse, unmarried, no kids.
1st Juror – Laura Miles, late 60s, writer, no children.

Court characters:
Judge James Campbell
Henry Bolt – prosecutor (assistant DA)
Patricia Preston - defense
Heidi Koslovsky – clerk
Miranda Ainsworth – court reporter
Bill Statford – Bailiff
John Hanson – original prosecutor for the Preliminary Hearing

Principals in the case:
Albert Daniel Flores – defendant
Alejandra Rivera – Albert's wife
Sandy Rivera – alleged rape victim
Mandy Rivera – older sister
Armando – Alejandra's son
Sonia Flores – Albert's sister
Carrie – driver

Witnesses:
Sandi Lock – Detective – sexual forensic expert
Sam Davenport – first officer on scene
Carlos Garcia – Bilingual officer on scene

Frank Lopez – Bilingual detective
Richard Finnegan – Lieutenant head of detectives
Bob Aragon – supervisor of SART team
Lieutenant/Sergeant Cardova – interviewed Alejandra at hospital
Deputy Condor – Field training officer (FTO) for the first arrivals on scene
Frank Macdonald – CSI deputy
Bernadette Ramsey Victim advocate called by defense out of order after Macdonald (CSI)
Mary Williams – SART nurse
Amanda Hernandez – SART nurse
Frieda Monroe – forensic expert
Dr. Caroline Marcus – DNA expert (defense)
Denise Farrow – DNA expert (state)
Margery Hampton – Mandy's teacher
Stephanie Phillips – Child Protective Services

Before diving into my story, I'd like to tell you a bit about the setting. The trial takes place in Santa Cruz, California.

Santa Cruz is a town of about sixty thousand people located on the north end of the Monterey Bay about sixty miles south of San Francisco. The surrounding twenty-nine or so communities in Santa Cruz County bring the total population of the local area to about two-hundred-sixty thousand.

The official primary industry of Santa Cruz is tourism, and on a given summer day, tens of thousands of people leave the heat of the Silicon and Central Valleys of California to visit the beaches of Santa Cruz. Unfortunately, most don't realize that summer has some of the worst weather of the year with night and morning fog clearing about noon, then rushing in again mid-afternoon with chilling winds chasing sunbathers back to their warmer locales.

The University of California at Santa Cruz (UCSC) is perched above the city in a redwood forest with spectacular views to the south across Monterey Bay, all the way to the Santa Lucia Mountains above Big Sur.

In addition to its over seventeen thousand students, UC Santa Cruz employs over twelve thousand full and part-time people. It brings over a billion dollars of revenue to the Monterey Bay Area.

With its proportionally large population of transient students, the University has significant political influence on the city. While Berkeley, California (home to the most famous of the University of California campuses) used to be considered the most liberal city in California, over the last several years, most would agree that Santa Cruz has taken that honor.

Agriculture is another major contributor to Santa Cruz County's economy. While surrounded by the Santa Cruz mountains, which rise to over thirty-five hundred feet, the majority of the flatlands are home to fields of Brussels' sprouts, artichokes, strawberries, lettuce, and countless other crops. This has brought in a huge influx of legal and illegal immigrant labor from Mexico and Central America.

In contrast to these struggling newcomers from the south, to the north, the Silicon Valley is overflowing with high tech companies and their financially successful employees. Tens of thousands have moved to Santa Cruz County, pushing home prices to dizzying levels, as they face the often treacherous commute over sinuous Highway 17 and the eighteen hundred foot summit that separates Santa Cruz from the Silicon Valley.

The area is one of the most beautiful in California and is home to the Monterey Bay Sanctuary, offering protection to sea otters, sea lions, harbor seals, elephant seals, several varieties of dolphins and whales, and countless species of birds.

Recreational opportunities abound with surfing, cycling, hiking in thousands of acres of parkland, wind and kite surfing, kayaking, fishing, swimming, and countless other activities to attract and entertain.

As our story begins, Santa Cruz is being pelted by torrential rains. After a five-year drought with water rationing for over four years, the citizens are glad to have the rain in spite of the flooded roads, landslides, and power outages which have become daily inconveniences in mid-January.

CHAPTER 1

THE JURY

"When you go into court you are putting your fate into the hands of twelve people who weren't smart enough to get out of jury duty."
- Norm Crosby

1

Juror 16: Mark, early 60's, retired ex-Silicon Valley startup CEO.

When I received my jury notice, I figured that this time would be like the dozens of others - I call in each day and am told to call the next. At the end of the week, the recording thanks me for my service and says that I have fulfilled my jury duty obligation and would not be called for the next two years.

But this time was different. It started out the same; I called in to see if I had to report the first day and as had happened literally dozens of times before, I was told to call back the next day. Same thing the following day. I was sure that this was going to be a repeat. What was the likelihood that I'd be called in the middle of the week for a DUI trial? Almost everyone I knew who was actually called to appear was impaneled on a three-day DUI trial. Only a couple of people had to serve longer - a week or so on civil suits.

On my next call, I was told to appear on Thursday. The fact that I was supposed to show up at two o'clock near the end of the week should have been my first clue that more was going on here.

After driving around the courthouse for thirty minutes in search of parking, I finally found a spot on Water Street. I walked into the Jury Assembly Room, dripping wet because of the raging storm, with barely ten minutes to spare. I filled out the basic questionnaire and took a seat among well over a hundred people. A few minutes later, a friendly Sheriff's Deputy led us through security and into the courtroom where we struggled to find seats. Judge James Campbell greeted us warmly and encouraged the stragglers (me among them) to sit in the jury box and to fill the six chairs in front of the box.

Once we'd all taken our seats, the judge began. Looking over at us in the jury box, then at the crowded courtroom, he said, "Now that we have filled the jury box and alternate seats, we have our jury, the rest of you can go home."

I looked at the people next to me and saw my own shocked face reflected back at me. Was this a new way to select a jury?

As a few people in the courtroom started to get up to leave, the judge stated seriously, "Not so fast! I was just joking. I'm sure most all of you have seen how TV thinks this works, and while they don't have it all correct, you should have a basic idea of how jury selections are done. There are a lot of you here for a reason. This is a very serious case. It may take us several days to finalize our jury. Let me thank you in advance for coming. You're now part of the most fundamental of our country's democratic process – right to trial by jury; presumed innocent until proven guilty."

Over the course of the next twenty to thirty minutes, Judge Campbell explained our responsibilities as jurors and how the process worked. He also made it very clear that no one was getting out of jury duty without a very good reason. Then he dropped the bombshell. This was a five week trial and the defendant was charged with raping his seven year-old daughter.

There were countless audible gasps in the courtroom, followed by an eerie silence as the significance of the case struck all of us.

Could I do this? My wife was sexually abused as a child. My ex-wife was sexually abused as a young teen and suffered horrible psychological damage leading to her violent death. And although I hate to think about it, when I was eight years old, I was molested by three teenaged boys. This case was going to bring up a lot of history that I didn't want to think about.

2

9th Juror – Erica Hesse, CEO of a rapidly growing high-tech company. Single, no kids.

Oh Fuck! A child sexual assault case? A father raping his daughter? No way I'm going give up five precious weeks for this. Not that it's not important. It's just very bad timing for me.

I have enough drama in my life. I didn't struggle all these years, giving up family, friends, and time off to get my company to this point only to miss out on its first steps into major success. There's just no way I can put in over a hundred hours a week at work and do a jury trial. It just can't be done.

I'm sure there's a way out.

Hopefully, the hardship questionnaire will work. After making his disruptive announcement about the nature of the case, the judge explained that we were all to complete a questionnaire. And for those of us who wanted to get out, we could also complete a hardship questionnaire. Full-time students and people with already-purchased tickets for overseas travel would be excused as would people with certain medical conditions (a doctor's certification would be required) and those who could prove that they had a financial hardship.

Certainly he'll see that a woman CEO of a Silicon Valley startup that has just received its Series A round of venture capital funding can't afford to leave her fledgling company at this critical time. If I could convince three venture capital firms dominated by Stanford-graduate old-boys to give us money, I can certainly write a persuasive argument to get out of jury duty. Clearly, it would be a hardship on my employees, my customers, and my investors if I weren't able to work these next five weeks.

Before we left the courtroom to fill out the questionnaires, the judge said, "Please do not discuss this case with anyone including each other, your family members or your friends. You must not conduct any independent research about this case, the matters in the case, and the individuals involved in the case. In other words, you should not consult dictionaries or reference materials, search the internet, websites, blogs, or use any other electronic tools to obtain information about this case or to help you decide the case. Please do not try to find out information from any source outside the confines of this courtroom.

"That said, I want to thank you all for your service thus far and I look forward to seeing you all here Monday morning at 10am."

I picked up one of the huge questionnaires – there were at least twenty double-sided pages – and asked the clerk for a hardship questionnaire. I stepped outside where dozens of people were rapidly scribbling responses. I wrote up a great argument for the hardship questionnaire then dove into the other one. As a single woman who has fought to succeed professionally, I've had to harden myself to most of the behaviors women encounter in the workplace. I must admit that I've ignored a lot of nasty shit to get where I am. And even worse, I've judged other women who I found to be too sensitive to succeed. But this questionnaire rattled me. I finished it over an hour later and saw tears streaming from several people's faces, and it wasn't just the women.

I had a bad feeling about this.

3

6th Juror – Andy Harrigan, early 50s, Supervisor, California EPA, daughter about to graduate from high school, other daughter away at college.

God! What a questionnaire. It took me nearly two hours to complete. I can only imagine what it might have been like for someone who'd experienced sexual assault. I guess I was lucky growing up. I'm from a big family where everyone looked out for each other. We're Irish and our family has been in Santa Cruz, on the Central California coast, for about one hundred fifty years. We started out in logging, developing what today would be called sustainable logging techniques long before anyone knew what that was. Although my great-great grandfather bought up most of the mountains surrounding Santa Cruz, he knew that he had a limited amount of land. If he cut trees, he replanted, rotating logging areas and scheduling his cutting so that there would always be trees. For him, this was farming with a crop that took a long time to get to harvest.

As generations came and went, we expanded into a lot of different business areas. Fishing became a big deal to the family and as we had great visibility into how different fish were doing, we moved quickly into conservation, building fish hatcheries on local creeks when stocks declined. My grandfather donated much of his landholdings to the State, forming a circle of parks around the city.

Don't get me wrong, I'm not one of the rich landed gentry. Our family has always been practical and down-to-earth. Each of us had to make our own way. Certainly there was family money if someone got into trouble, but almost all of us worked our way through college (for those of us who went), started our own businesses from scratch, or went to work for causes we believe in.

We were all raised with a strong sense of right and wrong, with a belief that hard work would bring value to our lives, that we could make a difference – make the world a better place. Sure, there were a few black sheep over the years, but it's funny how a strong family support system with beliefs in common ideals helps keep everyone in line or brings them back to the straight and narrow if they stray.

For me, it was the environment and conservation. I grew up fishing, diving, and surfing, and the ocean is my first love. I've seen the damage that people have done to this most precious of resources and I've seen almost miraculous recoveries. I think back to when I was a kid and sea otters were almost extinct. Same with brown pelicans. Now they're back; welcome companions that I get to see in the ocean every day.

But back to the questionnaire.

I've completed dozens of questionnaires, even written quite a few for my job at CalEPA. But this one was one of the best I've seen.

It started out pretty innocuously. There were several easy-to-answer personal questions – family, education, science background, work, have you ever been on a jury before, do you know any attorneys, do you know any judges, do you know the defendant, members of his family or anyone associated with this case. Each question also gave you a chance to explain in more detail Then it gradually progressed into asking about your feelings about the justice system. Did you believe that everyone had a right to a fair trial? Did you believe in 'innocent until proven guilty'? Questions like that.

Next it moved into questions where you answer on a graduated scale of strongly agree, to strongly disagree. Each of these REQUIRED an explanation. These got to be a bit more personal, like 'Children can be trusted'. The police are more likely to tell the truth than other people.' 'Someone who has been arrested is likely to be guilty.' 'Minorities are more likely to commit crimes.' - Lots of questions intended to get into your head about prejudices, your sense of honesty, trust in other people, police, lawyers, scientists and children(!), and about your faith in law and order and the justice system and how it works.

But the most challenging questions were about your own personal experiences with violence, sex, sexual abuse, sexual harassment, drugs, alcohol, and your friends' and families' experiences with violence and abuse. If you had a positive answer to a question like 'Do you know anyone who has experienced sexual abuse?', you had to describe this in detail.

Although I've bragged about my wonderful family, the truth is, there were some incidents. I've known a lot of women in my life, and a large percentage have experienced sexual abuse. Almost all have experienced sexual harassment through much of their lives.

By time I finished this section of the questionnaire, I found myself thinking about issues that I thought were settled for me years ago. I've been married for almost 25 years and have two nearly-grown daughters. And while there were some difficult times for my girls growing up, I've always thought Amy and I did a great job, preparing our girls to deal with the world. But this questionnaire made me rethink things. And after describing some of the incidents I'd seen and heard about in our family, I also began to ask myself just how wonderful my family actually was. Were we really better than most?

I turned in my questionnaire knowing that I was pretty qualified for this jury. I could be impartial and didn't have any personal history or strong biases that would disqualify me. I guess we'd find out on Monday. The judge and attorneys would take Friday and the weekend to go through all the questionnaires. We had Friday off. Still, I couldn't shake a truly ominous feeling about what I might get into here.

4

2nd Juror – Barbara Hatch, mid-40s, ER nurse, married, no kids.

It was raining hard Monday morning when I finally found a parking space in front of the County Building. I hoped that the parking pass which said it was valid for the previous week would still be good today.

I opened my umbrella and tried to get into the courthouse without getting soaked. But in spite of my raincoat, the bottom of my pants legs and shoes were soaked when I got to security. After more than four years of drought, it looked like Mother Nature had decided to be generous this year. I don't think we'd seen the sun in nearly two weeks. So, in spite of the fact that I'd spend most of the day with wet clothes, I, like everyone I knew, was grateful for the rain.

After my embarrassing fiasco getting through security the previous week when I had to pass through three times, holding everyone up, I'd decided to go without jewelry today and to put everything metallic into a large bag. I don't usually carry a purse. I don't like the constraints that come with one, and years ago, I had a few incidents where my purse was stolen. The worst though was in an upscale restaurant in San Francisco. I had put my overly-large purse on the floor next to my seat, and the woman behind me surreptitiously lifted my wallet from my bag. Since then, I've learned to live without a purse. However, I was pretty sure I could go a day with one to avoid problems getting through security.

I was sure it would only be a day. You see, I work as an ER nurse. Over the last twenty years, I've seen dozens of sexual assault victims come into the ER. After triage, I've worked with some of the sexual assault teams. And while I don't have any particular biases, I suspected that my background would disqualify me from the jury.

I made it through security with no problems, but didn't even get a returned smile from the sheriff's deputies. It was all routine for them and clearly they didn't remember me.

I joined the standing-room-only throng of jurors waiting in the hallway outside the courtroom watching the rain pellet the parking lot outside. Ten o'clock came and went. At ten-forty-five, a sheriff's deputy came out of the courtroom and invited everyone inside. The judge welcomed everyone back and thanked us for braving the weather to appear. He apologized for the delay, but said that he and the attorneys had several issues to resolve before opening the courtroom. He then stated that he had reviewed the hardship questionnaires. The court clerk would be reading the names of those who would be excused and thanked them in advance for their service. I started counting, and thirty-seven people were excused for hardship.

He then said that there were several potential jurors that he and the attorneys wanted to interview one-on-one. The court clerk read the list. My name was on it. As I suspected, I was going to get out. He asked everyone to wait outside. The bailiff would call each of the seven in individually.

The bailiff came out and called a name. An elderly woman limped into the courtroom and the door closed. Less than five minutes later, she exited with the bailiff, smiled at those of us waiting nearby and left the courthouse.

The second to be called in was a well-dressed man in his early thirties. That interview took about ten minutes and the young man came out, but didn't leave the courthouse.

I was next.

I followed the bailiff inside and walked up to where the attorneys seemed to be waiting for me. No one asked me to take a seat, or told me where to stand so I just approached the gate separating the spectator seats from the attorneys, the court clerk, and the judge. I'm not sure why, but I was a little nervous. I hadn't really looked at the attorneys before, but now both were only a few feet away. The defense attorney was impeccably dressed in a suit with a conservative blouse. Her very curly dark blond hair was pulled back almost severely. She looked like a high-powered lawyer from some big firm, not a public defender.

For his part, the Assistant District Attorney was lanky and of average height. His mouth was tight and his eyebrows furrowed, like someone who carries the weight of the world on his shoulders. He seemed a bit fidgety.

"Good morning Ms. Hatch," the judge began. "This is Ms. Preston, the defense attorney for Mr. Flores, and Mr. Bolt, representing the People for this case. We've reviewed your questionnaire and have a few questions for you. I'll start.

"We see you're an ER nurse at Community Hospital and that

you've seen numerous sexual assault victims during the course of your career. Have your experiences in the ER or with these patients in any way prejudiced you such that you wouldn't be able to render a fair verdict in this case? Could you presume Mr. Flores is innocent unless Mr. Bolt proves beyond a reasonable doubt that Mr. Flores is guilty?"

I thought about it only briefly. There was no question I could be fair and open-minded. I took a deep breath and responded, almost surprised at myself when I answered, "Your Honor, I've seen a lot in the ER and along the way, I've learned that you can't jump to conclusions based on the obvious."

I looked over at Mr. Flores. He was dressed in a dark suit with a conservative tie and his long dark hair pulled back in a low pony tail. The suit was a bit too big for him and he looked nervous, almost frightened. My reaction to him was more curious than sympathetic, and I didn't pick up any dangerous vibes. I hated to admit it to myself, but I wanted to do this. I wanted to be on this jury. Maybe my medical experience could come in handy.

I finished my answer, "So yes, Your Honor, I could certainly presume Mr. Flores is innocent until proven guilty beyond a reasonable doubt."

"Thank you, Ms. Hatch. Mr. Bolt, do you have any questions for Ms. Hatch?"

"Ah, yes, Your Honor."

"Please proceed."

"Good morning Ms. Hatch. I see from your questionnaire that you've had some training in handling sexual assault victims. Have you ever been part of a SART team?"

I almost chuckled at the use of 'SART Team' since SART stands for Sexual Assault Response Team, and he didn't need the extra 'team' but I knew what he meant.

"No. As you would expect, in the ER, we're focused on triage and emergency treatment. Sometimes we need to make decisions very quickly, without paying attention to what police or forensic examiners might want. My training is intended to minimize any loss of evidence that might need to be collected. That's not to say we can always do that – some situations require urgent, drastic care, but with most sexual assaults, we can preserve the evidence."

"Thank you Ms. Hatch."

Mr. Bolt paused, taking what for me was an uncomfortable minute to think about his next question.

"Ms. Hatch, do you think you'd be better able to assess forensic evidence than the average person?"

"Well, for forensic evidence like blood or DNA, I don't think so. I know about collection, but not about analysis. On the other hand, I've seen a lot of injuries and probably have more experience than most in assessing the nature and extent of injuries."

"Thank you Ms. Hatch. Your Honor, I have no other questions."

"Ms. Preston?" the judge asked.

"Thank you, Your Honor. Good morning Ms. Hatch. Have you ever collected evidence in a suspected sexual assault case?"

I noticed that right off the bat, she used the word 'suspected' I guessed this is how it would be throughout the case with the defense.

"I have never been the primary nurse for forensic collection. Although I do have the training, I never wanted to be part of a SART. However, there have been a handful of cases where I've been asked to assist in collection of evidence, following the instructions of the lead nurse."

"And did your training involve how to handle children as well?"

"Yes. It did. In addition to understanding the issues of collecting evidence, there's the issue of not contaminating the victim either physically or emotionally."

"What do you mean by contaminating the victim emotionally?"

"We have to be careful not to suggest causes, events, or reactions to victims during our examinations and treatments. We can all be susceptible to suggestions and this can taint what people remember and how they react. This is especially true for young children when they're being examined, treated, or interviewed by someone who is perceived as an authority figure. Most children want to please.

"Our training is to ask open-ended questions that are limited to what we need to know to provide treatment or to get an examination done."

I wondered if I went too far in my explanation. Ms. Preston smiled and thanked me, revealing nothing of her reaction to what

I'd said. The judge asked me to wait a moment while he and the two attorneys had a brief hushed discussion to the left of the judge's perch. The attorneys returned to their respective tables and the judge thanked me and asked me to join the other jurors outside. I wasn't going to be excused at this point.

5

15th Juror – Mathias Wright, Silicon Valley engineer, early-thirties with 2 children under 5.

I was one of the seven people called in for a private discussion with the Judge and the attorneys. I'm not really sure why they called me in. I don't have any previous experience with sexual assault. I do have two kids and am a fiercely protective father. My kids are only two and four years old. Both are girls. What kind of animal could rape his own daughter?

Maybe my questionnaire betrayed some of my bias against criminals. I do believe in the police and do think they have insane jobs, risking their lives with druggies, the mentally ill, the homeless and transients we have in Santa Cruz, and these sexual predators, to help keep us safe and society under control.

Yeah, it was probably that question – do you believe the police are more trustworthy than other people? And maybe the other one – do you believe a police officer is less likely to lie when testifying. And now that I think about it, yeah, there were probably several more.

The prosecutor seemed pretty happy with me. But that defense attorney. She's tough. She was very polite, but her questions were – what's a good word? Incisive. Yeah, incisive. They cut right to the issues. Ultimately I had to admit that the police could lie, that some people might be more trustworthy than a corrupt police officer, but in reality, I don't really believe that your average cop is a bad person. Your average cop is a hero in my eyes.

This didn't come up in their questioning, but I used to live in Brooklyn, near the old Navy Yard. If you know Brooklyn, then you know that twenty-odd years ago, Vinegar Hill, where we lived, was not a place you necessarily wanted to raise kids. Our neighborhood seemed nice enough, but we were only a street or two away from the Farragut Houses – the projects.

I was probably seven or eight years old. The school bus had dropped me off a couple of blocks from my house as usual. But on that day, a huge, beat-up car pulled up beside me as I walked home. A Puerto Rican guy, who seemed really nice, asked if I could help him. As my Mom had taught me, I told him that I couldn't talk to strangers. He then told me his name was Julio and that if I told him my name, we wouldn't be strangers anymore. I said, "Sorry, I gotta go home," and kept walking.

He pulled over, jumped out of the car and grabbed me by the arm. He tried to pull me into his car. I fought as hard as I could, kicking and hitting him, screaming all the time, but I was only a kid. Just then, God smiled upon me. A patrol car beeped its siren and pulled up behind Julio's car. Julio literally threw me across the street. I landed hard, the pavement tearing through my pants and ripping up my knees, hands, and forearms.

The police officers were out of the car before Julio could get his started. One pulled Julio's door open and dragged him from the car while the other tended to me. I'll never forget him. His name was Office Moody. He made sure that I was okay, aside from the scrapes. He invited me to sit in the front seat of his patrol car while he called for backup. He asked me what had happened, and I told him, though apparently, he had seen most of it.

Within a few minutes, two other police cars arrived. Officer Moody's partner stayed behind while Officer Moody took me home. He told my Mom that the man who had tried to hurt me would be going to jail and wouldn't hurt me or anyone in the neighborhood again. He explained that while I might have to make an official statement, he had taken down what had happened to me and he suspected Julio, who they'd been looking for, would spend a lot of time in jail for other crimes he'd committed.

So I do believe that I was telling the truth when I said on the questionnaire that I had never been the victim of a crime. That's why I didn't have to talk about this incident.

After the defense attorney for Mr. Flores had finished questioning me, and the prosecutor asked a few positive, encouraging questions, they went up to the judge and had a hushed discussion. I couldn't hear anything but since she kept looking over at me with an exasperated expression, it was clear that the defense attorney didn't want me there. In the end though, they didn't dismiss me. I'm glad they didn't.

After the rest of the seven were interviewed, they called all the jurors into the courtroom. They had already dismissed a few dozen people for hardships, leaving about sixty or seventy of us. They called twelve and the jury selection began. The judge spoke to the entire courtroom of potential jurors and told us that we needed to pay attention to the questions asked, particularly his questions as they were generic and asked of all the jurors. To avoid repetition, he would ask subsequent jurors if there was a specific reason from his list for why they couldn't serve. These included things like knowing the attorneys, knowing the defendant or the victims (I didn't know there were multiple victims!), knowing members of law enforcement or experts who might be working on the case, the willingness to follow the judge's instructions (when given) regarding the law, and the inability to render an impartial verdict. He went into detail on what that meant.

Several hands went up. One woman talked about the fact that her husband was a police officer on a Sexual Assault Team and that she had a lot of exposure to these types of cases. They discussed it for a while, but the Judge ended it by asking if she could render an impartial verdict in spite of what she'd heard from her husband. She thought about it and admitted she could.

Another said she had to get her children to school and pick them up. The judge told her that court started at ten most days and ended at four-thirty. Her excuse wasn't good enough.

There were a few who were excused and their seats were immediately filled by others.

One interesting case was a woman who said she had done a long jury trial a year before. After suffering for several weeks watching attorneys battle each other, ignoring facts, just trying to put points up on the board, she said she had become disgusted with the whole process. She couldn't support the adversary system of our courts by being a juror again. She didn't believe in the system, didn't believe that the truth could come out and said she wouldn't follow the Judge's instructions since the laws were often bogus and the arguments for getting to the decisions were bogus too. After many challenges from the Judge, she was excused.

The next step was for the attorneys to interview the potential jurors. They worked from their notes and questionnaires. If I remember correctly, the prosecutor started. He greeted the jurors and introduced himself. Then he picked specific jurors and asked them questions. The questions were similar to those I answered during my private interview. He asked about their work, how it affected their points of view about the law, but most of the time, it seemed like he was trying to see if the person could be impartial. I hadn't expected that.

When he was done, the defense attorney would ask her questions. Once again, I'll use that word, incisive. Her questions were much more probing. She seemed to be able to get into people's heads and to get them to say things they might not have said otherwise. I thanked God for my luck on that front.

When she was done, the Judge asked the prosecutor if he had more questions. He did. Then he asked the defense attorney. She did. Then the two attorneys joined the Judge on the side of the bench and conferred just like they did when I was interviewed. After much discussion, they returned to their tables. The judge excused two jurors for cause, thanking them for their service, then the prosecutor thanked three people who left, and the defense attorney thanked two who left.

They seated seven more and the judge announced the lunch break. We were to return by one-thirty and were not to discuss the case with each other or anyone else. Nor were we to form any opinions about the case.

I walked across the river in the pouring rain and went to Zoccoli's Deli for lunch. I noticed a couple of the other jurors there but we avoided eye contact.

When we returned, we waited outside for about ten minutes, then got called into the courtroom. That afternoon, we got through two more iterations, and it looked like they were close to having a jury.

"Okay," the Judge began. "It's almost four-thirty. I want to thank you all for your patience. It looks like we need to seat two more jurors and four alternates. We should be able to complete that tomorrow morning. However, I think we can excuse a fair number of you today. We'll call out the names of those who are excused. I'd like to thank you for your service."

You could hear the sighs of relief.

The Judge conferred with the Clerk for a few minutes as they went over a list. Then the Clerk stood up and called out about thirty names, leaving about twenty of us left, me among them.

"For the rest of you, please be here tomorrow morning at ten-thirty. Again, please don't discuss this case with anyone. Don't do any internet searches about the case or the law pertaining to the case. And please don't form any opinions in this matter. We'll see you tomorrow morning."

I left nervous but a little excited too.

The next morning went quickly. They seated two more in the jury box and I was included in the four alternates. There were a lot more questions. When one of the people in the jury box was excused, they randomly pulled an alternate into the jury box and seated another alternate. I thought I would have chance to get into the jury box, but no. I was juror number 15. An alternate. Unless someone dropped out, I'd be sitting through five weeks of trial and would have nothing to say about it. That isn't my plan. But I'll trust in God. If He wants me on this jury, I'll be on it.

CHAPTER 2

OPENING STATEMENTS

Note from the author: As mentioned in the Preface, what follows are edited court transcripts of the attorneys' opening statements.

1

Prosecutor's Opening Statement

Santa Cruz, California
January 30, 20XX
PROCEEDINGS

THE COURT: Let's go on the record, please, regarding People versus Albert Flores. Mr. Flores is present. Counsel are present. All of our jurors are present. Counsel and I have been working over the past two and a half working days on various issues. I appreciate your patience. We were working this morning for about two and a half hours and I do believe that that will save us time as we go through the trial. So I thank counsel for their efforts in that regard.

I appreciate everyone being so punctual this afternoon. We've picked a jury. You've received the initial instructions. Now we are going to proceed with opening statements.

Mr. Bolt, at your convenience please.

MR. BOLT: Thank you very much.

Welcome back. Good afternoon to you all. Sandy. Sandy Rivera. On November 1st, 20XX Sandy was just seven years old. Sandy had a sister. Her name is Mandy and Mandy is four years to the day older than Sandy. Seven-year-old Sandy has a mother and her name is Alejandra and she has a father.

November 1st, 20XX started out like a very typical and normal day for Sandy. When she was home from school she and her sister were at their residence and they were with her father and it was a normal day until the rule was broken. It was a normal day until the rule was broken. You see Mandy went to a friend's house. Sandy's older sister went to a friend's house for a play date but Sandy was not supposed to be alone with her father.

Now after Mandy left, Sandy was playing outside. Her dad wanted her to come inside. She didn't want to but she did. She didn't want to come into the bedroom but he counted and counting means you better not let him get to three. She wanted to play. She didn't want to lay on the bed but he made her. She didn't want to take her pants off and she struggled to keep them on but he overpowered her and forced them off and he raped her right then and there in her parents' bedroom at home.

It was painful. It hurt. At one point Sandy screamed and he covered her mouth to stop her and when it was over she was bleeding. The man who raped Sandy Rivera on November 1st, 20XX is in this courtroom and he is right over there. His name is Albert Daniel Flores. The man seated there is the man who raped Sandy. He is Sandy's father.

(Pause for effect)

After that sexual assault was over Sandy was cleaned up, washed off. Her father took her down to a beach area and fished. He went by a storage unit and ultimately that day they returned back to their home and when they got there Alejandra, Sandy's mother, was already home. But before they got home the defendant took Sandy's bloody underwear and got rid of them. He told her not to tell. He threatened that if she did he would hurt her.

And so there she is back at home. Sandy is sad. When her mother sees her it's obvious that there's something wrong, but she asks what's going on and Sandy doesn't say anything, glancing over at her father who glared at her. She hid in her room. Mandy came home not long after that. Sandy and Mandy were together in their room and guess what? It was obvious to Mandy that something was wrong. So Sandy - Mandy tried to get her younger sister to say what happened. She didn't want to say but ultimately she told Mandy what had happened. She showed her the blood that was now on the new panties that she had on, new underwear.

When Mandy heard what had happened, when she saw that her father had caused this injury to Sandy, she urged Sandy to tell their mom. Sandy was afraid. She didn't want to. She didn't want to tell but Mandy pressured her to tell. And so those girls got their mom away from the room where she was, where the defendant was also, got her in private and Sandy showed her mom. Alejandra became extremely mad. She immediately went and confronted the defendant demanding that he tell her what he had done to Sandy. And he was calm. He pretended to have no idea, to have no idea that there was anything wrong whatsoever.

She confronted him with Sandy's bleeding genitals and he remained calm, just pretended he didn't know what she was talking about, had no idea what happened. What could have caused this?

There was an argument as you might imagine. Alejandra was loud. She threatened to call the police if he didn't tell her what happened. She confronted him with sexually molesting their daughter. She accused him of this and he stayed calm and told her not to call the police and said he didn't know what happened. At one point he grabbed the phone that Alejandra had when she was threatening to call the police.

Mandy, who was with Sandy, could hear what was going on. Mandy took it upon herself to call 911. And before Mandy was off the phone with the 911 operator, the defendant had fled.

The police came as soon as they could, deputy sheriffs from Santa Cruz County Sheriff's Office. They talked to Alejandra, to Mandy. Sandy told the first officer that spoke with her what had happened. She appeared afraid. She was curled up. She was obviously distressed. Medical personnel were there and she was taken to the hospital just a short time after the horrible sexual assault. At the hospital many things happened.

There is a sexual assault response team examination, a S.A.R.T. exam performed by sexual assault nurse examiners or SANE nurses and in this particular case, which is common in situations like this, there were two S.A.R.T. nurses who took part in that exam. You're going to hear all about that and you're going to hear about their specialized training. You're going to hear about their experiences and you're going to hear how they performed this S.A.R.T. exam which includes talking with the child. It includes collecting evidence. It includes a physical examination where they make note of any findings that are in any possible way relevant to what this child is complaining of. And what you're going to learn is that she indeed had an injury and it was just the type of injury that's caused by a sexual assault like this.

Now at one point during the interview portion of this examination, Sandy relates that she thinks something like this has happened to her sister. So one of the nurses, named Amanda Hernandez, who you're going to meet and you're going to hear from, went and asked Mandy if Mandy would like some hot chocolate. She sat with Mandy and they talked a little bit. Eventually – eventually, Nurse Hernandez asked Mandy if anything like this had ever happened to her; if her father had ever done something like that to her. And Mandy said that a long time ago something did happen to her when she was little. She said that she had told her mom about it.

At the hospital, Alejandra was interviewed by a detective. She had also been interviewed at the house more briefly. Mandy had spoken with a deputy at the house and she had also spoken with a deputy at the hospital.

Alejandra told officers that none of her children had ever made any kind of complaint before this, that she never knew anything about it. She denied that the rule existed.

Now before Amanda Hernandez went and talked to Mandy, a detective had even asked Mandy if something has happened to her in the past. She said no.

When Mandy told Amanda Hernandez that something had happened to her when she was little, Amanda Hernandez immediately told Sergeant Bob Aragon and because so much had happened and all of this was so stressful, they made the decision that they wouldn't try and talk to Mandy any more that evening but they would investigate. And I'll get to that because eventually, on November 3rd, Mandy and Sandy came down to the sheriff's office and there's a detailed interview of both of them which you'll hear is common practice.

So now there was an investigation beyond just talking to people because when somebody makes a report and you're trying to determine whether or not it really happened, you try and collect evidence, you look for corroboration, and you try and see if what they say matches up. And so the police did that.

Deputies searched the house and, you know, one of the things that Sandy described was that her father had some little bottle and she described it was kind of clear. It had a green top and he put some of that on his penis and it was slippery. When they searched the house in a place way high up, there was like a basket that had like a pot in it and hidden in that pot was a bottle of Astroglide which looked pretty much just like what Sandy had described.

And later, an inspector by the name of Sandi Locke, who at that point in time was a detective with the Santa Cruz County Sheriff's Office working in sex crimes, took a photograph of that bottle of Astroglide and a whole bunch of different more or less similar looking containers. She showed the picture to Sandy a couple of weeks later and Sandy identified the Astroglide that was found as what her father had used.

You'll hear how the defendant would make deals, as Sandy

describes it, where he would buy you something or do something nice for you, but then you had to do something for him.

That's what the defendant was doing when he was trying to force Sandy to come into the bedroom. Sandy said that a little while back that her father had had bought her a big eraser that she wanted and now it was time for her to pay up for her part of the deal.

The investigators asked Sandy who she was with when he bought it for her and they tried to determine, you know, if that could be corroborated.

What they found was that, indeed, there's surveillance video and it shows the defendant with Mandy and Sandy and they go in the store and they go to the register and a receipt is recovered from that very day and time where he purchased the eraser as Sandy described.

You're going to learn that they collected other evidence at the house. Of course the child reported that this occurred on a bedspread on a bed. It had a bedspread. You're going to learn that there were blood stains that were analyzed using DNA technology, identifying that blood as Sandy's blood.

You'll hear that other DNA analysis was done. Some of it didn't prove anything one way or another. It didn't really provide evidence one way or another, but some of it did. And another thing that you are going to hear is that an analysis called a Y-STR analysis was done from evidence collected from the inside crotch area of the panties that Sandy had been wearing when the police encountered her and it's a partial four locus Y chromosome short tandem repeat of the interior crotch of her underwear.

You're going to learn about that test. It's a test that cannot distinguish between members of the same patrilineal heritage. What does that mean? It means that if a person, if a man has that profile his father would have that profile, his grandfather. And this particular partial four locus result occurs in one in 120 Hispanics. One in 120. The defendant has that profile. That's his profile. I don't think you're going to hear evidence in this case of anyone else in the defendant's patrilineal heritage who could have left his DNA on Sandy's underwear.

The defendant fled their home knowing that the police were being called. He was actually found in his car in the middle of the night on November 2nd, 20XX and he was arrested, brought to the sheriff's office, and Sergeant Carlos Garcia interviewed him.

It's in Spanish. It's on video. And so the defendant waives his Miranda rights and Sergeant Garcia asks him to tell him why he'd been arrested. And the defendant claimed that he was arrested over an argument with his wife.

Now they talk a little bit, you know, tell me what happened today. What happened? And so what he says is basically that he's home with the girls, Mandy and Sandy, and Sandy goes to a friend's house for a play date and he goes fishing and then - and then everybody kind of gets home in the evening. He tells it twice exactly the same way, exactly the same way. And the thing is neither time did he mention that Sandy actually went with him fishing. And when Sergeant Garcia eventually said, hey, did Sandy go fishing with you the defendant pretended like he had completely forgotten that.

So now Sergeant Garcia asked the defendant a lot of questions about what happened when he got home from fishing and when everybody was home. The defendant repeatedly claimed that there was an argument because his wife was jealous and he fled because he was afraid he was going to be arrested for domestic violence. He repeatedly insisted that she was jealous of his relationship with the girls. So Sergeant Garcia asked him, well, did you hit her? No. Well, why did you think you were going to get arrested for domestic violence? No explanation.

Sergeant Garcia confronts the defendant about the fact that Alejandra was accusing him of harming their daughter. He adamantly denied that that was true. That was absolutely not what any argument was about according to the defendant. Sergeant Garcia confronted him with Alejandra's statement that the argument was about you sexually assaulting Sandy. Absolutely not. It was not, according to the defendant. He absolutely denied that Alejandra was confronting him with having raped their daughter, absolutely denied it. That was not at all what it was about.

Sergeant Garcia confronted the defendant with the fact that Sandy had at that point repeatedly said that he had sexually assaulted her and the defendant pretended to have no idea what Sandy could have been talking about. He absolutely put himself with her all day once she got home from school. And what you're going to learn is that she was fine when she got home from school and she had bleeding genitals when she got home to her mom. The defendant was with her the whole time and the defendant - you know, you'd think if by some possibility these injuries to Sandy were not caused by the defendant forcing his penis into her vagina, then the guy who is with her all day would have some sort of answer or explanation for what in heaven's name could have caused that injury. But, no. No idea. No idea. No explanation at all.

Now November 3rd is the day that Sandy and Mandy came down to the sheriff's office for the detailed interview. This is very common. When a call comes in for service like this the police officers who are on patrol go and get information but then they turn it over to detectives and there always comes a point where if the charges are serious like this, they're not going to only rely on interviews that were done on scene or at a hospital.

They sit somebody down in a place where they're going to try to get them to relax and then try to get as much information as they can. That's the detailed interview which took place of both Sandy and Mandy on November 3rd.

The day before, Detective Locke and her partner Detective Frank Lopez, also of the sheriff's office assigned to investigate sex crimes, had tried to get Mandy and Sandy to come to be interviewed, but they were too exhausted, and so they arranged it for the next day. So let's just talk a little bit about what happened at the Sheriff's Office.

Alejandra shows up with Sandy and Mandy and Sandy is interviewed once again in a detailed interview. It's videotaped. They do it in what's called the soft room and then after Sandy is done, Mandy is interviewed. Now, Mandy tells all about what happened the day before, about the rule that the girls weren't supposed to be left alone with dad and that on this day she broke the rule because she went on a play date and left her sister. And then when she returned, she was with her sister in her room, saw how sad she was, knew something was wrong, got some information, tried to get her to tell mom, all of that stuff. That's what she'll tell you. That's what she told them.

And then at some point the detective asks her about anything happening to her and she says, "No, it didn't." She becomes quiet. She appears nervous.

Detective Locke reminded Mandy about Amanda Hernandez and Mandy said she didn't remember the details. She had told her mom and said that it happened so long ago and that that was the reason for the rule. The child was nervous.

Detective Locke stressed being honest and asked her if she had any memory of these events and Mandy told her that when her mom was pregnant, pregnant with Sandy, that she was home alone with dad and that she had just gotten out of a shower and had a towel on her and the defendant pulled her by the arm into their bedroom and he had his pants off but his underwear on and she was naked and she described how he fondled her genital area.

She described how he penetrated her vagina with his finger. She didn't want it to happen. She described how these events took place in her mind for about five minutes and then they heard the front door open and her father jumped up and that she told her mom what happened. She said that her mother confronted her father and that she said that she would call the cops if he didn't tell her what had happened and according to Mandy he had actually admitted that this was true. And she said from basically that point on she was never to be left alone with her father and that's the rule. Sandy knows the rule too she'll tell you about it.

The defendant was charged with crimes. He was jailed and you'll hear about how there was a lot of pressure, a lot of pressure placed on Mandy. A lot of pressure placed on Sandy. You'll hear some calls between the defendant in jail and Alejandra and how the girls actually got on the phone with him and were talking with him just a little bit. You'll hear about how later, in April of 20XX, there was a preliminary hearing where both Sandy and Mandy testified in court, not in front of a jury, but in court. And at a minimum you're going to get to see Mandy and she denies that father did anything to her. When she takes the stand and testifies she says nothing happened. I lied. I made it up. You'll see the weight that she carries in trying to talk about what happened and how she feels.

You're going to hear a lot of evidence in this case and you're going to hear from a lot of different witnesses. I don't know exactly what they're all going to tell you. It wouldn't be shocking if Mandy continues to recant, but you're going to get to look at all of the evidence to help you make a decision and you're going to see that at the end of this case what the evidence proves is that these charges are true and that the defendant committed some very horrible crimes against his daughters. Thank you very much.

2

Defense Opening Statement

THE COURT: Thank you, Mr. Bolt. Ms. Preston, opening statement at this time?
MS. PRESTON: Thank you.
THE COURT: Thank you. At your convenience.

MS. PRESTON: People lie to get out of things. They lie to protect themselves. They lie to protect each other. It's small lies they call big lies. Sometimes the lie is so big that they can't take it back. Sometimes the lie is so convincing that they start to believe it themselves and sometimes the lie is so powerful that it builds and grows and it spreads until it completely consumes the truth. That's what happened here.

Albert Daniel Flores did not sexually abuse his children but he was abusive. He created a toxic environment for his family. They couldn't stop the poison. They had to find a way out. This was a home where Albert and his wife Alejandra would fight in front of the girls, bitter angry fighting, screaming, yelling and cursing. It got so bad that Alejandra told her oldest daughter Mandy to call 911 if daddy ever hits me. In a small apartment with no privacy the girls were at the center of these frequent violent storms, scared.

Albert disciplined the girls in ways that scared them. He yelled a lot. He used a tone that they dreaded to hear. He would count to three and threaten to hit them with a shoe if they misbehaved and sometimes he'd get to three and sometimes he'd hit them. He'd hit them with that shoe. It was especially bad when he was drinking. They were frightened. They were anxious, walking on eggshells. They didn't know what to expect.

In the days leading up to the accusation things took a turn for the worse. Mr. Flores told Alejandra that he wanted a divorce. He told Alejandra: what's more I want custody of the children and what's more I'll probably get it because I make more money than you and I can better provide for them. The girls didn't want to live with their dad. The girls didn't want to lose their mother and you can imagine how Alejandra felt. She had given birth to these children. She worked night and day to provide for them. They were her life and now he's threatening to take it all away.

In the days leading up to the accusation, his family had another reason to feel desperate. Armando, Alejandra's adult son from another marriage, a son who the children adored, who Alejandra loved with all of her heart was in immigration proceedings. He was in danger of being sent back to El Salvador away from his mother. Alejandra couldn't turn to Albert for help because Albert and Armando didn't get along and in any case what could Albert to do to fix this? Alejandra needed official help. She needed the government's help.

Less than two weeks after this accusation is made Alejandra picked up the phone and she called the victim's assistance unit at the DA's office and she asked for a letter to help Armando in his immigration proceeding, a letter stating that now that Mr. Flores was in custody, Armando, and not Mr. Flores, was her sole source of support. The accusation gave her access to that official help that she needed.

This is a family with motives to lie, powerful motives. They lied to get out of a desperate situation to protect themselves and to protect each other. Like all infective lies, like all convincing lies, this lie was held together with bits of truth. Sandy did have an injury on her vagina but there were many other things that could have caused it. It wasn't Albert. She was bleeding but he didn't do it. He was abusive in ways but he did not sexually abuse these girls. The problem with a lie like this one is it builds and it grows and it spreads quickly. A small spark becomes a raging fire. When a child accuses an adult of sexually molesting her a team of professionals rush to her defense.

MR. BOLT: Objection; argument.

THE COURT: I'll overrule. You're expecting the evidence will show this. So that's the representation by counsel. Correct?

MS. PRESTON: Yes, Your Honor.

THE COURT: Please proceed.

MS. PRESTON: A team of professionals rushes to her defense, building and growing the accusation insulating it against attack, officers, detectives, victims' advocates, S.A.R.T. and SANE nurses, doctors prosecutors. It is not their job to be doubtful. It is not their job to be critical. It is not their job to be skeptical. It's their job to assume this is true and protect this little girl.

MR. BOLT: Objection. This is argument.

THE COURT: Again - well, I'm going to overrule that it's argument. It's simply an attorney indicating what she believes the evidence will show.

The jury has already been advised that nothing the attorneys say is evidence. You base your decision on what is evidence once we have the testimony that we will begin shortly. I'll allow it.

Please proceed.

MS. PRESTON: You have a different job because as horrible as it is when these accusations are true, how horrible is it when they're false? It is your job over the next few weeks to look at every piece of evidence in this case doubtfully, critically and analytically, to look at this evidence from the perspective that Mr. Flores is innocent and from that presumption to consider the accusations false. It is false. If you look at this evidence doubtfully, skeptically, critically, you will find stories that change to fit what the questioner wants to hear. You'll find Sandy stating first that she was assaulted on the bed and then later to her sister and mom that she was assaulted on the bed and then in the shed and then later at a preliminary hearing that she was raped on a bed and raped on a beach, not just inconsistencies but fabrications that don't add up and aren't supported by the evidence.

You'll see Mandy at first stating that, no, nothing happened to her. Well, okay, maybe they told me something happened. Later under pressure from a forensic examiner who is looking for a stronger case, she comes up with a fantastic story of abuse that happened when she was three. It's not a three-year-old's story. It's the story of an 11-year-old trying to please her questioner and when she gets up here at the preliminary hearing after taking that oath to tell the truth she says I made it up. I felt pressure to lie. I'm sorry I lied.

You'll see Alejandra's changing story as this case progresses from, no, there was no rule like that. What are you talking about a rule? No, nothing ever happened to Mandy. And then again as her questioner, really in her case an interrogator, the detective breaks her down and says, you know, this is the time to come clean to us so that we don't find a failure to protect. She starts to try to tell them what they want to hear and she comes up with a couple of fantastic stories about what happened with Mandy that don't match what anybody else has said and they don't match anything else because they're not the truth. It's an echo chamber of statements being thrown at all of these people and everyone trying desperately to get it right because they're afraid of what will happen to them if they don't.

You'll find physical evidence that doesn't add up and a lack of physical evidence where you would find it if these accusations were true. There's blood on the bed but nothing of Mr. Flores's. There's blood on the bed where they find Sandy lying when the EMTs and the officers show up. No DNA from Mr. Flores. No sperm.

In her underwear you've heard about this DNA that was found in her crotch. What you didn't hear and what you will hear is that it's an incredibly small amount and that also on her underwear is the DNA of her mother, her DNA, mixed DNA, DNA that could be there if he touched those panties, did the laundry. How much DNA would we expect there if he had done these horrible things? Much, much more. That tiny amount is actually evidence of innocence.

You will hear that there is no DNA from him in this girl's body. Not in. Not on. No sperm. No nothing. You will hear that they did a head-to-toe examination of this man, that he was unkempt. He was dirty. He was sleeping a few blocks away in front of Ben's Market trying to get some rest after this argument with his wife. They find him there. He clearly hasn't changed or bathed or washed and they do a head-to-toe examination of every part of his body.

This is a girl who is supposedly bleeding because he raped her - and yet they find not one molecule of blood on him. Nothing. Nothing of her. Nothing.

If you look at this evidence doubtfully, skeptically, critically - you're the lens of innocence - you will find lies that build and grow and spread until they consume the truth and in the end if you give this man the benefit of your every reasonable doubt there will be only one fair verdict and that verdict is that Mr. Flores is not guilty.

THE COURT: Thank you, Ms. Preston.

Your first witness, Mr. Bolt.

MR. BOLT: The People call Alejandra Rivera to the stand.

THE COURT: Thank you.

MR. BOLT: Your Honor, we need to call for an interpreter. Perhaps we could take the afternoon break right now and have the interpreter here in 15 minutes.

THE COURT: We can take our recess a little bit earlier. We'll recess until 3:05. We'll have an interpreter here also for this witness.

Please do not discuss this matter amongst yourselves or within anyone else. Please do not form or express any opinions concerning this matter. I'll look forward to seeing everyone at 3:05. We're off the record at this time. Thank you.
(Short recess.)

3

13th Juror – Maria Fugetti, retired physician's assistant, late 60s, 3 grown children.

I'm sure glad the judge gave an additional instruction before the opening statements because I tell you if it were up to me right now, I'd vote guilty.

"If the prosecutor makes a powerful opening statement which convinces you beyond a reasonable doubt that the defendant is guilty, the defense makes no opening statement, and the prosecution and defense rest without calling a single witness, what would your verdict be?"

I'm lucky he didn't ask me personally. He asked the group. I should have known that as he previously told us, opening statements are not evidence. The defendant is innocent until the State proves beyond a reasonable doubt, via evidence, that the defendant is guilty. Evidence is testimony and exhibits, not what the attorneys have to say.

So, the correct answer to the judge's question was: 'Not Guilty.' If no evidence has been presented, the assistant district attorney hasn't proven anything. We have to come back with a not-guilty verdict

Still, the prosecutor said he had evidence. He said he has the testimony of the little girl. He has the testimony of her sister and her mother, of forensic examiners, the police, all sorts of people. Plus, there's DNA evidence.

Even the defense attorney admitted that Mr. Flores drinks and is abusive. Her argument that lies build on lies is going to be hard to prove. If all the police, the forensic people, family, and the victim herself says he did it, he must have. They can't all be lying. Then again, I should stop myself. The judge has instructed us: the defense doesn't have to prove anything. It's up to the prosecution to bring proof. It sounds like it will be easy. Hopefully this case will be open and shut and won't keep us too long. The judge said five weeks. Almost a week has passed. Maybe the rest will go quickly. I'm sure our deliberations will.

4

7th Juror – Sue Markovsky, late 40s, unmarried, no children, recent arrival to the area. Political activist.

God! What kind of father rapes his seven-year old daughter? What kind of animal molests a three-year old? I know better than most that the law says innocent until proven guilty.

I don't have a lot of faith in the system. This is a system that persecutes minorities, especially immigrants. I've worked for years helping defend the rights of the poor and disaffected in our communities. But the truth is, there are also scumbags in any population. It certainly looks like we have one here.

I grew up in South Central Los Angeles. Yeah, that sounds strange. It has a reputation. Most of it deserved. But it wasn't always like that. As late as the 1970s when I was born, South Central was a middle-class neighborhood.

When my father took a job at USC, he decided he wanted to live in South Central. My dad is a sociologist. But unlike those who live in ivory towers and write papers and books about their ideas of what society is like, or who conduct arms-length studies, my dad lived his work. He believed he could make a difference in the community.

When he arrived, while a majority of the population was black, there were quite a few middle-class white families too. Local manufacturing provided jobs, and people of all colors lived relatively prosperous, productive lives.

That all changed in the 80s when the factories brought in cheap Hispanic labor, much of it illegal, and laid off countless workers. As you might expect, people lost homes, families were broken, and crime rates skyrocketed.

The demographics shifted too. Instead of a majority black population with a good number of whites, if you look at it today, you'll find almost eighty percent Hispanic, ten percent black, some Asians, and a few whites; my parents among them.

But my dad is respected. He has done good work in the community, and I've been at his side for a long time. Things are getting better.

I don't know if they're good enough for me to leave my dad on his own, but after a difficult divorce, and having spent my whole life in LA, I really needed a change. I moved to Santa Cruz six months ago.

I can't believe I got called for jury duty so quickly or that I was impaneled. In all my years in LA, that never happened. I must admit, though, that I was excused several times because of my position in the community. I was known; I knew both victims and accused, and the court was well aware of my biases. Santa Cruz is different though. I haven't quite gotten my head around the weird mix of students, Silicon Valley entrepreneurs, farmworkers, and transients.

I'm currently working as a consultant for social services. My clients are Hispanic. Most are immigrants, a few illegal. My Spanish is fluent, so I manage pretty well in most of the domestic situations I walk into.

I like it here. It's so different from LA. The pace is slower, and I have the impression that the police and local authorities are much more aware of community issues for the homeless and for immigrants. Of course, I don't have much experience with that yet. I guess this trial will give me a bit more perspective. But for now, I'm willing to give local law enforcement the benefit of the doubt. That certainly wasn't the case in LA. Yes, things have improved there over the last couple of decades, but you still can't trust the police.

As far as this case is concerned, I almost don't recognize myself. I always fight for the little guy or gal – the one that the system is burying. Maybe this one time, the system has it right. Maybe Albert Daniel Flores is the scumbag the prosecution says he is. I have an open mind, but I have to admit to an initial bias against him and his case.

How does a seven-year old who spent the entire day with her father get injuries consistent with rape if she wasn't raped?

I've had a chance to chat with a few of the other jurors in the hallway outside the courtroom. So far, we've scrupulously avoided discussing the trial. Most are fascinated by the fact that I'm from LA, and from South Central. And I'm learning a lot about Santa Cruz. Most of the others seem to be long time locals. Many are older. I guess that makes sense since they have the time to be on juries, particularly with a longer trial like this one.

So while we haven't talked about the trial at all, I've seen the faces of everyone outside the courtroom. After the opening statements, I'd be willing to bet that everyone thinks the defendant is guilty. While we all know that the defense doesn't have to prove innocence. The reality is that that's what it's going to take this time – even for me, the infernal liberal anti-establishment champion.

Sure. I'll do my job. I can assume innocent until proven guilty. I'll listen carefully. But there is one thing that stuck in my mind. The judge also gave an instruction about the fact that the defendant doesn't have to testify. He kept emphasizing that the defense doesn't have to prove anything. And as part of that, the defendant doesn't have to prove his innocence by testifying. He doesn't even have to say he's not guilty, even though I guess he's said that as part of his plea.

I remember the questions on the questionnaire regarding whether we believed the defendant should have to testify. I knew the correct answer. Of course not. But I have to admit that I really want him to. If he doesn't, in spite of myself, I have to ask what he might be hiding. Is he afraid the prosecutor will trip him up? That he won't come across as honest? Or maybe that no one will believe him anyway. Yeah, I want to hear from him, but from the statements by the judge, and some of the questions posed during voir dire, I think they're all trying to prepare us for the fact that we'll never see Flores on the stand or hear his side of the story. Then again, if the prosecutor has the evidence he claims, Mr. Flores is guilty as hell and nothing he might say on the stand is going to change that.

5

12th Juror – Steve Dietz, engineer in Santa Cruz startup, early-thirties no kids.

Yeah, he's guilty. I know. I'm not supposed to think that at this stage, but I have no doubts – no reasonable doubts. Sure, I'll do my job. I'll look at the facts and will decide accordingly, but I can't imagine that this guy is innocent. He's an alcoholic, abusive father with a history of violence who went too far and finally got caught. It's just too predictable. I'm surprised it made it to trial. The defense should have pled it out.

My father is an attorney. He works for the DA's office in San Francisco. He's seen more than his share of cases like this. I talked to him briefly about it – before he shut me down. In spite of his pessimism about the system and how easy it is for criminals to get off in our overly-liberal California courts, he does follow the rules and expects as much from his son. I'm not to discuss the case with anyone until deliberations start. Well, I won't be discussing it with him, but as for the rest, we'll see.

Of course, I don't want to get kicked off the jury. I want to do my part to put a child rapist away for life without the possibility of parole. I don't think most of the other jurors realize what this guy is looking at. Sure, the judge read the charges. And while we're not supposed to check out the case on the Internet or other sources, I did get the list of charges – it's a small stretch.

As I said, the judge read them to us anyway. For me, having the list is a good reminder of what this guy did. I suspect many of the others will forget until we get into the jury room. Most weren't taking notes when the judge read the charges. I think they were too shocked to do anything other than stare at Flores.

Okay, I admit it, I actually checked out the charges online before I was part of the jury. I wanted to see what I might be getting into. And here are the 14 counts (the first column is the charge number; the second is the charge; and the third is Felony/Misdemeanor). There are what appear to be duplicates for each charge, but these are just to let the jury associate the count with a more aggravated situation (e.g. requiring life without the possibility of parole).

Ch#	Charge	F/M
001	PC288.7(A)-F-SODOMY WITH VICTIM UNDER 10 YEARS	F
001	PC667.61(A)-FEL SEX OFFENSE (25 YEARS)	F
002	PC288.7(B)-F-ORAL COPULATION/10 YRS <	F
002	PC288.7(B)-F-ORAL COPULATION/10 YRS <	F
002	PC667.61(A)-FEL SEX OFFENSE (25 YEARS)	F
003	PC261(A)(2)-F-RAPE BY FORCE/FEAR	F
003	PC269(A)(1)-F-AGGRAVATED SEXUAL ASSAULT OF CHILD	F
003	PC667.61(A)-FEL SEX OFFENSE (25 YEARS)	F
004	PC261(A)(2)-F-RAPE BY FORCE/FEAR	F
004	PC261(A)(2)-F-RAPE BY FORCE/FEAR	F
004	PC667.61(A)-FEL SEX OFFENSE (25 YEARS)	F
005	PC288(B)(1)-F-LEWD ACT/CHILD UNDER 14/FORCE	F
005	PC288(B)(1)-F-LEWD ACT/CHILD UNDER 14/FORCE	F
005	PC667.61(A)-FEL SEX OFFENSE (25 YEARS)	F
006	PC288(B)(1)-F-LEWD ACT/CHILD UNDER 14/FORCE	F
006	PC288(B)(1)-F-LEWD ACT/CHILD UNDER 14/FORCE	F
006	PC667.61(A)-FEL SEX OFFENSE (25 YEARS)	F
007	PC236-M-FALSE IMPRISONMENT	F
007	PC236-M-FALSE IMPRISONMENT	M
008	PC135-M-DESTROYING/CONCEALING EVIDENCE	M
008	PC135-M-DESTROYING/CONCEALING EVIDENCE	M
009	PC289(A)-F-PENETRATION FORCE/OBJECT	M
009	PC289(A)-F-PENETRATION FORCE/OBJECT	F
009	PC667.61(A)-FEL SEX OFFENSE (25 YEARS)	F
010	PC289(A)(1)-F-PENETRATION W/FOREIGN OBJECT	F
010	PC289(A)(1)-F-PENETRATION W/FOREIGN OBJECT	F
010	PC667.61(A)-FEL SEX OFFENSE (25 YEARS)	F
011	PC288(B)(1)-F-LEWD ACT/CHILD UNDER 14/FORCE	F
011	PC288(B)(1)-F-LEWD ACT/CHILD UNDER 14/FORCE	F
011	PC667.61(A)-FEL SEX OFFENSE (25 YEARS)	F
012	PC288.7(A)-F-SODOMY WITH VICTIM UNDER 10 YEARS	F
013	PC288(B)(1)-F-LEWD ACT/CHILD UNDER 14/FORCE	F
014	PC269(A)(1)-F-AGGRAVATED SEXUAL ASSAULT OF CHILD	F
999	PC667.61(D)-F-SEX OFFENSE - LIFE SENTENCES	F
999	PC667.61(E)(4)-F-SEX OFFENSE-LIFE SENTENCES	F

It looks like a lot of charges, and it is. Charges one through six apply to Sandy, the little girl who was raped. I'm not sure where they get charges seven and eight. Apparently seven has something to do with Flores taking the phone away from his wife to prevent her from calling 911. Charges nine through eleven apply to Mandy, the older sister who the prosecutor says Flores molested when she was three years old. Charges 12, 13, and 14 apply to the rape of Sandy at the beach. The last two 999 charges are not really charges, but they can be added to others to invoke life without parole if there are multiple victims.

I've followed my father's cases most of my life, so I know that often the DA will throw in additional charges that have little bearing on the case. The prosecutor said nothing about sodomy or oral copulation so clearly these charges are there to make the DA look tough but also to give the jury something to feel better about if they find the defendant guilty – they can find him innocent on these bogus charges. According to my father, this often helps swing jurors who are reluctant to turn in a guilty verdict.

For this case, it's not going to be a problem. I don't think anyone feels sorry for an abusive, alcoholic father who molests his three-year old, then years later, rapes his seven-year old.

With the mother and both daughters saying he did it and the police backing them up, I don't see any way this guy is going to get off on any except perhaps those bogus counts. And I'm glad I get to be part of being tough on these criminals.

CHAPTER 3

THE PROSECUTION

"The prosecution has to go with the evidence and the facts and tell the story as it happened. The defense has more creative freedom. All you have to do is look for a defense that works. But it doesn't have to be the truth. Sometimes you get lucky and it is, but sometimes you don't, and either way, it doesn't matter."
- Marcia Clark

1

11th Juror – Brian Hamilton, early 50s, insurance broker, 2 kids in college.

This is going to be a long trial. I can tell. We've heard from one witness, the mother. It took two and a half days. Yeah, I guess using an interpreter is part of the reason it's so slow. The attorney asks a question in English. The translator re-asks it in Spanish. The witness responds in Spanish. Then the interpreter gives the witness' response in English.

Sometimes there are misunderstandings. The interpreter doesn't understand the lawyer or the witness doesn't understand the interpreter or the interpreter doesn't understand the witness. Sometimes the judge intervenes. Then, after every hour or so, they have to change translators. Yeah, that definitely drags out the process.

But for me, the real problem is the prosecutor. He stumbles, makes mistakes, backs up, asks the same question more than once, doesn't seem to be listening to the answers. Often he appears confused. He doesn't seem prepared. Hopefully it will get better with future witnesses. This one was confusing.

Yeah, it started out as you would expect. Alejandra, the mother, confirmed the story that Mr. Bolt, the prosecutor, told us during his opening statement. On the day of the incident, she went to work. Her husband called her about lunch time to find out if it was okay if Mandy (the older daughter) went on a play date with a friend. The friend's mother had called and this was the first he'd heard about it. He wanted to know what was supposed to happen with Sandy since he had planned to go fishing that afternoon.

They agreed that he would take Sandy fishing with him. Alejandra got home about 4:30. She called Flores and he told her he was heading home with Sandy. When they got home, Sandy seemed 'sad'. I got confused about this because there seemed to be some misunderstandings between sad and sick – in English, we often say 'not feeling well' and while usually that could be a physical illness, it could also be emotional. I got the impression that when Sandy came home, she didn't look 'well'. Alejandra knew that Sandy had a flu shot the day before and seemed a bit ill in the morning when she went to school.

Obviously, the prosecutor and Alejandra tried to build on this as indicating something had happened which had upset her that day, but the discussion seemed a bit confused.

Anyway, when they got home, Flores grabbed a beer, turned on the TV, and stretched out on the couch to watch. Sandy went to her room and came out to the dining room with her homework while Alejandra served her a snack and fixed dinner. According to Alejandra, this just seemed to be a normal afternoon.

When Mandy got home, Sandy joined her in their room. Sometime later, they asked to talk to Alejandra. At first they went to Alejandra and Albert's bedroom but the girls wanted to talk in their room. Upon entering (surprisingly, they left the door open), Mandy told Sandy to tell their mother what had happened.

Sandy dropped her pants, pulled down her underwear, pointed to the blood and said, "Father did this."

At that point, Alejandra ran into the living room screaming, "What happened to my daughter?"

Apparently Albert appeared confused and seemed to have no idea what Alejandra was talking about. When she confronted him with the fact that Sandy's genitals were bleeding, he asked her how that had happened. She told him that if he didn't tell her what had happened, she would call 911. She pulled out her phone and started to dial, all the time screaming in Spanish. He took the phone from her, hung it up and gave it back. In the other room, hearing the fighting between their parents, Mandy called 911.

Albert left the apartment and Alejandra called 911 and was told that Mandy was on the phone with them already. They dispatched the police and an ambulance.

Twenty minutes later, several police arrived and briefly interviewed Alejandra, Mandy, and Sandy. They were then taken to Community Hospital, to the sexual assault unit, where Sandy was examined in Alejandra's presence. At some point during their time at the hospital, Albert called Alejandra and asked where she was. She responded that she was at the hospital and he asked why. She said she wanted the nurses to tell her what had happened to Sandy. He asked what had happened to her and if she was okay.

Later that evening they went home. The next day, the girls both had fevers so they stayed in bed and sometime after that, they went down to the sheriff's office to be interviewed.

Mr. Bolt asked Alejandra about where she and the girls were living and she answered that they now live in Colorado. They moved to get a new start in a new state.

All of this made sense and seemed consistent with Mr. Bolt's opening statement. Then it started to unravel. Quite frankly, even before Ms. Preston, the defense attorney, took over, I must admit I was starting to get confused. I really wanted to talk with the other jurors about this. I really wanted to know if they had heard it the same way I did.

2

3rd Juror – Linda Lancaster, early 40s, personnel manager in a larger corporation, married, no kids.

What the hell was that? It all started out well enough. We got the basic story from the mom's perspective. She and the prosecutor seemed to be in synch, as you might expect. But then it went south. He started to ask questions about The Rule. You may remember from Bolt's opening statement that there was a rule in the household that neither girl was supposed to be alone with her father. From Bolt's argument, this was because Mandy had been molested as a child and the Rule was put in place to ensure it never happened again. He made a big deal about The Rule.

And now, I'm starting to wonder about the prosecution's case.

<From Court Transcript Testimony of Alejandra Rivera>

Q. Before your husband was arrested before you -
the police arrived at your house, was there a rule that
your daughters were supposed to stay together and not
be alone with your husband?
A. Yes.
Q. Where did that rule - who established that rule?
A. I did.
Q. When did you do that
A. Since they were little.
Q. Why did you do that?
A. Because that's how I was raised. My mother
always said you have to take care of each other and no
one should be alone with their dad.
Q. So as you were raised and became an adult and
imposed that rule upon your own children, why did you
have that rule?
A. I don't know. Because my parents brought me up
that way. I don't know why.

Q. Your daughters were aware of that rule?

A. I needed to always say to them take care of each other. Don't be alone.
Q. Why would you tell them to not be alone with their father?
A. I repeat. Because it was a rule that I acquired when I was a little girl too.
Q. When Mandy was a little girl did she ever complain to you that your husband had touched her genitals inappropriately?
A. No.
Q. Never happened?
A. No.
Q. When Mandy was a little girl did you ever see anything that caused you concern about how - about the appropriateness of the way your husband was interacting with Mandy?
A. No.
Q. Nothing at all?
A. Yes, nothing at all.
Q. Did you explain to your daughters, give them a reason why they would not be allowed to be alone with their father?
A. No.
Q. Do you have any idea what either one of them would believe that the reason was?

MS. PRESTON: Your Honor, I'm going to have to object on foundation and speculation at this point.
THE COURT: Sustained.
Please rephrase.
Q. (BY MR. BOLT) Has either Sandy or Mandy ever expressed to you a belief about why they are not supposed to be left alone with dad?
A. No.
Q. Now do you remember telling a law enforcement officer that in fact Mandy had complained to you that her father had touched her sexually on the genitals?
A. I don't remember.
Q. Wasn't there an interview on I believe November 3rd, 20XX where you in fact told a detective

that Mandy had complained that she had been inappropriately touched on her genitals when she was very young?
A. I don't remember that.
Q. Do you remember ever talking to anybody following your husband's arrest and the short period of time thereafter about having seen troubling things and about Mandy having complained of inappropriate sexual contact by your husband?
A. No.
Q. Are you saying you were never asked?
A. I don't remember.

Q. You don't remember whether you were asked?
A. I don't remember.
Q. What don't you remember?
A. What you are asking me.
Q. So at any time following you finding out about Sandy and your husband leaving do you remember speaking with somebody from law enforcement and them asking you questions about what had happened?
A. I don't remember.
Q. Do you remember in the time period following your husband's arrest speaking with any law enforcement person about anything involving Mandy and your husband?
A. I don't remember.
Q. Was there ever an occasion when Mandy was a young child and you were concerned that she had been touched sexually by your husband?
A. No.
Q. Was there ever a time when Mandy was very young when you laid her down on a bed and pulled down her pants and examined her privates to see if you could find any indication that your husband had touched her sexually?
A. No.
Q. There never was any occasion like that?
A. No.
Q. Didn't you tell a detective that in fact there was an occasion where you were concerned?

A. I don't remember having said that.
Q. Didn't you tell a law enforcement officer that you examined her privates because you were concerned that he had touched her inappropriately?
A. I don't remember.
Q. The first time any sort of child sexual abuse was reported from anyone in your household was November 1st, 20XX; right?
A. Yes.
Q. At the time that you were interacting with police weren't you concerned that you had never reported suspicions of your husband abusing - sexually abusing Mandy in years past?
MS. PRESTON: Your Honor, at this point I'm going to object on badgering this witness; leading, Fifth Amendment.
THE COURT: I'll overrule.
THE WITNESS: No.
Q. (BY MR. BOLT) At the time your husband was arrested did you have any concerns that your children may be taken away from you?
A. No.
Q. Didn't you tell a detective that in fact you were concerned that your children could be taken away from you?
A. I don't remember.

29

Q. So you remember - do you remember talking to a detective about these things?
MS. PRESTON: Objection; asked and answered.
THE COURT: I'll sustain on vague and ambiguous, the phrase about these things.
Please rephrase.
Q. (BY MR. BOLT) So then do you recall at least talking to a detective about the subject matter of - of being worried that your children could be taken away from you for not having reported suspicions of sexual abuse of Mandy by your husband?
A. I don't remember.
Q. You don't remember like that topic ever being

discussed?
A. No.
THE COURT: It's about two minutes to. Is this a good time to stop for lunch?
MR. BOLT: Yeah, it is.
THE COURT: All right.
MR. BOLT: Thank you.
THE COURT: We will take our noon recess at this point. I will look forward to seeing everyone at 1:30. Please do not discuss this matter amongst yourselves or with anyone else. Please do not form or express any opinions concerning this matter. Thank you for your attention and your patience. I'll see everyone at 1:30.

<End Transcript Excerpt of Testimony by Alejandra Rivera>

Yeah, it really went south. All of a sudden, any rapport between Bolt and Alejandra was gone. It was almost like he was the defense attorney, that he was cross-examining her. I was afraid that after lunch he was going to continue to badger her, but fortunately, he changed course. He asked about jail calls that she had with Mr. Flores and if she remembered him apologizing (she said he had), and then about his sister's children, and then about whether they had plans to divorce each other. It was all pretty innocuous, but it looked like Alejandra was now reluctant to answer any of Bolt's questions.

But without even asking a question or putting on a witness, a big part of Bolt's case just fell apart. According to Alejandra, nothing ever happened to Mandy when she was young and The Rule, was not what Bolt is trying to make it. I know quite a few Hispanic families, and this idea that girls need to stick together and that they shouldn't be alone with men, even their fathers, seems to be cultural, not specific to this family and Flores' alleged abuse of his older daughter – which now seems not to have happened. That calls into question a lot of the charges against Mr. Flores.

Still, the description of what happened to Sandy seems indisputable. We'll see if other witnesses back that story up. I really thought Bolt still had an iron-clad case, at least for the rape of Sandy.

And then Ms. Preston took over.

3

10th Juror – Amy Friar, late 60s, retired Child Protective Services (CPS) social worker.

Don't get me wrong, I'm sure he's guilty, but that Ms. Preston is impressive. It's good to see a young woman in such command of a situation. Of course after Mr. Bolt's performance, almost anyone would look good. He certainly doesn't seem to connect with people, even his own witness. And while Ms. Preston may have been adversarial, she introduced herself, and somehow made Ms. Rivera more comfortable, even apologizing for some of the detailed questions she would have to ask.

And when Ms. Rivera was clearly lying, Ms. Preston treated her nicely, just moving on and letting the inconsistencies speak to us, the jury. She's a very talented young woman, someone I'd enjoy knowing on a social basis. I bet her life is even more interesting than mine.

Me, I retired a few years ago and I must admit, I'm bored. I do some volunteer work for the homeless and for Habitat for Humanity, and I do have friends, a book club that I love, and Mandy (such a weird coincidence), my Australian Shephard that I take everywhere (except to court). But I miss my work. It was hard and often heartbreaking but I honestly felt like I made a difference in many lives.

I spent almost all of my career in Santa Cruz County doing social work, mostly with Child Protective Services. The vast majority of my cases were with Hispanic immigrants, and my work with the families and foster families was largely done in Spanish. So unlike most of the rest of the jury, I was able to understand Ms. Rivera's answers to the questions directly. I was probably also better able to discern when she was lying and when she was telling the truth. I don't know why she would lie about her son Armando, saying he never lived with them, and I don't know why she wouldn't admit that she wasn't sure it was her in the video and audio recordings of police interviews that were presented in court. I also don't understand why she would lie about her relationship with her husband. She claimed they hadn't fought in years, but that certainly wasn't true. She said he only drank on weekends. And she was clearly lying when Ms. Preston pushed her on their home life, asking about the social worker from CPS who came to visit the house. We really don't go out unless there is some real concern about the safety of the children in a household.

But I do believe her when she described her anguish over discovering her daughter's injuries, and I do believe that she thinks her husband raped her daughter. I really don't care if they fought before the incident with Sandy. I'm sure the other jurors don't either. If anything, it supports the idea that her husband is a violent alcoholic who abuses his family.

As I think about it, it almost seems backwards. Why would Ms. Preston be trying to convince us that Mr. Flores and his wife had marital problems, that he was abusive, that he was an alcoholic, and that CPS was called because of the problems in the home? It almost seems like she's proving Mr. Bolt's case.

Unfortunately, what we're seeing in this court case is not that unusual. Alcoholic fathers who abuse their wives and children were the main reasons I was brought into these complex family situations. I do have sympathy for immigrants who work ridiculous hours to make better homes for their families than they could have elsewhere, but quite frankly, in spite of my very liberal leanings on most issues, my experience has shown me that in many Hispanic families, the men's attitudes towards their wives and daughters seem to come out of the dark ages. Wives and female children are property, the relationships bordering on master and slaves. Wives are expected to cook, clean, and take care of the children. Children are expected to obey their fathers' rules. For female children, it's worse. Historically, they've had little value in the family other than to help the mother with household chores. They have no voice, no future. And so, it becomes easy for a father to abuse his family. It's tolerated, even praised in many of their homelands, but should be punished here in the United States.

4

4th Juror – Evan Garcia, mid-40s, Hispanic, Silicon Valley Entrepreneur, film fanatic. Unmarried, no children.

That was really tough. I knew from the minute I was impaneled, that this was going to be difficult, but I couldn't imagine how hard it would be to listen to a ten-year old recount how her father raped her when she was seven years old. She seemed surprisingly calm and collected about it. I guess I expected tears. I also thought she'd have difficulty describing the gruesome details about lubrication, penetration and her father's orgasm. Still, I don't see how she could have made this stuff up.

Sure, Ms. Preston made some good points by getting Sandy to admit that she actually didn't remember anything about the incident, that her testimony today was based on the tapes of her previous testimony at the preliminary hearing and the tapes of her interviews with the police. But even though I'm doing my best to assume Flores is innocent until proven guilty, looking at the guy, listening to his wife, and now hearing the testimony of the kids, it's going to be hard to prove him innocent. I know. I know. He shouldn't have to prove his innocence. But you know, the reality in our society is that with this type of offense, you are guilty until proven innocent. Plus, there seems to be a ton of evidence against this guy.

Don't get me wrong. I have some sympathy. He's an immigrant. As you might guess from my name, I have a Hispanic heritage. My parents worked in the fields near Watsonville after coming here from Mexico. They wanted a better life for their kids. My dad was much like Flores, or at least what we've heard so far about Flores. He worked hard, drank beer every night, and treated my mom and us kids like slaves. Still, I know he loved us. It was just that culture. Wives and kids were there to serve the man so he could do the work to support the family. It didn't matter that my mom worked in the fields too. Making his life easier was her role.

And look at me. Here I am, mid-40s and semi-retired. Unlike many of the Mexican families whose kids I went to school with, my parents emphasized education. My father literally beat me the first time I hung out with a gang. I was afraid he'd kill me – for real. But I stayed on the straight and narrow while many of my friends ended up in gangs or were just too lazy to do what it took to change their lives.

Me, I graduated at the top of my high school class (it wasn't that hard, given the competition), got a full ride scholarship to Stanford, met some good white fraternity guys who didn't hold my heritage against me, and founded a software startup. Our first one went belly up after two years of ridiculously hard work: sixteen-hour days, working weekends, no holidays or vacations. The Venture Capitalists that gave us our seed round had found something more interesting than what we had prototyped and we were unable to get a Series A round (the first real round of investment) from them. Since our original investors weren't interested in funding us further, no one else would jump in. We (or at least I) learned some lessons about the cutthroat VC world. It was truly 'go big or go home.'

Sick of VCs, I pushed the other guys to bootstrap a company on our own. They were skeptical. They had MBAs and were true believers that venture investment was the only way to go. And to some degree, they're right. If you want to make hundreds of millions, or billions, you need investment to grow rapidly. As I said, from the VCs' point of view, you've got to bet it all. Fewer than one in ten VC-funded startups succeed. Four or five fail outright, and the rest get sold off for pennies or forced out of business like we were – the VCs don't want them in their portfolios if they aren't going to be billion dollar successes 'overnight'.

I convinced the guys that if we built a sustainable business on our own, we could either sell it, or take investment at a later date, and we'd be in a better place to negotiate terms of the investment at much higher valuations. They finally agreed.

We worked even harder, took out loans and ran our credit cards to the max. But we were profitable within the first year, and by the end of the second, we were making decent money. By the end of the third year, we started taking vacations, and then we took a step back to look at where we wanted to go longer term.

Quite frankly, I didn't want to take investment and go public. Sure, we could have done it and I might have made hundreds of millions off of it, but maybe it's having grown up in a tiny apartment sharing a room with my brothers and sisters – I just didn't need that much money.

So, we started talking to our customers about the possibility of them owning our technology all for themselves. When one larger customer got wind of the fact that we were offering to sell our technology to their largest competitor (gee, I wonder how they found out ☺), a bidding war followed. We sold for just over a hundred million dollars with an earn-out over three years. Even better for me, they made me CTO – Chief Technical Officer of their company.

Five years have passed and I'm still there. I say semi-retired, because aside from trade shows and conferences, and setting up quarterly technology strategy plans, my time is my own. I have to admit that I go to more movies than I should. I'm a film fanatic and love almost everything you can see in a theatre.

As for relationships, I'm divorced. It was rough. I don't think marriage and startups are a good idea. I spent far too much time at work, and even when I wasn't AT work, I was working or thinking about work. If there was a crisis (which seemed to happen every day), I'd drop everything. I missed birthdays, anniversaries, and even jumped out of bed more than once, leaving my ex frustrated. No, I wasn't a good husband. And I probably got what I deserved in the divorce. Somehow though, it caught me by surprise. I really thought she'd be there for me and that once I made us comfortably rich, we could have the life of leisure that we'd only dreamed of. Clearly she wasn't patient enough or I wasn't smart enough to see that relationships need as much nurturing as startups. I admit to not being over that, so right now, I don't think I'm going there again. I'm happy with my work, my movies and my family. I bought my parents a nice but modest house in a good area. I've helped my brothers and sisters with their studies and with getting their careers going. And, I'm Uncle Ev to my 6 nieces and nephews. I make time for them so their parents can work as they need to and get away from the kids from time to time. I feel like I'm doing a good job with my family.

But back to the trial.

We had a very long day. It ran well past the five o'clock ending time. The judge wanted both sides to complete the testimony from the two girls, Sandy and Mandy.

Like I said, Sandy's testimony was excruciatingly hard to hear. And being from a similar family, I guess I understand a bit about Mandy's testimony.

Apparently during the forensic examination, Sandy mentioned

to a nurse that her sister had been molested by her father some years before. The nurse mentioned this to the forensic detective who questioned Mandy after she finished with Sandy.

Mandy claimed that when she was almost three years old, her father had removed her underwear and molested her. The police jumped on this as proof of a pattern and brought charges against Flores around that incident in addition to the charges about Sandy. Then, during the preliminary hearing a few months after the incident with Sandy occurred, Mandy recanted, saying she had made it all up. Today, she admitted that she did this to be supportive of her sister. I guess she wanted to be sure her abusive dad would be put away, so she embellished.

I liked her though. She's a really spunky kid of fourteen who wouldn't take any shit from the prosecutor or the defense attorneys. She kind of flirted with the judge and charmed the courtroom. It's funny how we'll all probably just accept the fact that she lied about being molested. Of course, what kid actually remembers what happened to them before they were three years old. But as the judge said in his instructions, it's up to us to decide whether to believe some of the testimony of a witness if we know that they've lied about other things. I think that's the case here. We're going to believe her.

5

1st Juror – Laura Miles - late 60s – writer - no children.

What an intriguing young lady! I really liked Mandy. She's got spirit. She seemed so confident. I would have been a nervous wreck on the stand in her situation. Still, I'm not sure I believe her. I'm not sure that she wasn't abused as a young child or that her story of her sister's rape is accurate. She's a deft liar and would be a perfect character for one of my upcoming novels – someone who's so charming, you just accept whatever she says, discounting untruths in favor of her approval. It's hard to believe she's only fourteen.

Yes, Mandy had the judge, attorneys, and all of us wrapped around her little finger to deploy an over-used cliché. On the one hand, she tells us how kids today, even kids her sister's age when the alleged incident occurred, know much more about sex than anyone thinks, that while there's standard sex-ed in schools, between friends and the internet, they know it all. In the next breath, she's coy about mentioning body parts. You can't say vagina or penis to her, and she certainly won't use these embarrassing words. It's 'private parts', as in "my sister said my father put his private part in her private part." And even then, just using the words 'private parts' made her giggle nervously. Utterly charming and disarming. Yep, I think everyone on the jury believed her and accepted that although she lied before about being molested, she is telling the truth about what happened with her sister.

Don't get me wrong. I'm not saying she lied about that. No. I'm just skeptical. I'll be looking at other evidence to see if all of these different accounts line up with the police evidence.

Perhaps I'm just too jaded. I've read and written too many stories to not look for more than the obvious. They say that in real life, the simplest answer is usually the right one. I've found that to be a complete crock. People are much more complicated than we imagine. Their motivations go well beyond the what we see on the surface. What tangled webs we weave.

I certainly hope that at least a few of the other jurors are asking themselves questions, that they're not just assuming that

Mr. Flores is guilty. I know that's hard in a case like this, but I do wonder why it has taken three years to get to trial and why, if he is guilty, he hasn't taken a plea bargain. I'm sure with the court backlog, it was offered.

And now, even as the case is just beginning, we have a mother who lied about many things not directly connected to the case, as well as about her perfect relationship with her husband, the older sister who admitted she lied to police about being molested before, and even little Sandy. She seems to have changed her story about what happened and where and when. Okay, the part about the rape in the house is consistent, though she admitted she doesn't actually remember it happening. Aside from trauma-induced amnesia which didn't seem to be present for the preliminary hearing, I'm struggling to understand how she could forget such a traumatic event.

But what is this story about a second rape on the beach? And was there a third at Mr. Flores' storage locker where he stopped on the way home after speaking with his wife on the phone? No, in spite of the credible nature of the charges and the circumstances, it's going to be easy for me to continue to assume 'innocent until proven guilty'. I'm just very surprised to see the prosecution's case looking this weak just a few days into the trial. Quite frankly, my writer's nose smells something fishy. Sorry for the clichés. I usually avoid them in my books.

6

5th Juror – Melissa Duplisse, early 70s, retired nurse.

What a horrible night! I didn't get more than a few hours of sleep. Nightmares kept me up. I can't believe I'm on this jury. I did try to get out of it. I told the judge that I was a retired nurse and had seen too much of this in my career. That's part of why I retired. I couldn't take it anymore. People just seem to be getting worse and worse. There's violence everywhere. It almost seems to be accepted.

Children and even adults play violent video games. Movies have become more and more violent. There's sex everywhere. It's little wonder that our quiet little town of Santa Cruz has become the home to gangs and the 'homeless'.

Just last year, a young woman who ran a small business downtown was shot in the head by a 'homeless' man. She was walking to lunch in broad daylight in a perfectly good part of town (if that exists anywhere), and this man walked up behind her, put a gun to her head and pulled the trigger. She died instantly. He was arrested, but will probably get off for being homeless. I don't know why this town tolerates these people. I know part of it is the University. We have too many students here. But a bigger problem is the immigrants. Because of them, we have gangs and gangs have been killing not only each other, but innocent bystanders. I wish they'd just all go away. I want the Santa Cruz of the sixties. Yes, there were hippies, but it was a peaceful place. You felt safe here. No more. I'm afraid to go out.

You'd think that with my obvious biases, the judge would have let me go. Or that the defense attorney, that nice Ms. Preston would have challenged me. But no. I'm here. And now I'm having nightmares.

Last night I kept dreaming about this little girl being raped by her father. I kept hearing her words – he put his private parts in my private parts and he kept moving in and out for a long time. I heard the prosecutor ask her for details and heard that when he was done, she had a sticky white fluid on her and it was on his private part too. How would a seven-year old know about this if it didn't happen.

But just look at the family. Immigrants. A hard-working

mother, an abusive drunk for a father – even Ms. Preston made that point. It's almost like she thinks he's guilty too.

And those poor children. The oldest is smart, really smart. The younger one is so shy. I can't help but feel sorry for them. They're going to be traumatized for the rest of their lives over this incident – both of them. Maybe the older one will get over it, but the younger one seems so fragile. Imagine! Raped at seven years old by her own father. How do you get over that?

Well, if the other jurors see it like I do, and I can't imagine that they don't, at least the father will be going away for the rest of his life. I just hope my nightmares go away. But I have a feeling it's just going to get worse. We'll soon be hearing all the details from the police point of view. I understand we'll have to look at pictures of the injured little girl. That's going to give me never-ending nightmares. How can they do this to people? How can they pick average, good people and ask them to participate in gruesome trials. Shouldn't there be a better way? Shouldn't the courts just hire professional jurors – people who are prepared to deal with these horrible crimes. I know I don't want it invading my life. But now it has.

7 From the trial transcript just before police testimony began:

THE COURT: Let's go on the record, please, regarding People versus Mr. Flores. Mr. Flores is present. Counsel are present. All of our jurors are present.

We had marked as Court Exhibit 14 last week a couple of questions from one of our jurors. And I have discussed these with counsel.

And the first question is: Since the first witness who testified, the ex-wife of the defendant, denied knowledge of statements made to law enforcement during interviews recorded after the accusations, the facts presented in those interviews are not facts at this point; correct?

And that is correct.

All we know is what the attorneys have stated in questioning. But if the witness denies knowledge or recollection of those interviews, we cannot consider them facts unless they are presented later in testimony from the law enforcement officer; is that correct?

That is correct. A question offered by an attorney is not evidence. It's the response offered.

Now the response offered, for example, if a response is, "I don't recall," that may possess some evidentiary value for you folks. You'll have to listen to all of the evidence that's presented in the case and make a decision in that regard.

But a representation as to something that was said previously, where there's a lack of recollection in court or a denial of that, that lack of recollection or denial may have evidentiary value for you.

But the facts, as the question, are not facts at this point. You may receive something later on in the trial from a law enforcement officer as to prior statements. I don't know. I'll leave that in the hands of the attorneys.

Okay? So is that clear?

Those were good questions. Thank you very much.

I mean, all of the questions have been very good questions up to this point.

8

8th Juror – Ben Singleton, mid-30s, state park ranger, 2 kids under 10.

Wow! That jury asking questions thing is new to me. I'd never heard of it before, but it really gets us involved in the process. We're almost like mini-lawyers.

Those were my questions that got asked today and I think they were important. If we have questions that we think the attorneys should ask a witness, we write them down on a piece of paper and signal Bill, the Bailiff. He comes over, takes the question or questions, gives them to Heidi, the clerk, who passes them to the judge. At some point, the judge calls the attorneys over and in a whispered side-bar, discusses the questions with them. They decide whether any of the questions have merit and if so who gets to ask them. Mine were more for the court than for a witness, but I'm impressed with this option.

Judge Campbell walked by us in the hallway outside the courtroom at the end of the lunch break yesterday and I asked him about this. Apparently, some states allow judges to optionally give an instruction letting jurors pose questions. California is one of them. He doesn't do it in every trial, but felt that as complicated as this one was (I wonder what's coming), it was important.

Apparently we can't rely on the video transcripts of Alejandra's testimony themselves as evidence since she denies knowledge of them even though it's obvious that it was her on the tapes. I like the judge's answer that her denying may have evidentiary value to us. It's kind of interesting. We can't rely on the tapes, but we can consider the fact that she denies their existence as evidence about her. I probably shouldn't be jumping to conclusions, but it appears the judge is saying that we can use the fact that she's lying to make judgments about her other testimony. But at this point, I can't imagine why she'd be lying about anything. She certainly wants her husband convicted for raping her daughter so what is it she has to hide? It seems like it might be unrelated. Maybe it has something to do with her son, who she claims never lived with her. Maybe it's some immigration issue.

I really don't envy these immigrants. I work as a State Park

Ranger. Currently I'm assigned to Mount Madonna Park just above the town of Watsonville. Watsonville has a huge immigrant population. Whites are definitely in the minority there and somewhere I read that almost 80% of the population is either Hispanic or of Hispanic descent.

Anyway, on weekends, these Hispanic families come to the park. I've always found them to be respectful, and unlike many of the white families that come, they usually clean up after themselves. As families, they also seem to have better food and more fun. I've talked with many of them (my Spanish is okay but not perfect), and I see just how hard they work during the week. Many of them are illegals. I'm glad I don't have to turn them over to ICE. They bring a lot to our community with their hard work.

Sure, I have to deal with some of their kids who have gone astray and yes, we have our share of drunks to deal with. But fortunately for me, most of the gang members avoid the park. I've got to say, I love my job.

As it turns out, though, with the heavy rains this season, roads in and out of the park are blocked with mudslides. I can't really get to work anyway, so this is a great time for me to have jury duty. I'd always dreaded it before, but I'm fascinated by this case. I love detective shows and read a lot of detective and legal novels. And while I see similarities, it's far from what I expected. I mentioned the questions from the jury. What I didn't know is that examination, cross-examination, redirect, re-cross, etc. can go on forever (or until the judge loses patience). And I'm still surprised at how the defense and prosecution work so well together. TV would have us believe that this is battle between adversaries who hate each other. That's certainly not the case here. But as I saw today, fireworks are possible, though they're a bit more subtle than on TV.

Yesterday we had testimony from Sandi Locke, the detective who did the forensic interviews of the girls and one of the detectives who conducted the search of the apartment. She's also the one who found the bottle of Astroglide hidden in a plant inside a ceramic swan on a shelf high above the toilet in the bathroom. I can't help wondering how it got there or why it would have been hidden there, or for that matter, how Detective Locke found it.

I'm not sure I like Detective Locke. There's something

strange about her. She's small and thin with stringy blonde hair. Her face is a bit mousey and she seems very introverted (unlike me). It's clear she takes herself and her work very seriously but I guess in that business, where you're dealing with the sexual assault of children day in and day out, you'd become pretty jaded about people. Still, she's not very forthcoming. Mr. Bolt had to drag things out of her. Then again, she's a cop and doesn't want to make a mistake by saying too much. She really tried to be very concise with all of her answers and interrupted Mr. Bolt when he said something that wasn't as exactly correct as she thought it should be. I guess that's how it should be. Still, though…

Anyway, her testimony for Mr. Bolt went very much as expected. He had her talk about her work history and her training in interviewing children. He then played tapes of the interviews as we followed along reading the transcripts. That took pretty much all day.

I'm not sure what goes on behind closed doors in the courtroom, but it sure seems like we spend a lot of time outside the courtroom waiting. We normally start at ten or ten-thirty, break for lunch from noon to one-thirty, then get a short break about three o'clock before adjourning at about five pm. But so far, we've been asked to leave the courtroom countless times and have had to wait for anywhere from ten to forty-five minutes.

Today, Detective Locke continued her testimony. Mr. Bolt took her through her interviews with the two girls, Sandy and Mandy. What was weird was that the family had agreed to meet with her and the other detective at one pm the day after the assault. Then they just didn't show. Weird! Detective Locke and her partner then went to the family's house and convinced them to come in the next day. That's when the tapes were recorded.

I must admit, the tape of Sandy really bothered me. It's just that she was so matter-of-fact about what had happened. She didn't seem particularly upset about it. Obviously, I've never been a seven-year old girl, but I have a seven-year old daughter and I can't imagine she would react this way. Maybe it's cultural.

After discussing the tapes, and in particular, The Rule, Mr. Bolt took the detective through the search of the house where she found the Astroglide, and of the fact that a search had been conducted of Mr. Flores' storage locker.

As he wrapped up his direct examination, it seemed like Detective Locke had pretty much confirmed the events as Mr.

Bolt presented them in his opening statement. I didn't have much doubt about Flores' guilt.

And then, Ms. Preston began her very subtle cross-examination.

9

14th Juror – Jonathan Comstock, retired, early 70s, ex-engineer.

It's amazing how much time we spend out of the courtroom. In general, we're supposed to be her at 10am, take an hour and a half lunch, then have a fifteen minute break at about three-thirty.

But the reality is quite different. Often we don't start until eleven, and we're often sent out of the courtroom for as much as an hour or more.

I'm actually glad for these breaks. Aside from a bit of relief from the intense testimony, it gives me a chance to walk. I've always thought of myself as pretty fit, but a year ago, I was diagnosed with type 2 diabetes. I changed my diet and made sure I did at least an hour of walking each day. I've been able to avoid medication and my doctor is quite pleased that I'm one of the few (of his patients) that seem to have the discipline to change their lifestyles. For me, if your life is threatened, it's time to change.

When the trial started, I was worried that I wouldn't have the time to walk, especially with the horrible weather. I appreciate the drought-ending rains we're having, but it's actually dangerous to be outside.

The good news is that with the breaks, I get plenty of walking time. The courthouse is a giant rectangular block. Some might say it's ugly, but in fact, it's a classic example of Brutalist Architecture. Okay. I'm not really a fan. In the 50s and 60s, government buildings were mostly Brutalist. In spite of being built almost entirely of cement, the courthouse has huge windows that surround the building. There really aren't what you'd think of as external walls – they're pretty much all glass.

The courtrooms are also part of a rectangular structure on the inside with a huge, wide hallways separating them from the windows.

There are also giant glass panels in the roof which allow natural light into each of the courtrooms. Although it may be ugly, it's very practical. And for me, the rectangular shape and wide hallways make for great walks.

I've measured it, and it's exactly two hundred yards around. So, I do plenty of walking and actually the views aren't bad. The back of the courthouse faces the river and San Lorenzo Park, with lots of different kinds of seabirds, hawks, and river birds swimming, fishing, or seeking shelter. These walks also let me step away from the stress of the trial multiple times a day.

As an alternate, I'll probably never make it into the jury room. It's tough. As an engineer, I think I'm pretty well equipped to analyze facts, discard the chaff, and make good decisions. But for this case, my opinions won't matter. The only real influence I can have is with my submitted questions. So far, I've submitted two, one of which was asked of Alejandra, but I have a feeling I'm going to be asking a lot more.

What looked like an open and shut case is beginning to show a few holes. I suspect the other jurors don't see them yet, but if they don't, I have a feeling they will soon. Hopefully my questions will help elucidate the flaws that I'm beginning to see. And if I'm right, particularly after today's testimony, that Ms. Preston is a force to be reckoned with. She's going to undermine Mr. Bolt's case just a little at a time, here and there until the whole thing comes crashing down. I could be wrong, but at my age, I'm a pretty good judge of people and Mr. Bolt is no match for Ms. Preston. Also, in my opinion, so far, every witness has lied. That's a weak foundation on which to build a case.

The past two days, we heard testimony from Sandi Locke, the detective who conducted the forensic interviews with the two girls and did the search of their apartment.

After Mr. Bolt's examination, things looked pretty good for him. Everything she said supported his case. But then Ms. Preston took over. At first, I didn't see anything. She was subtle. She went through Detective Locke's qualifications, then drilled down into how she handled children, flattering her expertise and reinforcing everything she had said about how important it is that the number of interviews are minimized, that you have to ask open-ended questions, that it's important not to suggest answers, that it's critical not to ask a question more than once because it suggests you didn't like the answer given, that referring to another answer from someone else influences a child's answer, etc. Detective Locke agreed enthusiastically with Ms. Preston's understanding of what was required as a sexual assault team member who conducts these types of child interviews.

It was all very friendly at first.

Referring to the interview with Mandy, Ms. Preston inquired

as to why the detective had asked specific questions. These were good examples of proper interviewing techniques and rapport between the two was building. Then it started to go south. In the same vein and same tone of voice, she asked why Detective Locke had asked the previous question again – this was about Mandy having been molested as a young child, to which she had said she hadn't. The detective tried to explain. Then Ms. Preston asked why she had asked a third time and the detective fumbled a bit. Then she asked why she had then suggested that someone else had said that the molestation had occurred and when Mandy said she didn't know, but that maybe something happened that she didn't remember, the detective continued to press. Worse, when Ms. Preston asked the detective where she had heard about Mandy having been molested as a child, Detective Locke couldn't remember where she'd heard it, thinking one of the other detectives might have heard it from the nurse who did the physical examination of Sandy.

If that wasn't bad enough, Ms. Preston then brought out text from Sandy's testimony that showed she didn't clearly understand the difference between a lie and saying something that her mother had asked her to say.

Then, they talked about the search of the apartment. This happened several days after the incident. Ostensibly this was because it took that long to get a search warrant, but as Ms. Preston pointed out, they didn't need a search warrant since Alejandra had given permission for the police to search her home. Detective Locke also admitted that they had no record of who might have come and gone to the apartment during those several days before the search.

Okay. The prosecution still has a strong case. I suspect we're going to see a lot more damning evidence in the coming days. But Ms. Preston is a powerhouse and she has begun chipping away at Mr. Bolt's foundation. We'll see where it goes.

10

15th Juror – Mathias Wright, Silicon Valley engineer, early-thirties with 2 children under 5.

I'd like to kill the son-of-a-bitch with my own two hands. He's a wimpy little guy so it would be easy to do. Maybe just a swift kick to the head. I have a black belt in mixed martial arts. One kick to the head and it would be over. We'd save the government a lot of money – they wouldn't have to pay for years in jail, and certainly, the world would be a safer place.

I guess when we convict, he'll get life without parole in a high security institution where hopefully the bigger inmates will give him a regular taste of what he did to his seven-year old. I've heard it's bad news for child molesters. It's still not enough. He ruined this little girl's life.

This morning's testimony was pretty predictable. The first witness was Sam Davenport, a very professional police officer who took us through his arrival at the apartment after the 911 call. He interviewed Sandy for several minutes in her parent's room while another officer, Carlos Garcia, interviewed Alejandra in Spanish.

It sounded like Officer Davenport was very diplomatic in talking to Sandy and getting her to tell what happened. We got to listen to a recording of the interview and of a conversation he had with the detective on the SART team when they reached the hospital.

Even Ms. Preston seemed to appreciate Officer Davenport's professionalism. She had very few questions, most spent on the layout of the house and where Sandy was on the bed when the interview was conducted. I'm not sure what that was about.

Anyway, the big show came in the afternoon. We came back from lunch and had to wait quite a while after 1:30. Apparently there were a number of evidence issues the judge needed to discuss with the attorneys.

But then Mr. Bolt called nurse Mary Williams who did Sandy's physical exam at the hospital.

I like to think I'm tough. I play a lot of violent video games, love action films, and as I said, I do mixed martial arts. But after seeing the photos of that little girl's vagina with the laceration clearly caused by the rape, I just wanted to cry.

Looking back at the jury box, a few of the women were crying as nurse Mary Williams went through her testimony about the SART exam she performed on little Sandy. I felt sorry for them. Nobody wants to see that. It something you just can't get out of your head.

Mr. Bolt was excellent in leading nurse Williams through her testimony and helped her explain what might have appeared to be inconsistencies in her SART report. They spent a lot of time talking about the peer review where other doctors and nurses go through her exam results. I guess there was some confusion about whether the injury could have been caused by a finger. That seemed to have been noted in the report. But in the end, it was clear Flores raped little Sandy.

Ms. Preston didn't have much success trying to get nurse Williams to recant or admit a mistake. She did spend quite a bit of time asking about the other nurse – the Spanish speaking nurse who assisted with the exam. I'm not sure what that was about either.

There's absolutely no doubt in my mind that Flores is guilty. It's all there. How else would the little girl get such an injury? How could she know about what sex is like and describe her father's animal thrusting and orgasm if she hadn't experienced it? She was seven years old for heaven's sake!

I've been keeping my wife, Joan, up to date on the case. I'm glad to have someone to talk to about it. I know that officially, I shouldn't, but how can you not tell your life partner about an experience that consumes your entire day for what will be weeks on end. Joan is right with me on this one. Flores raped his little girl. We look at our two blessings from God and can't imagine that anyone would violate such innocence. Flores will burn in Hell. Now if only I could get on the main jury so that I can help make sure this scum is gets punished on earth as well. Joan and I are both praying for it.

11

16th Juror – Mark Mentor early 60s, retired ex-Silicon Valley startup CEO.

I'm an active guy. I spend between one and four hours each day doing something physical. Most days it's surfing in the amazing waves we have here in and around Santa Cruz. I started surfing in the 60s as a kid. We thought it was crowded then. But now that surfing has gone mainstream in commercials, advertising, and social media, the sport has exploded. In what used to be empty breaks you find hundreds of surfers, even at dawn.

But I'm lucky. Living here in Santa Cruz, we have the cold water and ever-present fear of sharks to keep the crowds down – not so much in town, but I often surf alone in obscure spots north of Santa Cruz.

One of the nice things about surfing is that early morning is usually best. Even when I was working ridiculously hard in my startups, averaging over one hundred hours a week, I found time to get an hour or two of surf at first light. People love sunsets over the ocean. For me, a sunrise over the water is almost a spiritual experience.

Surfing keeps me sane when stress is trying to kill me. I usually do quite well emotionally. I'm considered very even-tempered. If the surf is flat, I can always run, bike, kayak, hang glide, ski, or do other countless activities that a California lifestyle offers us. These alternative physical activities usually do the job if the surf is unavailable.

But right now, I'm struggling. Maybe it's the incessant rain. I love the rain. I don't find it depressing even when it doesn't stop. No, it's the lack of physical activity. The surf has been junk with the storms. Running and biking trails have been reduced to flowing muck, and the rivers and ocean are out of control. Yeah, maybe that's it. Then again, maybe not.

This trial is killing me. Yeah, we've only been at it a couple of weeks, but the stress is unreal. The subject matter is bad enough. Who wants to live through the excruciating details of a child rape? The fact that so many witnesses are lying makes it really hard. I guess it would be interesting as a novel or a movie. You'd want to figure out why all this is happening. But there are real lives involved here. This guy Flores has already had his life ruined, just with the accusation. And whether her story is true or not, little Sandy is permanently damaged, and I see what the situation and the lies have done to the very engaging Mandy. She's trying to ride above it all, but you can see the underlying stress.

The worst is that I can't talk about this. I'd love to step out of the courtroom during a break and turn to another juror and say, "Did you hear what I heard?" That would help a lot. There's just so much conflicting information, and we have a long way to go.

Did I say 'worst'? No. That's not the worst. The worst is I can't talk to my wife about the case. We have a great marriage because we talk about everything. But now, I come home stressed out and can't tell her why. I wake her up with my screaming from a nightmare and I can't tell her what the dream was about. My mind is back on the trial at dinner, during our regular games of scrabble, and even in mid-conversation. This trial is putting a real strain on our relationship and it's just going to get worse. We have weeks to go and I'm sure it's going to get even more complex.

Right now, my only physical activity is walking around the interior of the rectangular courthouse during each break and each time we're sent out of the courtroom, which seems to be happening with increasing frequency. The attorneys seem to get along in court, but I suspect there's a lot of argument going on behind the scenes that we'll never know about.

I'm not the only one who walks. There's a very focused woman in her late thirties or early forties who walks almost as fast as I do but with her cell phone glued to her ear as she talks animatedly, complete with gestures. I don't even know if she sees me or the somewhat elderly gentleman who sits beside me in the alternates box. He and I walk counter clockwise while she goes clockwise. He probably completes one lap for every two of mine.

Today, I slowed down and walked with him a bit and he told me about the history of the courthouse and about its 'Brutalist' architecture. I always thought it was a particularly ugly building, especially for a beautiful place like Santa Cruz, but he explained how it was built and how it maximized the use of light. Apparently construction in concrete is durable. This courthouse is actually fifty years old. But it doesn't look it.

When he said 'Brutalist', I thought he was just being derogatory. But no. It's actually an architectural style. I looked it up. I guess I'm looking for just about anything to take my mind off the case, even obscure, ugly architectural styles.

Anyway, enough about me.

We had a big surprise in the trial today.

As I understand it, normally you have opening statements, then the prosecution presents their case, then the defense does theirs, then closing arguments followed by the judge's instructions, and finally the jury gets to decide the outcome.

But today, things went out of order. Apparently, because the prosecution has gone on longer than expected, one of the defense expert witnesses couldn't be available any longer. She was leaving town.

So, here we are in the middle of the prosecution's case, and we get a defense witness who was going to refute testimony from a prosecution witness we haven't heard from yet. And this was big. It's about DNA.

Dr. Caroline Marcus actually wrote the standards that the FBI uses for their DNA testing. She's clearly at the top of the field as she has written countless papers on DNA forensics, consults to law enforcement at all levels, and teaches techniques and procedures for handling and testing DNA evidence.

Particularly interesting was the fact that when she's called in to review DNA testing results, she uses the same software and the same data that the other labs have used. She inputs the data from the other labs and analyzes it differently using the same software but with different parameters. This gives her more ways to look at the data – something the police labs typically don't have time to do. In other words, she just does a more in-depth examination of the data.

Most of the time this just goes further in confirming the police labs' analyses. But not this time.

If the prosecution DNA expert had testified first, we would have been educated by that person on what DNA is, how testing works, and the reliability of DNA testing in evidence. Instead, we got all of that from the defense witness. I'm not sure if our perspectives would have been different with the prosecution going first, but instead of a refutation, Dr. Marcus gave us a pretty thorough education on DNA and that became our base for understanding DNA evidence.

Sorry to go into detail but I found this stuff fascinating. The older gentleman next to me obviously did as well, but looking around the jury box, I could see that several people were completely lost. My guess is that my neighbor, like me, comes from a science or engineering background.

Anyway, here's a quick summary of what we learned about DNA:

First, as most everyone knows, we get our DNA from our parents – half from our mother and half from our father. DNA determines all sorts of things about us, eye color, hair color, blood type, all sorts of things, even propensities for diseases.

DNA is found almost everywhere, in pretty much all bodily fluids like blood, semen, sweat, tears, and in our skin, hair, et cetera – like I said, almost everywhere.

It transfers easily, and hence, it's become a major tool in crime scene forensics. Criminals usually leave some DNA behind.

But the analysis is not all that simple. Dr. Marcus always talked in terms of probabilities, not certainties, which to my mind, made her more credible.

So basically, analysis goes like this. The DNA lab gets a sample. They have to be very careful not to contaminate the sample with the technician's DNA (apparently this happens often). They then extract the DNA from the samples. In this case, the DNA samples came from scrotal swab from Mr. Flores, and from the crotch of Sandy's underwear.

For each sample, they do three extractions that they call injections and the put them into a machine called a genetic analyzer. The genetic analyzer generates a lot of data about the DNA. They then take the data from each extraction and feed it into a software program that produces a graph called an electropherogram. It looks a bit like an electrocardiogram except instead of indicating the strength of your heartbeat, the height of the line on the electropherogram indicates the amount of a particular type of DNA found. These DNA types are called alleles. In the tests that most labs do, they check for fifteen alleles and that is apparently enough to uniquely identify an individual.

If you're comfortable with graphs, visualize the y-axis as the amount of a particular allele found and the x-axis as the list of the fifteen alleles they looking for.

One of the challenges they have in analyzing DNA comes

when there are multiple sources of DNA – you may see multiple alleles in the graph – genetic material from multiple people. And obviously, people share some alleles, particularly family members.

We also learned about thresholds. The labs set a threshold for the amount of DNA they'll consider worth looking at. According to Dr. Marcus, there is no official standard for what the minimum should be – how high a peak you need to pay attention to. The idea is that the genetic analyzer produces a bit of noise, kind of like static in a radio signal. You don't want to misinterpret static as something significant, so you need to set a threshold above the 'noise level'.

For her analyses, Dr. Marcus uses a complex formula unique to each machine to determine what threshold to use. She analyzes all the injections and from her formula, can determine the noise level for each machine. She then sets her threshold above that level – accounting for the noise the machine is actually generating. She doesn't use an arbitrary level across the board.

I'm trying not to get too esoteric here, but what happened with Dr. Marcus' testimony got really interesting once we understood how all this worked.

Apparently, the crime lab did, indeed find Mr. Flores' DNA on the scrotal swab, and they also found one allele that could have belonged to either Sandy or Alejandra. Since the two share DNA, they couldn't say which. This suggested that it was possible that Sandy's DNA was found on Mr. Flores scrotum.

But using exactly the same data (before seeing the crime labs conclusions), Dr. Marcus looked a bit further. Apparently the height threshold for the crime lab's test was 150 RFUs – Relative Fluoresced Units. Both Mr. Flores' alleles and the one that belonged to either Alejandra or Sandy were at or above that threshold on the graph. In fact, that allele was at exactly 150 RFUs.

But what Dr. Marcus found was that there was another allele that had a peak of 143 RFUs on the graph. Since this was far above the noise threshold for the machine, it clearly identified the second allele as belonging to Alejandra, NOT Sandy.

More interesting, it turns out that the crime lab only used one of the three injections. In the first one, the shared allele was at 133 RFUs meaning if the lab had used that one, it wouldn't have found anything connecting Sandy or Alejandra to the scrotal swab. In the third one, the additional allele that belonged to

Alejandra showed up at 153 RFUs – above the threshold, so if they'd used that one, they would have concluded that it was Alejandra's DNA on the scrotal swab.

This was pretty convincing to me. Mr. Flores hadn't washed since the alleged incident and hadn't changed clothes. There was no DNA from Sandy found on him.

As far as DNA found on the crotch of Sandy's underwear, they found a tiny bit of male DNA there but not enough to associate with anyone. It might have been touched by Mr. Flores or by someone else. Ms. Preston asked if folding laundry could have left this amount and Dr. Marcus confirmed that it could have.

Mr. Bolt tried to challenge Dr. Marcus on her threshold saying she should have used 150 RFUs since the lab did, but she explained that this just resulted in the falling-off-the-cliff phenomenon. She understood why labs did this – they don't have time to do her level of custom analysis for each run of the machine, but that sometimes, they miss some things.

She also pointed out that the vast majority of the time that she's called in on a case like this, she just confirms the crime labs conclusions. This time it was different.

He also tried to challenge her on something he clearly didn't understand too clearly, the SWGDAM guidelines. SWGDAM stands for Scientific Working Group for DNA Analysis Methods. Apparently these are guidelines for DNA analysis that all labs use. Mr. Bolt asked Dr. Marcus why she didn't use them. She stated that she did, that in fact, she'd helped write them.

He then asked how that could be true if several labs used 150 RFUs as a threshold but she didn't. She tried to explain that SWGDAM doesn't specify thresholds – that thresholds are left to the individual labs since equipment, ambient conditions, and testing procedures varied somewhat from place to place. Somehow he didn't understand that. He seemed convinced that SWGDAM specified 150 RFUs, which it's pretty clear it couldn't – according to Dr. Marcus, it's a set of guidelines, not a list of absolute numbers. The labs work within the guidelines, just as she did. Having worked with a number of engineering working groups, like the Internet Engineering Task Force, I understand that this is common. You want to standardize, but you need to leave room for differences in specific environments, and you want to leave room for new technologies.

During part of this, Mr. Bolt deviated from just these two DNA analyses and asked about sperm and semen. I'm not sure why he brought this up as it turned out there was zero sperm and zero semen found on either Mr. Flores or on the crotch of Sandy's underwear. For me, I'd think there would be something – particularly on Mr. Flores.

Frustrated here, Mr. Bolt went back to the DNA analysis techniques, thresholds, SWGDAM, credibility of the crime lab, et cetera, and the cross examination went on for the afternoon with Mr. Bolt vainly trying to find a hole in Dr. Marcus' testimony. From my point of view his cross was often confused and he seemed unprepared and uninformed.

Ms. Preston did a redirect that fully shot down Mr. Bolt's proposals.

Mr. Bolt lost a lot of credibility in my eyes today.

12

9th Juror – Erica Hesse, early 40s, CEO of a rapidly growing high-tech company. Single no children.

Well, we're back. Unfortunately. I must admit to being grateful for the long break from court. It was Lincoln's Birthday on Monday, so in spite of the fact that no one in the business world gets this day off, it was a court holiday. I actually was able to spend an entire work day with my team. It seems like the first since we closed our Series A round of investment. In fact, it was. I reported for jury duty the day after we signed with the VCs (Venture Capitalists).

The evening before, I took our team to Café Sparrow in Aptos. We reserved the entire restaurant for the evening and I had a small string quartet join us. We had an excellent dinner and perhaps a bit too much wine. But after two years of non-stop hundred-plus-hour weeks on a very tight budget, my team deserved to splurge a bit and blow off a bit of steam.

Unfortunately, as they all know, the hard work has just begun. Right now, we're a small team. We have seven engineers, a tech writer, a social media expert, a VP of engineering, two salespeople and a VP of Marketing and Sales, my trusted CFO who also heads up Human Resources (HR) and administration, and me – fifteen in all.

We've developed a unique software product that identifies fake news. I know. After the election of Donald Trump, all of the social media networks are talking about stopping fake news, but claim there is no realistic way to do this. We've come up with a sophisticated, effective mechanism not too different from the models that filter email spam. I won't go into the details, but suffice it to say that the VCs thought it was good enough to give us fifty million dollars, and aside from a board seat, and a growth plan which they imposed, they're leaving us alone to use the cash to accelerate our success – no new VC-stipulated CEO, no new CFO, not even a VP of Marketing. They trust us – at least until next year when we'd better hit our first milestone.

Until now, we've paid our way through a combination of sweat equity – all the employees worked for free or very little for quite a while, cash that I, my CFO, VP of Marketing and Sales, and VP of Engineering put in, as well as some income we earned through consulting contracts and some funding by one of our new customers. But to grow, we needed money. We have to be able to reach markets worldwide. And realistically, in spite of our success in trials with our one large customer, it's a completely different story to scale to the point where our software works on millions of servers, computers, tablets, and phones. To be most effective, the more users, the more accurate we are.

We'll be adding quite a few people and it's going to be a real challenge to keep our company culture. I need to supervise this transition and be part of every hiring decision.

I guess the trial hasn't had as big an impact on my time as I thought. I still can work from about six am to ten am most mornings, all of the weekends, and from five thirty in the afternoon until late in the evening. I'm also on my computer or on the phone at every break and during our hour and a half long lunches. And although I hate to admit it, and will probably never let it be known to my team or investors (and reluctantly to myself), the reality is that having my mind on something else for several hours a day is a break I really need. Focusing on this case gives me better clarity when I come back to work issues. Who would have thought?

So I guess it's a good thing that this case is so consuming. I really can't think about work when I'm in court. Quite frankly, there are times I can't think about work even when I'm working.

I hope this isn't visible to my team. They are my family – actually they're closer to me than my 'real' family.

I know I'm not at one hundred percent. But I guess it's better than zero percent, which is what I feared when I didn't get excused. Then again, and I know I don't want to admit it, the hours I am working are not as effective as they used to be. I'm not as effective as I used to be. And it's not just the time. It is the case.

For the first time since I started on this career path, something is distracting me. I don't like it. I prefer to be in control. But how can you be in control when you're thrown into a court case about child rape? You can try to imagine that you're just watching a TV series or a movie, but it doesn't last long. This is real. These are real people. Worse, they don't behave like you'd expect them to. And whether Flores is guilty or not, real lives have been ruined. This poor little girl. Her sister.

I'm not sleeping well.

At least today was an easy one in court. It seemed a bit repetitive to me. We heard testimony from two police officers. The first was the one who interviewed Sandy in the apartment. He recorded his conversation and we read the transcript as Mr. Bolt took him through his testimony. I didn't really see much difference between what he said and what previous first-responders said earlier.

I was a bit surprised by Ms. Preston's cross. She spent a fair amount of time confirming the layout of the apartment and the position of Sandy on the bed when the officer arrived – propped up against the pillows of the bed with her hand on her groin area, obviously in pain. She also confirmed that the CSI team came and searched the house for evidence. I'm not even sure why she bothered to do this. There was nothing of interest there that we hadn't already heard. Even though it was a non-event, I wrote this down in my notes because it was so unusual. Ms. Preston is usually a tiger on cross. Maybe I'm missing something here.

The second officer was the lieutenant who headed up the SART team. He interviewed Mandy at the hospital. We went through those transcripts as, once again, Mr. Bolt led him through his testimony. This was a bit more interesting as there were numerous objections from Ms. Preston about hearsay – Mr. Bolt repeatedly asked the lieutenant if he had heard something from the forensic nurse about Mandy being molested as a child. The judge sustained most of the objections but Mr. Bolt kept trying to get this testimony in.

During her cross, Ms. Preston focused on the lieutenant's training in questioning young children. She was quite adept at flattering him and getting him to relax before forcing him to admit that Mandy never said anything about being molested when she was younger and said that as far as she knew, there had never been a previous incident with her sister.

I'm still not sure where this is supposed to go. I think everyone would agree that Mandy wasn't molested as a child. She recanted her story, saying she was just trying to support her sister, and she has stood by that. Her mother also agrees that nothing happened before to either Sandy or Mandy. So those charges are pretty much shot. Still, that doesn't mean that Flores didn't rape Sandy. In spite of the lack of DNA evidence, I'm still leaning for guilty. I don't see how else she could have gotten this injury or why she, her mother, and her sister would have lied about such a traumatic event that has ruined so many lives.

13

6th Juror – Andy Harrigan, early 50s, Supervisor at the California EPA, one daughter about to graduate from high school, another daughter away at college.

I have a love-hate relationship with this case. I'm really suffering with the thought of this poor little girl and all she's gone through. I really need to talk to someone about the case but I can't. Before court while we wait to be called in and during breaks, I've started having non-case conversations with Mark, one of the alternates, and Ben, the State Park Ranger and sometimes Sue, the woman who just moved here from southern California.

We talk about the rain, the floods, the landslides, the inconvenience of getting here, politics, and a bit about our families, but we've been studiously avoiding anything concerning the case, except complaints about the long waits in the hallway, and we did talk about the fact that we get to ask questions. But nothing about the case itself.

I can see that everyone is stressed out over the case. We've all made comments about not sleeping, being overly emotional, not being able to talk to our spouses about what's going on, and about hoping the trial will be over soon. At its current pace, it's hard to believe they'll be finishing next week as promised. So the stress and agony will continue.

On the other hand, I have to admit, I'm fascinated by the process and I'm learning things I never knew about police procedures, rules of evidence, DNA, and criminology.

Today we heard from the criminologist who examined all the collected forensic evidence from the scene, from Sandy, and from Mr. Flores.

I cringed as she described the tests she did on Sandy's vestibular swabs, her anal swabs, her vulvar swabs, and her underwear. I just couldn't stop thinking about what this poor little girl went through. She was seven years old for God's sake and she has to have her body poked and probed? I know it's important, but I imagine my girls having to go through something like this. Just the exams alone would be traumatic and would have lasting repercussions.

But the science part was fascinating. The test for semen is

complex, involving three components that have to be found. The tests for blood are almost as complex, and the DNA collection is scrupulous. Like I said, it's love-hate for me. I really don't want to be here. I really don't want to hear about what happened to Sandy. I don't want to think about what's happened to Mr. Flores if by some remote chance he's innocent. But it's like you can't stop watching. Nobody is falling asleep in the jury box, even after lunch, even after hours of video tapes or ridiculously detailed testimony.

Then again, you don't stop watching or thinking about it even when you're home. That part is torture. I keep seeing the pictures, imagining what happened, trying to put it all together, the lies, the facts, and all this evidence. I hope I get through this and that it really will be over soon. Maybe then I'll be able to get it out of my head and actually get a good night's sleep again.

But enough about my over-reactions. You probably want to know about the results of the forensic tests. I certainly did.

Mr. Bolt conducted the direct examination of Ms. Monroe, the forensic expert. He led her through her credentials, then had her explain the science behind each of the tests she performed. It took quite a while to get to each result, but the bottom line was confusing.

There was no semen found anywhere on Sandy or her underwear. There was no semen found on the bedspread. There was no blood on Mr. Flores' apparently dirty underwear or on the swabs from his penis or scrotum. That sounded pretty bad for Mr. Bolt's case, but he continued his methodic questioning.

Apparently several months later, Ms. Monroe was asked to examine some additional evidence from the crime scene. These included a wash cloth and the bottle of lubricant found hidden in the planter on the shelf above the toilet in the bathroom.

For the wash cloth, she used a fluorescent light and spotted stains. She meticulously removed a tiny sample from the stain area and tested for something called AP and P30 – components of seminal fluid, but nothing showed up. Then she tested for sperm which did show up in a very small quantity. She took some larger samples from the wash cloth and sent it to the DNA lab.

Once again, I was a bit disappointed in Mr. Bolt. After getting what he needed from Ms. Monroe, he kept going on and on about why she didn't test the entire washcloth or the entire stain, and why she didn't send the entire stain to the DNA lab. She explained all of this – how their procedures work and why it's not necessary, but he just wouldn't let it go. At one point he actually said, "I'm not suggesting you're not doing your job correctly." But he clearly was. By the end, she was getting pretty annoyed with him and from what I could see, the judge and the rest of the jury were as well.

Finally, after probably an hour of this, he moved on to the lubricant bottle which she just swabbed for DNA, and then to the comforter. This also took some time. She explained how she handled such a large piece of evidence, splitting it into sections and then uniquely identifying and examining both sides of each section, for blood and semen.

They spent a lot of time discussing how stains are identified, why one is sampled over another, why darker blood that transfers has more evidentiary value, and much more. And while it was all very interesting, at some point it became repetitive again. Mr. Bolt doesn't seem to know when to stop pushing, even his own witnesses. Bottom line, she found blood on the comforter but no semen.

When Ms. Preston took over, she was, as usual very professional and friendly. She basically took Ms. Monroe through each semen/sperm test on each swab and each piece of evidence. It was repetitive and we got the point quickly, but it was effective. There was no semen found anywhere on the swabs, on Sandy's underwear, or on Mr. Flores' underwear. There was also no blood on his underwear. Throughout the process, Ms. Preston was complimentary to Ms. Monroe and her professionalism.

I was a bit surprised when Mr. Bolt decided to redirect. This time he spent over an hour trying to get something out of Ms. Monroe about the lack of semen and the lack of a mix of semen and blood on the comforter as not being exonerating. Ms. Preston and the judge just wouldn't have it. Clearly, Ms. Monroe is someone who collects and analyses evidence. It's not her role to come to the conclusions that Mr. Bolt wanted.

Then Ms. Preston did a re-cross. Again, it was largely complementary about her procedures, but also got into how the DA's office can request additional testing. As it turns out, they requested a lot of additional testing on these and other pieces of evidence, but unfortunately, the tests proved fruitless. They didn't find anything new.

Then Mr. Bolt did another redirect and Ms. Preston did another re-cross and Mr. Bolt did another redirect and Ms. Preston did a short re-cross. It seemed like it would never end. These were all focused on the requests for additional testing and where they came from. I must admit to being confused about why they spent so much time going back and forth on this point.

One last note on Ms. Monroe's testimony. We had five questions from the jury. All of them were very helpful in understanding the process of getting evidence from the comforter.

So, at this point, we have tiny traces of sperm (but no semen) on the wash cloth. I guess we'll see where that goes. As we know, these particular wash cloths were used by Mr. Flores and his wife after sex – they keep them in their nightstand next to the bed. Then again, this one might have been used by Sandy to wash up afterwards.

14

2nd Juror – Barbara Hatch, mid-40s, ER nurse married, no kids.

I almost didn't make it to court today. I live in the Santa Cruz mountains and we had a mudslide on our road. There were also mudslides on San Jose – Soquel Road, my usual route into town. Our power was out and there's no cell service there, so I couldn't even call the court. We moved there 5 years ago and with the drought, we didn't fully realize what a 'normal' winter could be like. I'm definitely going to order a land line for the house. Little did I know that mobile and internet can't be relied on in the mountains.

With the road closures, I had to go thirty miles out of the way to get to court. Fortunately, part way there I was able to call the court and they held up the trial for me. I felt really guilty about that.

Arriving in Santa Cruz, I saw that the San Lorenzo river had overflowed its banks. The park next to the courthouse was several feet underwater and I was worried that the courthouse itself would get flooded. I decided to park on the upper level of a parking garage further away from the river. Of course I was soaked before I made it to court.

We still had to wait to get started since there was another juror stuck in the mountains. Ultimately, the judge decided to hold off until after lunch to start today's session.

All that stress this morning, only to wait to get started. But the trial has been like that. I'm sure other jurors wonder what goes on in the courtroom when we're asked to leave. Okay. It wasn't the case this time, but we do spend an awful lot of time in the hallway. At least today, it was fascinating to watch gigantic logs race by in the flooded river just outside the courthouse.

When court finally convened, we got to hear from the State's DNA expert witness, Denise Farrow.

Unlike Dr. Marcus, Denise Farrow doesn't have a PhD. She didn't help write the standards for DNA analysis, and clearly isn't as experienced as Dr. Marcus. Still, she seemed very competent and professional.

Mr. Bolt began his questioning, focusing on the SWGDAM standards for DNA analysis. He tried to talk about thresholds and how Ms. Farrow's lab uses 150 RFUs as their threshold, suggesting that a lower level might cause false results based on noise. But even without Ms. Preston's cross-examination, Ms. Farrow made it pretty clear that the 150 level selected by her lab was not necessarily perfect – that sometimes they could miss some DNA. I think Mr. Bolt was disappointed. He wasted a lot of time with Dr. Marcus, trying to impeach the idea of using something other than a 150 threshold, but anyone with any common sense could see that Dr. Marcus' more detailed analysis was just that.

Fortunately, seeing that he was getting nowhere on that front, this time, Mr. Bolt moved on and soon after establishing the fact that there was none of Sandy's DNA on any of Mr. Flores' samples, he focused on Sandy's underwear.

Apparently, Ms. Farrow found some male DNA on the front of the underwear. It didn't uniquely identify Mr. Flores, but it was a type of y-str male-only DNA found in about 1 in 120 Hispanic males. It follows family lines so any male relative of Mr. Flores would definitely have it. Still, for me, this looked pretty damning for Mr. Flores. That initial testimony took all of the afternoon and as we left the courtroom, I sensed that Mr. Bolt's case, which seemed to have been slipping, was back on track. It was most likely Mr. Flores' DNA on Sandy's underwear, not a male relative (we haven't heard about any relatives), and probably not some random Hispanic male with a 1 in 120 chance of sharing this particular feature.

The next morning, we started a bit late (again). After we were seated in the jury box, the judge announced that he had received a call from juror number 11, and that he was very ill. We had noticed him coughing for the past few days, and this week, it seemed to be getting worse. As a nurse, my guess was that he might have picked up pneumonia.

Anyway, he was excused, and a nice looking young man from the alternates was seated in his spot as the new juror number 11.

Apparently, when a juror is excused, they put the names of all the alternates in a hat and do a random draw. When he was announced, juror number 15 looked very happy. The other alternates seemed disappointed.

Of course if I were an alternate, I'd be happy to get on the main jury. I couldn't imagine going through all that we're going through, seeing all the evidence over the course of weeks, only to have zero input in the final outcome. Worse, there might not be closure.

I know that for me, and I'm sure it's true for most of us on the jury, including the alternates, this has been one of the most difficult experiences of my life. I've seen a lot in the ER, gunshot wounds, drug overdoses, suicide attempts, horrible accidents, as well as some of the impact on family and loved-ones of the victims. Watching young children suffer is always the worst. I've shed a lot of tears over the years, but at least I've had my colleagues and my husband to talk to. Talking really helps put things in perspective. You get to let go of it all, at least a bit.

But with the confidentiality orders that come with the trial, you see all these horrible things – pictures of a young girl's damaged genitals, close ups of the interior of her vagina and of her anal area. You think about what she went through, not just the alleged rape, but even if it didn't happen, the exams, the probing.

You add the family drama, an alcoholic father, a much older mother, the mother's phantom brother, the lies by the mother, but the young girls – it's just too much.

Sure, you think you could step back. We see violent movies and drama on TV all the time. But it's not like TV where you watch a show for at most an hour or two. You're living this most of your waking hours, five days a week and it's real. These are real people. Multiple lives are at stake.

I feel tremendous pressure to do the right thing – whatever that is. At the same time, I'm afraid I'll make a mistake, that I'll miss something. Maybe some of the others see what I might be missing. That's why talking about it would really help. But we can't.

If it's bad for me, I can't imagine what it's like for those who don't live with tragedy every day. At least I'm somewhat used to that part. I can get past that. For me it's the rest. Quite frankly, this trial scares me. I'm not sure why, but it does.

15

15th Juror – Mathias Wright, Silicon Valley engineer, early-thirties with 2 children under 5.

I'm in. I'm in!

God smiled upon me today and I see this as a clear sign. Flores is guilty. He's going to prison where he'll get what he deserves from the other inmates, then he'll burn in hell for all eternity. Yes!

I don't feel bad about the other juror number 11, but I must admit that I was a bit nervous about taking his seat. He'd been sick for quite a while and I certainly don't want to catch anything now.

I actually asked the judge if I could stay where I was in the alternate seat. He reluctantly agreed, but I have to go up into the box after lunch. I'll wipe down the seat with some disinfectant just to be on the safe side.

Today, we continued with the testimony from the State's DNA expert.

Mr. Bolt immediately jumped on the DNA testing threshold thing. Standards are standards. If the lab says you use 150 RFUs, you use 150 RFUs. That Dr. Marcus may very well have picked up noise by lowering her threshold. It doesn't prove that it was Alejandra's DNA on Flores' underwear. It could have been Sandy's.

But ultimately, that didn't matter. It's clear that male DNA that matches Flores was found on Sandy's underwear. If it wasn't sewn up for me before, it certainly is now and I'm sure most of the other jurors see it the same way.

Sure, that clever Ms. Preston tried to shoot down the evidence by pointing at other members of the family and even at one of the other DNA analysts who handled the samples. The expert testified that she herself had contaminated a few of the samples and that a male Hispanic expert had handled the one sample that showed male DNA, but that was just smoke.

I'm a bit worried about the quantity though. Ms. Preston got the expert to admit that of all the samples she tested, there was this marker on only one and that the quantity was so small that she had to use special equipment to see it at all.

Ms. Preston also got her to say that usually there is a lot more

DNA, particularly if fluids were involved, if there was rubbing, or significant touching.

She then pressed on where this was found, and it was on the outside of the underwear, not on the inside.

It was a good cross-examination, but hey, there was male y-str DNA indicators consistent with Flores on Sandy's underwear.

I guess the cross-examination about Flores' underwear was bothersome too. The expert confirmed that the only other DNA on that underwear (other than Flores') was Alejandra's.

She also had to admit that if she had chosen other samples or injections as she called them, they would have definitively excluded Sandy because the peak that showed up as either Sandy or Alejandra in the one she used for her findings was the only sample to have this ambiguity. The other two didn't. Ms. Preston didn't ask why she had chosen that particular one or why she didn't look at the others, but I'm afraid that some of the other jury members might look at it as a bias.

Then, one-by-one, she went through each swab taken from Sandy and the expert confirmed that there was no male DNA found.

As a final exclamation point, Ms. Preston got the expert to talk about the thresholds and after a long, drawn-out exchange, she admitted that the process used by Dr. Marcus was more thorough than hers, that Dr. Marcus used some sophisticated color filter that she has never used but had heard about to establish the thresholds. Any noise from the environment or equipment or chemicals would always be below that threshold. So, basically although the State's expert couldn't change her findings because she followed the rigorous procedures required by her lab, she couldn't contest Marcus' conclusions.

On redirect, Mr. Bolt emphasized the procedures that the expert followed and that her lab does so many DNA analyses, so they're the real experts. He also pointed out that her results were reviewed by her peers – other experts from the lab and that they were verified. Then he asked if she knew if Marcus's results were peer reviewed. Obviously, she didn't know. But he tried to sow some doubt about Marcus' conclusions. Lastly, Mr. Bolt tried to show that there were a lot of possibilities. I hate to admit it, but all he did was create some doubt about the DNA results – that there are a number of scenarios where DNA could have been transferred – or not. So Flores could have done it.

And then, Ms. Preston shot him down again. She got the expert to admit that she wasn't as familiar with more modern procedures that are part of SWGDAM. She referred her to several papers about setting thresholds and definitely threw some shade on the procedures of the lab itself, suggesting they could use an update. At the same time, she acknowledged that with the budgets and work load, it would be impossible for an expert like her to do the same job as Marcus did. Then, gene by gene (or peak by peak in the electropherograms, she went back through the analysis and compared Marcus' results to the expert's.

It took most of the afternoon, but in the end, the expert left feeling she had done her job but that her results were limited by her lab's procedures.

That Ms. Preston is smart. She dismantles a witness while the witness thinks she's been hugged by someone so terribly understanding. Preston is dangerous.

We spent the rest of the afternoon on the other State expert – the male Hispanic who did the sample from Sandy's swabs. He also did the DNA tests from the lubricant bottle, the bedspread, and the washcloth. Mr. Bolt took him through the same discussion about test procedures, injections, and thresholds and he came off as a bit more credible than the other expert. But I think Mr. Bolt blew it again.

It's almost as if he didn't know what the expert was going to say. He asked about the lubricant bottle. The expert said there wasn't enough DNA to reach any conclusions about it. Mr. Bolt pressed saying he couldn't exclude Flores. But the expert wouldn't have it. In spite of testifying for the State, he wouldn't let Mr. Bolt lead the jury to a conclusion based on non-evidence. He reiterated that there wasn't enough DNA to perform any valid tests.

For the bedspread, only Sandy's DNA was found, and for the washcloth, only Flores' and Alejandra's DNA were found. Nothing at all from Sandy on the washcloth. Mr. Bolt tried to make a point that DNA testing can't tell when the DNA was deposited so that it was possible that the DNA from Alejandra happened at a different time, but even to me, this was a stretch.

Obviously, Ms. Preston took him through all the details again, one-by-one, showing no DNA from Flores on anything. It was long and repetitive, but Preston got her point across.

Okay. Most of the DNA evidence isn't solid. But it doesn't

prove he didn't do it either. After all, Sandy washed up and changed her underwear, so it's not surprising none of Flores' DNA would be found on her or her underwear. The washcloth may not have been the one that Sandy used. If it had Alejandra and Flores' DNA on it, they had probably used it to clean up after one of their many sexual escapades. Flores probably got rid of the one that Sandy used just like he did with her underwear.

You know, at some point, you just have to believe a seven-year-old girl, her sister, and her mother. The lack of DNA doesn't prove anything. Even if it did, it doesn't matter. I'm on the real jury now and I'm not going to change my mind no matter what. Flores is toast.

16

13th Juror – Maria Fugetti, retired physician's assistant, late 60s, 3 grown children.

Even though we got out early, today seemed like one of the longest days of the trial.

It started out with cross-examination of that nice DNA expert, Ms. Farrow. She certainly has a difficult job, but she seems very good at it. Plus, she's testified in dozens of cases. I think she said she'd worked on over sixty. She's clearly the expert and she knows how to follow rules. I agree that Ms. Preston's questions about Dr. Marcus' techniques called into question some of the results, but the bottom line is what the Department of Justice lab concluded. Those are Ms. Farrow's results. While there wasn't much DNA, what they did find was consistent with Mr. Flores having raped poor little Sandy.

Our next witness was Frank Macdonald, the CSI officer. He explained how he collected all the forensic evidence from the apartment – the bedspread, the washcloth, the sheets, and everything they found during the search the evening they were called. He also talked about the techniques for using his ultraviolet lights, and how he packaged everything up for the lab. For me, it all was a bit boring. There were just too many details. Worse, several of the other members of the jury had questions, so he and the attorneys went into even more detail about what was examined, where he searched, what the bed looked like, how he found the washcloth and more. I'm not sure why they asked these questions or why the judge and the attorneys thought they were important enough to ask.

The next witness was a defense witness called out of order. The judge explained that this happens because of witness scheduling. It's clear this trial is running longer than expected and some of the witnesses now have scheduling conflicts.

Anyway, the next witness was Bernadette Ramsey, a victim advocate. I'm surprised she was a defense witness because she really just testified about how she tried to help the family after Mr. Flores was arrested.

Ms. Preston did make a point about the fact that Alejandra asked Ms. Ramsey for help with immigration problems that her son had saying that with her husband in jail, her son was her only support, so he couldn't be deported.

But again, almost all of the questions from Ms. Preston and Mr. Bolt were about her role and who she talked to. Officially, she represented Sandy, but since Sandy is a minor, she had to work through Alejandra who often asked for things that Ms. Ramsey couldn't provide.

I feel sorry for Ms. Ramsey. She's supposed to help these victims, but the State gives her no budget, no authority, and no real guidance for these horribly difficult situations.

I guess there was actually something to all of this. I now realize that Ms. Ramsey mentioned something about being able to request a letter to immigration for people who hadn't committed felonies.

During the re-direct-examination, Ms. Preston asked if they had provided a letter and her answer was no. Although it wasn't explicitly stated, it kind of implied that Alejandra's son Armando may have committed a felony.

During the re-cross-examination (I never realized this could go on and on), Mr. Bolt asked about the family's relocation, and although Ms. Ramsey said she wasn't involved in this one, she said that it was only done if there seemed to be a real threat to the safety, stability, or mental health of the victims. I guess that implied that the prosecution, the advocates, and the State felt that it was important to move the family.

For me, this was a lot to digest for the day.

But after lunch, the judge gave us the bad news. Because of the delays with the weather, with jurors being unable to get to court, and with availability of witnesses, the trial would likely go on a week longer than expected. He asked that if anyone had scheduling conflicts, we let the clerk know. I heard a lot of grumbling, but from what I could see, no one talked to the clerk at the end of the day.

Of course, it was a long time until the end of the day.

The first witness called in the afternoon was Margery Hampton, Mandy's teacher. She was another out-of-order defense witness. She testified that she had informed Child Protective Services about possible violence in Mandy's home. She described Mandy and also talked about having met Sandy. She did have some problems remembering details because this all happened more than two years before the rape – that's over five years ago.

Ms. Preston got her to describe Mandy and her changes in attitude over the first few months of the school year. She had her explain why she'd contacted CPS – that there was physical fighting going on where Albert and Alejandra would shout at each other and kick and hit each other. They argued about divorce and Mandy didn't feel safe. I understand that Ms. Preston was trying to make the point that this was an unhappy marriage and that divorce had been discussed even though in her testimony, Alejandra said they were happily married. But at the same time, I think Mr. Flores came off pretty bad. Ms. Preston seemed to emphasize that he was probably an abusive husband and father.

Mr. Bolt's questioning was even more confusing. He tried to make Alejandra look bad – like she was the cause of the fights. I really don't know what he was trying to accomplish. If anything, both Ms. Preston and Mr. Bolt seemed to be working against their own interests.

That wasn't enough for the day. The next witness was another out-of-order defense witness. This was Carrie, the driver. I'm not sure why she was called at all.

She was clearly hostile to both Mr. Bolt and to Ms. Preston. She couldn't remember anything. It appears that Mr. Bolt and Ms. Preston had previously talked with her in front of the judge and that she had told them that she had driven Sandy and Mandy home from school on the day that Sandy was raped. But now, she said she couldn't remember what day she drove them home. They also both asked her about how often she had driven the girls home, and while she apparently had previously told them and the judge that it was almost every day, now she was saying it was rare.

She denied being close friends with Alejandra until after the rape. As a final question, Ms. Preston asked her if she had been coming to court since the beginning of the trial to support Alejandra. She replied that she had.

I have no idea what that had to do with anything.

I think both attorneys were frustrated with her testimony and I think that I, along with the other jurors, was very confused about her. Why would she lie? She's not involved. She just drove the girls home from school. Then again, why did Alejandra lie? It just doesn't make any sense.

This case is very confusing. Mr. Flores is clearly guilty. Poor little Sandy was raped. No one is suggesting anyone else did it. But why are all these people telling lies? It just makes the overall case weaker. It might even give some of the other jurors reasonable doubt. But these lies are coming from the prosecution witnesses. Don't they see that they're hurting the case against Mr. Flores. They clearly want him convicted. I admit. I just don't get it.

And, we still weren't done for the day – at least not officially. We took our afternoon break, and when we returned, Mr. Bolt called Nurse Hernandez. She's the Spanish-speaking nurse that assisted in the physical exam of Sandy. She's also the nurse that spoke to Mandy and who Mandy told about being abused when she was younger.

After going through the preliminaries of getting her background and experience, Mr. Bolt started asking questions about Nurse Hernandez's role in the physical exam of Sandy. She said she just assisted with positioning. He then asked if Sandy had said anything about something similar happening to Mandy and before she could answer, the judge stopped everything. He sent the jury out of the courtroom and said they needed ten minutes. But it wasn't ten minutes.

An hour later, the Bailiff called us back in and the judge told us that their discussions were more complicated than they'd thought and would likely take the rest of the afternoon and part of the morning. We were to return at 10:30 the next morning, not 10am as usual.

What could be going on there? This case just gets stranger and stranger.

17

12th Juror – Steve Dietz, engineer in Santa Cruz startup, early-thirties no kids. Father is a lawyer.

What a waste of time. I know I'm biased against defense attorneys. But I'll tell you. I'm really biased against good defense attorneys. And after following my father's cases over the years. I can tell you that this Patricia Preston is definitely one of the best. I'm really surprised she's working for the Public Defender's Office. She could easily be making seven figures doing litigation defense with a private law firm.

She's smart. Very smart. She's also prepared. Bolt looks like a buffoon compared to her. He stumbles over questions, doesn't listen to responses from the witnesses, backtracks and asks the same questions over again, and often undermines his own case with his stupidity. Still, when you've got a rock-solid case on such an emotional issue, conviction is a slam dunk, even with all the mistakes.

But that Ms. Preston. She never hesitates. She listens to answers and follows up brilliantly. She is also ridiculously good at making a hostile witness comfortable, then getting them to cut their own throats. That's what happened today.

Bolt called Nurse Hernandez, the nurse who assisted with Sandy's exam and who talked to Mandy afterward. She is the one who got the whole Mandy thing going. I'm not sure if anything actually happened there, but it certainly added fire to the accusations about Sandy. And, as I mentioned before, is one of the ways the jury can get to life in prison without the possibility of parole – that's if the State proves that he's done this more than once with multiple victims.

Something happened yesterday. Nurse Hernandez was called, then the judge asked to speak with the attorneys outside the presence of the jury. We left the courtroom for what was supposed to be a ten minute break.

I had a feeling it was going to be longer. Normally, it's the attorneys who ask for a sidebar or a conversation with the judge. Part of the fun for me in this trial is guessing what goes on in the sidebars and behind closed door. I think I'm pretty good at it because when an attorney requests a sidebar, usually testimony resumes in the same direction, or it stops and changes direction.

It's obvious what happened and what was discussed – usually evidentiary rules – things which are excluded from the trial.

But when it's the judge, it's usually something pretty serious. It's not just a disagreement between the attorneys, it's something the court is concerned about. Something that goes directly to the law in the case or to the possibility that a mistake has been made that could cause a reversal on appeal.

With Nurse Hernandez, I have no idea what it could have been. And I was right. Not only did we wait more than promised ten minutes, after an hour, we were called back in only to be sent home (and asked to return in the morning later than normal).

I followed the testimony closely the next day and I still don't have a clue.

Bolt took Nurse Hernandez through her interview in Spanish with Alejandra before the SART exam, then her role in the exam itself. He had her explain how Sandy had told her that her sister Mandy had been molested by Flores and how she came to interview Mandy.

One new piece of information, which wasn't that significant, was that she was the one who did the SART exam on Flores.

That took the morning since we started late. At the lunch break, I walked out with Matt, who now sits next to me in the jury box. We've had lunch together a few times since the beginning of the trial. He's about my age and we have a common love of World of Warcraft which we play remotely some evenings. We're also on the same side in this case.

I've heard some grumbling from other jurors that leads me to believe that some of them may think that Bolt is incompetent. I may agree, but as I said, this is a slam-dunk case for the prosecution.

Matt and I have discussed it at length over lunches. Yeah, I know. We're not supposed to do that but hey, why not? We're just clarifying testimony. We spent most of today's lunch talking about what happened behind closed doors, so this conversation was completely innocuous. Since neither of us has the faintest idea, in spite of several far-fetched theories, our discussion clearly doesn't affect the outcome of the case or our decisions on how to vote in the jury box.

On that note, I'm glad Matt is now on the main panel. He may be a bit too religious, but at least he's not one of these crazy progressives who think the courts are there to persecute poor minorities. Like me, he believes in law and order.

After lunch, it was Preston's turn to cross examine Nurse Hernandez. It started off pretty innocuously as Preston got her to confirm that Flores clearly hadn't showered in a while, that his clothes were dirty, and that she had swabbed him thoroughly. This was her way of saying that there should have been DNA found on him.

She then tried to confuse us, the jury, and Nurse Hernandez with the forms from the interview with Alejandra. From her testimony, it was obvious that Alejandra was being honest (for once) during the interview when she told Nurse Hernandez that she didn't know what had happened between Flores and Sandy; that Sandy said that Flores had 'touched' her. When asked whether it was a finger, a penis, or an object, Alejandra said she didn't know. But on the form, Hernandez checked "Don't Know' for the penis and object, but checked yes for finger.

She tried to explain that Alejandra never said 'finger' but that she'd checked that box because by the process of elimination, 'touched' implied 'finger'.

Okay. It was pretty weak. The woman made a mistake for God's sake. It doesn't change the fact that Alejandra saw that her daughter was bleeding from her vaginal area.

I don't think many of the other jurors latched onto this as some sort of incompetence or a change in the facts – 'finger' to penetration with a penis.

If anything, I suspect Preston just used that to shake Hernandez's confidence as she moved into the more sensitive area.

You know, these nurses have a tough job. They look at sexual assault victims and they want to help them. They want to make sure that the perpetrators are stopped so the children can be protected from them.

If I were a nurse and saw what was obviously an injury consistent with rape and if the seven-year-old victim said that her father did it, I'd certainly ask if anything like this had happened before to her or her sister. And, if the victim responded that it might have happened to her sister, I'd certainly follow up with the sister.

Yeah, I know that there are rules about contamination – predisposing people, particularly children, to tell you what you want to hear. And I know that it does require special training to deal with situations like this – Ms. Preston made it abundantly clear that Nurse Hernandez lacked that training – but come on. This is a kid who's been raped by her father. Her sister has been molested by him. Do you just let it go? Restrict yourself to the physical exam? Sometimes doing your job is more than that. And sometimes, you just have to do the right thing, even if it means breaking some overly restrictive rules.

And as I said, Preston is very good. I'm sure most of the jury thinks that Nurse Hernandez was wrong in what she did – that she contaminated Mandy and got her to say what Nurse Hernandez wanted to hear.

But for me, what was worse was that Preston dismantled Nurse Hernandez. The poor nurse left the stand feeling incompetent in spite of Bolt's feeble attempts to shore her up.

Like I said, Preston is dangerous. Nurse Hernandez is just one of many who have cut their own throats under Preston's incisive cross-examinations.

18

7th Juror – Sue Markovsky, late 40s, unmarried, no children, recent arrival to the area. Political activist.

Am I back in LA? Is it the last century?

I thought this was Santa Cruz, one of the most liberal cities in the country. I thought the Santa Cruz police were there to help people, that they had a good understanding of the plight of immigrants because there are so many here.

Yes, I was pleased with how the police handled the family when called upon the scene. Even in the hospital, their behavior was impeccable. They were thorough and fair, doing their best to objectively collect information.

And you know, even after the testimony of Lieutenant Cardova, formerly Sergeant Cordova and the testimony of Detective Frank Lopez, I must say that these officers are very good at their jobs. But still, that interrogation, I can't believe what I saw. If it had been me instead of Albert Flores, I would have confessed to putting my penis into my daughter's vagina, and I'm a woman.

Sorry. Let me back up. I'm just so outraged at what we've seen the past two days. I've been involved in a lot of police interrogations in my role as advocate and while working for my father, but the interrogations of Albert were the roughest I've ever seen. I'll get back to that in a few minutes.

The last few days have been tough. We spent the majority of our time watching interviews of Albert by Lieutenant Cardova, Lieutenant Finnegan, and Detective Lopez. Interestingly though, Both Lieutenant Cardova and Detective Lopez interviewed Alejandra as well. Lieutenant Cardova interviewed Alejandra in the hospital, and Detective Lopez interviewed her and Sandy and Mandy a few days later along with Detective Locke.

I guess the only real revelation in those interviews was that once again, Alejandra changed her story. With Lieutenant Cardova at the hospital, she said that Albert had never molested Mandy and that there had never been any incidents of that type with the family. There was no 'rule'.

With Detective Lopez, all that changed. I think Ms. Preston did a great job of once again showing Alejandra's inconsistency, or perhaps that Alejandra's story evolved over time.

Okay. So on with the interrogations.

The first interrogation happened the morning after the alleged incident. They picked up Albert and Nurse Hernandez conducted the SART exam and evidence collection. Then he was taken to the Santa Cruz jail where unfortunately, there were no cells or beds or cots available. At a little after 4am, he was taken to an interrogation cell where he was handcuffed to a metal chair. They left him alone for an hour before Lieutenant (then Sergeant) Cordova came in. Both had been up all night with no sleep and it showed.

As Lieutenant Cordova began his interview in Spanish, he came off as Albert's best friend. Obviously, Albert was a hard working good father who had started with nothing when he came to the States. Lieutenant Cordova seemed like he admired Albert. He joked around and established solid rapport. This continued as the conversation moved to the events of the previous evening.

Lieutenant Cordova seemed honestly surprised by what Alejandra and Sandy had said. Albert appeared confused. After the first few hours, it seemed to me that Albert had no idea what had happened. He thought that Alejandra had claimed spousal abuse and that was why he'd been arrested. Watching him closely and using my fluent Spanish to fully understand not just the words, but the tone, I believed him.

Over the course of the next several hours, Lieutenant Cordova employed what he and Mr. Bolt called ruses (and what Ms. Preston called lies) to try to get Albert to confess. He even promised him that if Albert just admitted what he'd done, he could be home with his family for Christmas.

Of course it didn't stop there. Towards the end of the six hours of interrogation, Lieutenant Cordova brought in the 'bad' cop: Lieutenant Aragon, the head of the SART team.

He told Albert that they had proof that he had raped Sandy and would spend the rest of his life in prison. Lieutenant Cordova then told Albert that if he just admitted his mistake, all would be forgiven. After all, it was just a mistake but as police, they just needed to be thorough and confirm that Sandy wasn't lying. Through it all, through countless ruses, and even more threats from Lieutenant Aragon, Albert said he never harmed his daughter. He honestly believed that Alejandra was accusing him of this because of their fight about divorce and custody of the children.

So okay, this was a 'reasonable' interrogation. I'm well aware of the techniques the police use to interrogate suspects. But the interrogation that really got my blood boiling was the one with Detective Lopez.

Like Lieutenant Cordova, Detective Lopez started out as Albert's best friend. But seeing he wasn't going to get too far, it quickly turned confrontational. In spite of the fact that he had no evidence, Detective Lopez told Albert that in addition to what Alejandra and Sandy had said, that they had found his semen in Sandy's vagina and that they had verified that his DNA was all over Sandy. He was guilty. Now he needed to be a man, and admit his mistake.

But Albert wouldn't have it. He said it was impossible. There couldn't be any evidence because he didn't do anything to Sandy.

There's a fine line between interrogation and coercion and Detective Lopez walked it very well. But it was close. I found him verbally abusive, and the interrogation went on and on. When Detective Lopez got tired or needed a break, he brought in Lieutenant Finnegan who proceeded to interrogate Albert in English.

Albert did his best to answer all the questions. He tried to be helpful, but it was clear that his English was not up to par. At one point, Lieutenant Finnegan asked Albert about his kids schooling, and Albert responded about his own schooling in El Salvador.

Through most of the interrogation, the two policemen ganged up on Albert going back and forth between Spanish and English in non-stop accusations. Oh, and did I mention that they had Albert in shackles? His hands and feet were cuffed and chained together and this lasted for ten – TEN – hours.

A few things stood out.

During the middle of the interrogation when they weren't getting anywhere, Detective Lopez suggested that Albert take a lie detector test. Although it's not admissible in court, the offer is a technique used to put the suspect in a difficult position – if he doesn't take it, he must be lying. But in spite of his obvious exhaustion, Albert asked for the lie detector test. He said it would prove his innocence. But since the policemen were bluffing, there was no test.

Then there was the recurrent questioning about whether Sandy was a liar. Over and over they reiterated Sandy's story.

Often they embellished it. Then they'd ask if Sandy was a liar and every time Albert would reply that of course she was not a liar. They'd then press and ask that if she wasn't lying then he must have raped her and that if he was a real man, an honest man, he'd admit to it. But he didn't.

For me, they missed something critical about many Hispanic cultures. I was kind of surprised that Detective Lopez didn't get it, but maybe it's because he's first generation – he was raised here and maybe his parents didn't push Catholic upbringing.

But in my experience, no parent is going to call his or her child a liar. Lying is a sin in the Catholic Church and it made sense to me that Albert refused to call Sandy a liar.

Perhaps if they'd played it a little softer they might have gotten a better response. But as it was, it did seem confusing – Albert claimed he didn't do it, but he wouldn't say his daughter was lying when she accused him of raping her.

I suspect this was lost on most of the other jurors. Not calling his daughter a liar suggests that she wasn't lying and that he might be guilty.

Towards the end of the interrogation, after nearly ten hours, Albert was very confused. He made a statement that the prosecution seized on. After being inundated with the 'evidence' that they had against him, all the forensic proof, the DNA, his semen, all of the evidence they had against him, Albert said that if they really had all this evidence, he might have forgotten that he did it since there was no other way to explain the evidence.

Me, I saw it as exhaustion, confusion, and frustration, and to some degree a challenge – show me the evidence. But, others might have seen it as the first break in Albert's unshakeable story.

Like I said, if I had gone through ten hours of abusive interrogation, in two languages, one of which I barely understood, if I had been doing my best to cooperate, to get to the truth, and if I'd been confronted with 'proof', I too would have begun to question my sanity, or at least what I knew to be true.

I don't know. I started out believing Albert was guilty. The prosecution has had so many witnesses who seemed convinced and who did a good job of convincing us.

On the other hand, Ms. Preston has impeached quite a few and has certainly cast some doubt.

And now, after watching Albert stand up to this heavy

interrogation, I'm leaning towards innocent. I'll try to keep an open mind. He may be guilty. After all, why would Alejandra and the girls have stood by such a horrendous accusation if it isn't true.

Then again, Albert certainly doesn't behave like a guilty man.

19

5th Juror – Melissa Duplisse , early 70s, retired nurse.

Watching these videos is really hard. The ones with Alejandra were all in Spanish. We're given transcripts with translations, but they're very hard to follow. I mean, the person being interviewed is speaking in Spanish. How are we expected to match words we don't understand with written English? I found it confusing with Alejandra, and even more confusing with Mr. Flores.

At least for Mr. Flores' interrogations, the officers who conducted them were present. As they played the videos in Spanish, we tried to read the English translation while simultaneously watching the videos to see Mr. Flores' demeanor. I don't think it worked very well, particularly since the interrogations went on for so long. It took us almost two days to get through the two interrogations.

That poor man. I do feel sorry for him. Those interrogations were horrible. I know that I couldn't have maintained my innocence under that kind of abuse. But Mr. Flores did. Not only did he not give in to the verbal challenges and abuse, he remained calm throughout. That was impressive.

But maybe Mr. Flores was too calm. As I think about it, it was like he'd done this before and understood police tactics during an interrogation. In spite of being shackled hand and feet, he kind of sat back and let them play their good cop – bad cop routines for hours on end. Me, I found it exhausting just to watch, but it didn't seem to affect him.

I think maybe he's just a great actor and a great liar. I still find it hard to believe he's not guilty.

CHAPTER 4

THE DEFENSE

"The prosecution wants to make sure the process by which the evidence was obtained is not truthfully presented, because, as often as not, that process will raise questions."
- Alan Dershowitz

1

4th Juror – Evan Garcia, mid-40s, Hispanic, Silicon Valley Entrepreneur, film fanatic. Unmarried no children.

I can't believe it's almost over.

After more than seven weeks of the prosecution's case with just a few defense witnesses, Ms. Preston's defense consisted of just one witness, Albert Flores.

Throughout the trial, I was pretty convinced that Albert would not take the stand. I don't know if you remember, but the questionnaires we filled out at the beginning of jury selection placed a lot of emphasis on the fact that it is up to the prosecution to prove guilt beyond a reasonable doubt and that the defense doesn't have to prove anything.

During voir dire, Ms. Preston asked almost everyone if they thought the defendant needed to testify to prove his innocence. I think that a few people were excused over their answers to that question. So clearly, we were being prepped for no testimony from Albert.

Today, we learned a lot more about Albert. Yes, we had heard bits and pieces, but they were always from other people's perspectives. This time, we heard directly from Albert, or, perhaps more correctly, most of the jury heard directly from the translator.

Ms. Preston led him through his life story.

Albert dropped out of school in the 5th grade (we'd heard about this during the cross examination of Lieutenant Cardova when Ms. Preston basically asked if it was fair to have someone with an advanced degree use interrogations techniques on someone with a 5th grade education).

Anyway, Albert worked in the fields of El Salvador. He was afraid of the police and learned that you never contradicted the police or you could disappear forever.

When he was fifteen, Albert's uncle helped him move to Santa Cruz where Albert began working for a landscaping service with his uncle.

A year later, a family friend moved to Santa Cruz from El Salvador. Her name was Alejandra and she was thirty-three years old at the time. Within a year, they were married, and two years later Alejandra gave birth to Mandy followed by Sandy three years after that.

Albert worked hard at the landscaping service while Alejandra worked for a housecleaning company. They had a very active sex life. When Albert was in his late twenties and Alejandra was in her forties, they started having problems. Alejandra was jealous. She wore the pants in the family.

Albert became a supervisor in the landscaping company, managing a team, but at home, he did Alejandra's bidding. This got increasingly frustrating for him, especially with her jealous rages.

At some point, Armando, Alejandra's son from a former marriage, who was the same age as Albert, left El Salvador and moved in with them. He and Albert did not get along. During this time, Mandy and Sandy slept in the same room as their parents while Armando took the other bedroom.

One day, Albert came home early from work and found Armando smoking weed with the girls in the same room. He threw Armando out of the house. The problems with Alejandra worsened.

Armando was arrested multiple times and Albert forbade him from coming to the apartment or seeing the girls.

One Halloween, a couple of years before the incident with Sandy, Albert had gone trick-or-treating with the girls, then after they got home, he went to a party with some friends who lived nearby. While he was walking home, he was shot in a drive-by by someone who mistakenly thought he was a gang member. After that, Albert refused to go out on Halloween.

This apparently led to the fight on the night before the incident with Sandy. Albert refused to go out with Alejandra and the girls. But, what may have triggered all of this is that some friends came by and dragged Albert to a party. When he got home, Alejandra attacked him – verbally and physically.

They eventually made it to bed and even had sex in the morning (apparently they did this every day whether they were speaking to each other or not (and Alejandra confirmed this)).

For the rest, the events were as you may have heard.

Alejandra was running late in the morning so Albert took the girls to school. When Albert got a call from Mandy's friend's mother asking if Mandy could join them on a play date, Albert called Alejandra who said that this was all arranged, that Carrie would bring the girls home.

They agreed that Albert would take Sandy fishing with him near the harbor and would bring her home a bit after five pm. He needed to stop at his storage unit to pick up some tools for a job he'd be doing on Saturday for his nascent new startup business.

All went as planned. He got home. Alejandra was there. He grabbed another beer and started watching television.

At some point, Alejandra attacked him again, saying that she knew he'd been with a woman the night before. The fighting escalated as it always did with each slapping and kicking the other. Albert threatened to divorce her and to take the children.

Alejandra started to dial 911 saying she was going to report Albert for spousal abuse. He took the phone from her, hung it up, gave it back to her and left the apartment as he always did when they had these kinds of fights.

He drove to Ben's Market, bought a twelve pack and sat in his car drinking until he fell asleep.

He woke up later and called Alejandra to see if it was okay if he came home. She told him she was at the hospital with Sandy and he wanted to know why. She hung up on him.

Not long afterwards, the police knocked on his window and arrested him. He thought that Alejandra had called them and claimed spousal abuse.

Ms. Preston asked the expected questions: She asked about the jail calls. She asked about the 'not remembering' during the interrogation. And, of course, she asked, Did you rape Sandy? Did you molest Mandy? As you'd expect, Albert said with conviction that he hadn't. That he still didn't understand why he'd been accused of this and had his life ruined.

You know, I believed him.

And then Mr. Bolt started his cross-examination.

I think he knew that he had to break Albert, that Albert had come across as credible. He went after him hard with Ms. Preston frequently objecting saying that Mr. Bolt was badgering the witness. He was and these objections were usually sustained.

Mr. Bolt attacked Albert for not asking the police why he was being arrested. Obviously he knew. Albert responded that he thought he was being arrested for spousal abuse, something Alejandra had threatened to do before.

Mr. Bolt tried to get Albert to say that he and Alejandra had a good marriage, that they didn't fight and that they certainly hadn't discussed divorce. Again, no luck.

He pressed on the jail calls where Albert seemed to admit guilt. Was he recanting now? Albert stated that he would have said anything to get Alejandra to post bail and to let him come home – that they could get past the arguments and that he wouldn't threaten divorce or to take the kids away from her – that's what he was talking about when he asked her to forgive him.

Mr. Bolt threatened Albert with having violated the restraining orders by calling Alejandra. Albert said that he was desperate, and worried about his family and how they would pay the bills. During one of the calls, he advised Alejandra to sell his truck and tools to pay the rent.

Mr. Bolt then focused on the interrogations: why he wouldn't say Sandy was a liar – that must mean that Albert was guilty. But Albert wouldn't say anything negative about any of his family, even Alejandra. And Mr. Bolt pressed hard on that, trying to get him to say anything negative.

Then, when things weren't going as he expected, Mr. Bolt made the mistake that for me lost him all credibility. He accused Albert of pretending he didn't understand English. He accused him of not needing a translator that Albert was just playing at being the ignorant immigrant. And he started badgering him, saying that Albert clearly understood everything he was saying, that during the interrogations, he understood English – he was nodding his head when Lieutenant Aragon was talking to him in English. There were objections galore which were sustained, and at one point, the judge admonished Mr. Bolt, reminding him and us, the jury, that the defendant had the right to a translator.

I admit, this pissed me off. I looked around the jury box and even those jurors that I'm pretty sure believe Albert is guilty were looking at their shoes. They were embarrassed for Mr. Bolt.

I don't know if you speak another language. I'm bilingual in Spanish and English. I also speak pretty good French and German. I can get by in those countries when travelling.

But you know, I have to admit that a lot of the time, I don't understand everything. And what do I do when I don't understand? I nod my head as if I do. It's only natural. I'd be willing to bet that Mr. Bolt only speaks English. Otherwise, he wouldn't have made such a huge, embarrassing mistake which, I don't think I mentioned, went on for almost an hour.

Ms. Preston did a redirect, reemphasizing Albert's responses and taking any of Mr. Bolts minor points off the board. And of course, Mr. Bolt tried to re-cross, but it didn't go well. There's a lot of evidence that points to guilt, but I can tell you, Mr. Bolt seemed almost like he wanted to sabotage his own case with this abusive cross-examination of a man who certainly appears to be doing his best to tell the truth.

From my point of view, the prosecution's case in in tatters.

CHAPTER 5

CLOSING ARGUMENTS

Note from the author: Once again, I've included actual transcripts. I thought it was important for you to see the actual closing words of the attorneys, particularly the prosecutor's. He made a strong case in closing. He does go a bit long though. I've tried to break it up with some jurors thoughts during the closing, but you might want to skip ahead if it gets too slow for you. At that point, you'll have a good handle on the prosecutor and how he's arguing his case. Plus, since he gets to do a final closing after the defense closing, you can get the really important points there. In other words, don't be afraid to skip ahead.

Also, I've included the Judge's instructions because they give detailed explanations of the charges and how they're to be judged by the law. You may want to skim or skip the judge's instructions because the prosecutor pretty much repeats them in his closing argument and because you may find the detailed definitions either boring or perhaps too explicit. Then again, I found them useful to refer back to, particularly during deliberations. And as before, I've removed line and page numbers from the transcripts for readability.

1

THE COURT: Let's go on the record, please, regarding People versus Mr. Flores. Mr. Flores is present. Counsel are present. All of our jurors are present.

You have received the initial set of instructions. I will now provide you with the balance of the instructions that relate to the counts themselves.

The defendant is charged in **Count 1**, at the apartment, and **12,** while fishing, with engaging in sexual intercourse with a child under ten years of age or younger.

To prove that the defendant is guilty of this crime, the People must prove that: Number one, the defendant engaged in an act of sexual intercourse with Sandy; number two, when the defendant did so Sandy was ten years of age or younger; number three, at the time of the act the defendant was at least 18 years old.

Under the law, a person becomes one year older as soon as the first minute of his or her birthday has begun.

"Sexual intercourse" means any penetration, no matter how slight, of the vagina or genitalia by the penis. Ejaculation is not required.

The defendant is charged in **Count 2** with engaging in sexual penetration with a child under ten years of age or younger at the apartment.

To prove that the defendant is guilty of this crime, the People must prove that: Number one, the defendant engaged in an act of sexual penetration with Sandy; number two, when the defendant did so Sandy was ten years of age or younger; number three, at the time of the act the defendant was at least 18 years old.

Under the law, a person becomes one year older as soon as the first minute of his or her birthday has begun.

"Sexual penetration" means penetration, however slight, of the genital or anal opening of the other person by any foreign object, substance, instrument or device, or by any unknown object, for the purpose of sexual abuse, arousal or gratification. "Penetration for sexual abuse" means penetration for the purpose of causing pain, injury or discomfort.

An unknown object includes any foreign object, substance,

instrument or device, or any part of the body, including a penis, if it is not known what object penetrated the opening.

A foreign object, substance, instrument or device includes any part of the body except a sexual organ.

The defendant is charged in **Counts 3**, at the apartment, and **14**, while fishing, with aggravated sexual assault, forcible rape, of a child who is under the age of 14 years and at least seven years younger than the defendant.

To prove that the defendant is guilty of this crime, the People must prove that: Number one, the defendant committed rape by force or fear on Sandy; and, two, when the defendant acted Sandy was under the age of 14 years and was at least seven years younger than the defendant.

To decide whether the defendant committed rape by force or fear, please refer to the separate instructions that I will give you on that crime.

Under the law, a person becomes one year older as soon as the first minute of his or her birthday has begun.

The defendant is charged in **Count 4** with rape by force. Rape by force is charged as the lesser included offense to aggravated sexual assault upon a child as charge in Count 3. Rape by force is also a lesser included offense to aggravated sexual assault upon a child as charged in Count 14.

To prove that the defendant is guilty of rape by force, the People must prove that: Number one, the defendant had sexual intercourse with Sandy; number two, he and Sandy were not married to each other at the time of the intercourse; number three, Sandy did not consent to the intercourse; and number four, the defendant accomplished the intercourse by force, violence, duress menace or fear of immediate and unlawful bodily injury to Sandy or to someone else.

"Sexual intercourse" means any penetration, no matter how slight, of the vagina or genitalia by the penis. Ejaculation is not required.

To consent, a woman must act freely and voluntarily and know the nature of the act.

Intercourse is accomplished by force if a person uses enough physical force to overcome the woman's will.

"Duress" means a direct or implied threat of force, violence, danger or retribution that would cause a reasonable person to do or submit to something that she would not do or submit to otherwise.

When deciding whether the act was accomplished by duress, consider all the circumstances, including the woman's age and relationship to the defendant.

"Retribution" is a form of payback or revenge. "Menace" means a threat, statement or act showing an intent to injure someone.

Intercourse is accomplished by fear if the woman is actually and reasonably afraid, or she is actually, but unreasonably, afraid and the defendant knows of her fear and takes advantage of it

The defendant is charged in **Counts 5**, Sandy at the apartment, **6**, Sandy at the apartment, **11**, Mandy, and **13**, Sandy while fishing, with a lewd or lascivious act by force or fear on a child under the age of 14 years.

To prove that the defendant is guilty of this crime, the People must prove that: Number one, the defendant willfully touched any part of a child's body, either on the bare skin or through the clothing; number two, in committing the act the defendant used force, violence, duress, menace or fear of immediate and unlawful bodily injury to the child or someone else; number three, the defendant committed the act with the intent of arousing, appealing to or gratifying the lusts, passions or sexual desires of himself or the child; and, four, the child was under the age of 14 years at the time of the act.

Someone commits an act willfully when he or she does it willingly or on purpose. It is not required that he or she intend to break the law, hurt someone else, or gain any advantage. Actually arousing, appealing to, or gratifying the lusts, passions or sexual desires of the perpetrator or child is not required for lewd or lascivious conduct.

The force used must be substantially different from or substantially greater than the force needed to accomplish the act itself.

"Duress" mean the use of a direct or implied threat of force, violence, danger, hardship or retribution sufficient to cause a reasonable person to do or submit to something that he or she would otherwise – would not otherwise do or submit to. When deciding whether the act was accomplished by duress, consider all the circumstances, including age of the child and his relationship - or her relationship to the defendant. "Retribution" is a form of payback or revenge.

"Menace" means a threat, statement or act showing an intend to injury someone.

An act is accomplished by fear if the child is actually and reasonably afraid, or he or she is actually but unreasonably afraid and the defendant knows of this fear and takes advantage of it. It is not a defense that the child may have consented to the act. Unless the law, a person becomes one year older as soon as the first minute of his or her birthday has begun.

The crime of lewd or lascivious act on a child under the age of 14 years is a lesser included offense to the crime of lewd or lascivious act by force or fear on a child under the age of 14 years, as charged in **Counts 5, 6, 11 and 13**:

To prove that the defendant is guilty of this crime, the People must prove that: Number one, the defendant willfully touched any part of a child's body, either on the bare skin or through the clothing; number two, the defendant committed the act with the intent of arousing, appealing to or gratifying the lusts, passions or sexual desires of himself or the child; and number three, the child was under the age of 14 years at the time of the act.

The touching need not be done in a lewd or sexual manner. Someone commits an act willfully when he or she does it willingly or on purpose. It is not required that he or she intend to break the law, hurt someone else or gain any advantage.

Actually arousing, appealing to or gratifying the lusts, passions or sexual desires of the perpetrator or child is not required for lewd or lascivious conduct.

It is not a defense that the child may have consented to the act.

Under the law, a person becomes one year older as soon as the first minute of his or her birthday has begun.

The defendant is charged in **Count 7** with false imprisonment of Alejandra Rivera. To prove that the defendant is guilty of this crime, the People prove that: Number one, the defendant intentionally and unlawfully confined Alejandra Rivera; and, number two, the defendant's act made Alejandra Rivera stay or go somewhere against her will.

An act is done against a person's will if that person does not consent to the act. In order to consent, a person must act freely and voluntarily and know the nature of the act.

False imprisonment does not require that the person be restrained or detained or confined in jail or prison.

The defendant is charged in **Count 8** with concealing or destroying evidence. To prove that the defendant is guilty of this crime, the People must prove that: Number one, the defendant intentionally and unlawfully destroyed or concealed any object, matter, thing, record; and, number two, the defendant acted with the intent to prevent the item from being produced in evidence at any trial, inquiry or investigation authorized by law.

The defendant is charged in **Count 9** with aggravated sexual assault, sexual penetration of a child who is under the age of 14 years and at least seven years younger than the defendant. To prove that the defendant is guilty of this crime, the People must prove that: Number one, the defendant committed sexual penetration by force on Mandy; and two, when the defendant acted, Mandy was under the age of 14 years and was at least seven years younger than the defendant.

To decide whether the defendant committed an aggravated sexual assault of a child, sexual penetration, who is under the age of 14 years and at least seven years younger than the defendant, please refer to the separate instructions that I will give you on that crime.

Under the law, a person becomes one year older as soon as the first minute of his or her birthday has begun.

The defendant is charged in **Count 10** with sexual penetration by force. Sexual penetration by force as charged in Count 10 is a lesser included offense to aggravated sexual assault upon a child as charged in Count 9.

To prove that the defendant is guilty of sexual penetration by force, the People must prove that: Number one, the defendant committed an act of sexual penetration with Mandy; two, the penetration was accomplished by using a foreign object; three, Mandy did not consent to the act; and, four, the defendant accomplished the act by force, violence, duress, menace or fear of immediate and unlawful bodily injury to another person. "Sexual penetration" means penetration, however slight, of the genital or anal opening of the other person for the purpose of sexual abuse, arousal or gratification.

A foreign object, substance, instrument or device includes any part of the body except a sexual organ.

In order to consent, a person must act freely and voluntarily and know the nature of the act.

An act is accomplished by force if a person uses enough

physical force to overcome the other person's will. "Duress" means the direct or implied threat of force, violence, danger, hardship or retribution that is enough to cause a reasonable person of ordinary sensitivity to do or submit to something that he or she would not otherwise do or submit. When deciding whether the act was accomplished by duress, consider all of the circumstances, including the age of the other person and her relationship to the defendant.

"Retribution" is a form of payback or revenge. "Menace" means a threat, statement or act showing an intent to injure someone. An act is accomplished by fear if the other person is actually and reasonably afraid, or if she is actually but unreasonably afraid and the defendant knows of her fear and takes advantage of it.

If you find the defendant guilty of two or more sex offenses as charged in Counts 1, 2, 3, 4, 5, 6, 9, 10, 11, 12, 13 and 14, you must then decide whether the People have proved the additional allegation that those crimes were committed against more than one victim.

The People have the burden of proving this allegation beyond a reasonable doubt. If the People have not met this burden, you must find this allegation has not been proved.

If you find the defendant guilty of the crimes charged in Counts 1, 2, 3, 4, 5 and 6, you must decide whether, for each crime, the People have proved the additional allegation that the defendant personally inflicted bodily harm on Sandy in the commission of that crime. You must decide whether the People have proved this allegation for each crime and return a separate finding for each crime.

"Bodily harm" means any substantial physical injury resulting from the use of force that is more than the force necessary to commit the offense.

The People have the burden of proving each allegation beyond a reasonable doubt. If the People have not met this burden, you must find that the allegation has not been proved. The defendant is charged with concealing or destroying evidence in Count 8, and lewd or lascivious act by force upon a child under 14 in Counts 5 and 6.

The People have presented evidence of more than one act to prove that the defendant committed these offenses. For these offenses, you must not find the defendant guilty unless you all agree that the People have proved that defendant committed at least one of these acts, one distinct act per count, and you all agree on which act he committed.

Each of the counts charged in this case is a separate crime. You must consider each count separately and return a separate verdict for each one.

If you find that the defendant is not guilty of a greater crime, you may find him guilty of a lesser crime, if you are convinced beyond a reasonable doubt that the defendant is guilty of that lesser crime. A defendant may not be convicted of both a greater and a lesser crime for the same conduct.

It is up to you to decide the order in which you consider each crime and the relevant evidence, but I can accept a verdict of guilty of a lesser crime only if you have found the defendant not guilty of the corresponding greater crime. You will receive a form for indicating your verdict on both the greater crime and the lesser crime. The greater crime is listed first. When you've reached a verdict, have the foreperson complete the form, sign it and date it.

Follow these instructions before writing anything on the form:

Number one: If all of you agree that the People have proved beyond a reasonable doubt that the defendant is guilty of the greater crime as charged, write "guilty" in the blank for that crime, then sign, date and return the form. Do not write anything for the lesser crime.

Number two: If all of you cannot agree whether the People have proved beyond a reasonable doubt that the defendant is guilty of the greater crime as charged, inform me only that you cannot reach an agreement and do not write anything on the verdict form.

Number three: If all of you agree that the People have not proved beyond a reasonable doubt that the defendant is guilty of the greater crime, and you also agree that the People have proved beyond a reasonable doubt that he is guilty of the lesser crime, write "not guilty" in the blank for the greater crime and write "guilty" in the blank for the lesser crime. You must not write anything for the lesser crime unless you have written "not guilty" for the great crime.

Number four: If all of you agree that the People have not proved beyond a reasonable doubt that the defendant is guilty of either the greater or the lesser crime, write "not guilty" in the blank for both the greater crime and the lesser crime.

And number five: If all of you agree that the People have not proved beyond a reasonable doubt that the defendant is guilty of the greater crime, but all of you cannot agree on the verdict for the lesser crime, write "not guilty" in the blank for the greater crime, then sign, date and return the form. Do not write anything for the lesser, and inform me only that you cannot reach an agreement about that crime.

There are a few other instructions I'll give after argument. One is the predeliberation instruction. The second one is the instruction that I'll give to our alternates.

Again, you will have copies of all of these instructions, actually a couple of sets that you folks will have in the deliberation room.

So we will proceed with closing argument at this time.

2

5th Juror – Melissa Duplisse , early 70s, retired nurse.

I can't do this. I really can't!

Rape is rape. I don't care whether it's actual intercourse, penetration by an object, whether it was 'aggravated' or 'rape by force'. They're all rape.

I don't want to go through every count and discuss the details of the type and depth of penetration or the depth of depravity of little Sandy's father. I just want to walk away.

Seeing the photos of the injury was bad enough. Then the videos, then the testimony. I suppose I thought we were past all of that. But now, with the judge's instructions, he's brought it all back. It's too horrible!

Next we'll get the details again from Mr. Bolt. It will be graphic and horrible.

That nice Ms. Preston will focus on other things. But then we'll have to deliberate every count. We'll talk about details. I can't. I really can't. I know it's late, but maybe I can be excused. I'll talk to the judge.

3

Closing arguments from the transcripts:

THE COURT: Mr. Bolt, please proceed.
MR. BOLT: Yes, Your Honor. Thank you.

Good morning everyone. I want to take a moment to thank you. This has been a long trial. It's been impossible not to notice how engaged you all have been. There's been lots of starts and stops, time waiting outside, and your patience is very much appreciated, and your attention is very much appreciated as well. And so thank you.

And here we are. You have heard all of the evidence that you will hear in this case. And this evidence is convincing. It is compelling. The evidence that you've heard is overwhelming evidence of guilt, evidence of guilt that is absolutely impossible to ignore.

And after hearing all this evidence, now you know that seven-year-old Sandy was raped. She was raped by her own father, the one man in this world who, more than any other man, should have been her protector. But he abused her. And you know that now.

You've heard how, November 1st, 20XX, the fateful Friday started out so typical, started out so usual, ended up changing people's lives forever.

You've heard how a seven-year-old child trusted her big sister enough to share a horrible truth. And you heard how these girls watched their parents argue over little Sandy having been raped by her father. You've heard them describe how that situation was spinning out of control.

You've heard how, in those tense and fearful moments, Mandy took it upon herself to call for help. Mandy took it upon herself to break that family silence.

Sandy couldn't know how everything would unfold when she decided to tell her big sister. Mandy couldn't know how her decision to call 911 would result in their world spinning out of control. Neither girl, neither girl could have known that a chain of events had started that would force their dark family secrets from years ago even, into the harsh light of day, force those secrets into public view into this courtroom in front of each of you. Because you've all been witnesses to a tragedy that has been years in the making in this case.

Now it took weeks to hear all this evidence. And it's a complex, messy, at times disorganized process. But now you've heard it and the truth is, in a way, very simple, because it all comes down to a simple fact: If you believe Sandy, then the defendant is guilty. If you believe that she was telling the truth about her father putting his penis in her, then he's guilty. If you believe that Mandy was also abused, he's guilty.

And there is so much evidence, but it really is that simple. And you do believe Sandy. You do. That poor kid is a victim of sexual assault and she's been through a lot. That was very clear. And so all this time, all that evidence, it really comes down to something that is just that simple. Each of you believes Sandy, and that the defendant is guilty.

And we're going to talk about that evidence and why the evidence really is overwhelming, how that evidence proves beyond a reasonable doubt that Mandy was also a victim of child molestation. And so let's get to it.

Now how does that evidence prove guilt?

Now, first off, let's talk about Sandy and let's talk about, sort of, how the evidence in a broad range lays out here. Because either the defendant is guilty or the defendant is innocent and wrongfully accused. Either he raped Sandy or Sandy is lying about being raped.

Oftentimes there's a middle ground. Not here. Oftentimes there can be a mistake. Maybe the wrong guy gets identified. Not here. There's no mistake. There's no mistake in identification. There's no mistake about anything else. Sometimes something is accidental. Somebody didn't intend, perhaps, to do something. Not here. There's no accident. There's no middle ground, not in this case.

For starters, that's because Sandy was clear about what happened. Her father forced sexual intercourse against her will. He forced her onto the bed. He pulled her pants off, while she tugged against him. He overcame her resistance.

He made his penis slippery. The defendant penetrated her genitals with his penis. It hurt. It bled. She wiped with a towel. She washed with warm water, changed her underwear. She is clear about those things. I mean there's no mistake. There's no accident.

She disclosed almost immediately. Really, even though the

defendant told her to remain quiet, even though he made her pinky swear, even though he threatened to hurt her if she told anyone, even still she took her first opportunity to share with her big sister what her dad had done to her.

And, of course, Mandy wanted to tell Alejandra immediately. Sandy was afraid. Mandy insisted.

It's very clear.

Now Sandy has remained consistent as far as the core substance of what she has always said happened. It's been more than three years. She told Mandy. She told her mother. She told Deputy Davenport, Sergeant - or Deputy Davenport and Detective Locke. She testified at the preliminary hearing. She testified in front of you all.

The core substance of what she has said has always remained consistent and clear. She testified before you that she has no doubt that she is 100 percent certain that her father forced his penis into her private parts.

And she's got lots of details at times that sound a little different. But when you look at that in the context of the evidence in the case, none of it is anything that the People need to rely upon to prove these charges beyond a reasonable doubt. She's always been absolutely rock solid and consistent on the core of what she says occurred, which is proven beyond a reasonable doubt.

And so, again, this is just a case where there is absolutely no middle ground. She didn't accuse her father of raping her by accident or by mistake.

And the defendant, because of that, you have to ask yourselves, he is either the victim of an intentional and knowing false accusation or he committed a horrible crime against his own innocent daughter. And I do submit to you that the evidence of guilt is overwhelming. Let's consider some of that, because the evidence proves that the defendant raped his daughter.

We are going to talk about a couple different categories of that evidence. We will talk about the injury itself. We will talk about the nature of the disclosure. And we will talk about corroboration for what Sandy says happened, before we move on to some other areas.

The first thing about the injury is that when you look at the injury, the evidence about the injury to Sandy's private parts, and you consider it in absolute isolation, completely separate from all the other evidence in the case, by itself it's strong evidence of guilt, strong evidence that, indeed, Sandy was raped.

You heard from Nurse Mary Williams. You heard from Nurse Amanda Hernandez. You have the stipulation from Dr. Sharpe. And, really, all of that testimony is - and all of that evidence is very much internally consistent. It's not really subject to a lot of dispute.

And you remember, what were the conclusions that could have been reached in that sexual assault examination on November 1st at Dominican Hospital that Sandy went through?

One possible conclusion would be that there were no findings. That's a common conclusion.

Another possible conclusion would be that there are some findings, but they are sort of nonspecific. It's like it's impossible to really say whether it's the type of thing that's caused by a sexual assault, versus the type of thing that is commonly occurring in another way.

But that's not what we have here. What we have here is a laceration caused by blunt force trauma. It's a very specific thing. And a laceration like this, by itself, causes medical personnel, medical professionals, to be highly suspicious that the person with this injury has been the victim of a sexual assault. The injury, by itself, causes medical professionals to think, "Yeah, this is probably a child who has been sexually abused." And why? And what does that mean?

Well, for starters, someone, some thing, penetrated Sandy's genitals in order to cause that injury.

Injuries like this, the evidence has established, they are just not common. It's inside the genitals. And let just break that down for a second.

This injury is inside the genitals, which means that it is 100 percent for sure, no ifs ands or buts, no way around it, this child was penetrated in her genitals.

That matters in the jury instructions, and it's important to make that point; 100 percent, that is a fact. An object simply cannot cause this injury without penetration. This injury is a blunt force trauma injury.

So the laceration to the inside of Sandy's genitals, it's not a scratch caused by like a fingernail or some other object like that. It's not a cut from a sharp object. It's not like that at all. This type of injury is caused by an object like a penis. Something has pressed hard enough against the tissue that it actually causes the tissue to split, like a boxer when he gets hit on a cheekbone and a cut occurs. Blunt force trauma.

And you could tell that, and all the testimony, all the evidence supports that. Nothing is weighing on the opposite side. You can tell that because of how it's jagged, how the redness, how the laceration appears.

So to stop for a second and think: Okay, well, that by itself, that's highly suspicious. But what if this wasn't caused by a sexual assault? What's the innocent explanation? And is there even a way to get this kind of injury some other way?

And the answer is, sure, you can get this injury other ways. They are just not likely. They are not likely at all. And it's not common.

And to see how unlikely it is, let's consider what wouldn't cause this type of injury. And this is coming from both the testimony of the S.A.R.T. nurses, but also from the stipulation about Dr. Sharpe.

Because this is not a straddle injury. Straddle injuries are caused by falls, usually, onto horizontal objects, things like bathtub rims or bicycle frames or playground equipment or things like this. These are horizontal objects, and they can cause injuries to the genital area.

But none of those types of causes would penetrate the genitals, cause an injury to the outside. None of those types of things can cause the type of injury that Sandy suffered. And so what could cause it? Well, something like a fall onto a vertical object.

And what does that mean? So, basically, Sandy has got to accidentally or intentionally fall onto something like a broom handle, some other object, any object that is of the right size that if she fell just on it as it sat vertically, that it could penetrate her genital opening and cause the injury. She's got to land on it just right. It's got to be just perfect for blunt force trauma to cause this type of injury, the type of force that would result in this type of a laceration. But when you think about it and you start thinking about what sorts of mechanisms can cause these types of injuries, you start realizing that the idea that Sandy's injury was caused by something other than a sexual assault, it's really quite remote.

And you remember the example that Nurse Williams

provided? And this was not in her capacity as a sexual assault nurse examiner. This was in her capacity as an EMT. So she responded to a call for an ambulance and she came upon the skateboard accident. And that was a situation where something that was a freak accident caused essentially a penetration injury not entirely unlike this.

So, yeah, it's possible. But no, it's not likely. And the evidence in this case is that nothing at all like what happened here, nothing at all.

And so what does that mean for the notion that the defendant is innocent? For the defense, it means that there better be some pretty good evidence that someone - or that something else caused this injury. But there isn't. There just isn't.

MS. PRESTON: I'm going to object; burden shifting; Fifth Amendment.

THE COURT: I'll overrule.

But the jury has been advised that the burden of proof rests strictly and solely with the People.

Please continue.

MR. BOLT: It's true, the burden of proof is with the People, and we're going to talk about that. And the People have the burden of proving each and every element of the offense beyond a reasonable doubt.

The other thing that it could mean, if - for the defense, it better mean that there's some pretty good evidence that someone other than the defendant caused that injury. And again –

MS. PRESTON: Objection, Your Honor; Fifth Amendment; burden shifting.

THE COURT: Let's keep the burden of proof on the People, please.

Please continue, Mr. Bolt.

MR. BOLT: The thing is, what you know is that there's absolutely no evidence that anyone else caused this injury, because the defendant is the one who was alone with Sandy. She was fine and then she wasn't.

Of course, the defendant says she was fine when he left the house that evening. But we'll get to that. But these reasons it's an uncommon injury. It's a specific injury. It's only caused by certain types of things. And, by itself, it provides strong evidence which corroborates Sandy, strong evidence, that she was raped and the defendant is guilty.

Let's just talk about Sandy's account with a little bit more specificity. Sandy has given a lot of statements. The first time she spoke about this was to Mandy after she had returned to the apartment with her father. Eventually, Mandy comes home and they are alone in their bedroom and Sandy discloses.

Now according to Mandy - and she's clear - statements made very close in time, she's clear, Sandy says, "Dad put his private part in my private part. It caused pain. It hurt. It bled." And so this - which is essentially what Mandy eventually testified to in this courtroom as well, that's expressly consistent with statements that Mandy made to Deputy Garcia, to Sergeant Aragon, and to Detective Sandi Locke, as well as her testimony at trial.

It's worth just taking a moment to think about her 911 call. You can tell the child doesn't like to talk about sexual things. She's really clear why she's calling; and the fundamental gravamen of what is going on there.

But the next statement Sandy makes is to her mother. And I put an asterisk by that because Alejandra is much more vague to - and consistently vague to different people, whereas Mandy is not.

So Alejandra testified Sandy says that she was touched in her private parts, causing pain and bleeding, or indicates that she was touched there which caused pain and bleeding.

And, of course, it's very clear that Alejandra never claims that Sandy said that she was touched with a hand or touched with a finger or that she was penetrated, at least according to Alejandra. But Mandy describes that conversation, also. And according to Mandy, that when Alejandra comes into the - when they meet in that bedroom, Sandy tells her mom in Spanish that her private parts were penetrated by the defendant's private parts.

And Mandy, as reflected in the recording, she was not sure whether her mother understood exactly what Sandy was telling her. And because of that, Mandy took it upon herself to explain to her mother exactly that, in Spanish, that the defendant put his private part in Sandy's private part.

Now, of course, Deputy Davenport gets there. It's a very short statement. There's hardly any questions. It's very open-ended.

But what do you get out of that? In about two minutes, two and a half minutes, maybe, Sandy describes getting forced into the bedroom. She describes being afraid that she's going to get hit, and definitely being grabbed. She describes these things.

And the officer asked, "Are you hurt?" And she's, yeah, she's hurt and she's pointing down to her genital area.

And the officer is like, "Why does that hurt? What happened?"

And they it comes out, "Dad, like he was squeezing me so much." And then, "it hurt," and then, "it bled. He put his thing in my private part."

So right there she's very clear, very clear. She really isn't interviewed specifically, although she does make further statements. At the hospital Davenport asked her, "Where did this happen?"

And she identifies the bed in her parent's room.

She talks about underwear getting taken.

It's really not until two days later, when Detective Locke interviews her at the Sheriff's Office - it's a detailed interview. It's all recorded, and all kinds of details come out, what led up to this, the deal, the counting, the lube, the description, which is a very credible description from a child who doesn't have a full understanding of what it is she's describing. It’s still expressly consistent.

She testified at the preliminary hearing. And you looked at her. You know, who was nervous testifying? She was nervous. How difficult that must have been, talking about these things in front of people, speaking out about - these things about your father, who you love.

And you saw her at jury trial. A lot of time has passed. Some memories have faded or details have been mixed up. But fundamentally, totally consistent.

And you watched her. After all this time, is she faking it?

Does she present like a little ten-year-old on a quest to wrongfully convict her father of raping her?

No. That's not what she looked like. She looked like somebody who was doing her best to be honest in a situation that she was very uncomfortable with.

But you could also see, through the course of her testimony, that some of the apprehension, some of the nervousness, some of the anxiety, as the questions wore on some of that started to subside. And she even remarked at one point late in her examination that she was feeling a little bit better. But she was absolutely clear, fundamentally, about what happened to her, what her dad did to her. The most rich, the most detailed and the most accurate account - not surprisingly though - is the one that you see from November 3rd during the Sheriff's Office detailed interview. If you want to know what happened to Sandy, what really happened to Sandy, that's the best place to look. That's the best place to look.

And what she describes is a terrible, terrible experience: the force that was used, the anger that she could see in her father's face, sweating, the use of this lubricant, this substance that she didn't even know what it was, when it hurt so bad that she screamed out and he is covering her mouth, it's horrendous, it's horrible, and it's the most accurate expression of what she suffered.

And how do we know that? A large part of the reason we know that is because her account is corroborated in so many ways. Because as the investigation wore on and as the evidence and information starts coming in, lots of aspects of her account are directly corroborated.

I mean, obviously, we talked about the laceration, obviously. It's inside her genitals. It's a penetration injury caused by blunt force trauma. And again, that's profound evidence. She mentions the storage unit in her account of what took place. What she says is that the defendant had her change her bloody underwear for fresh underwear at the storage unit. It happens in a sequence of events.

Now after Sandy tells this to Detective Locke, Detective Locke successfully goes and gets records from the storage unit which - that's right - reflect that the storage unit had been accessed at just the right time.

Now, by contrast, you know, when the defendant is interviewed and given every chance in the world to explain what happened, to explain what he did in detail that day, he leaves out - he doesn't mention - he never mentions the storage unit, where some important stuff happened. He never mentions it throughout the whole interview with Sergeant Cardova. And conveniently, to Detective Lopez the next day, when they know to ask about it, he forgot. How coincidental and convenient to forget to relay that this was part of your activities. It just so happened that the victim of this crime tells us that something important happened there. And it did. He took her bloody underwear, gave her fresh underwear, hiding the crime.

But that's not where it ends. There is the lubricant. And again, this comes up just because Detective Locke is asking questions, and she describes how there is this little bottle and it made his penis slippery.

What do you know? Three days later, in a search warrant, a bottle of Astroglide is found hidden in the bathroom.

And then, again, what do you know? Two weeks after the crime, Sandy is shown a photograph by Detective Locke, and out of five different containers found at the house, she picks out the Astroglide. No mistake, no accident; she picks it out, she describes it, and then the police corroborate it.

The jumbo eraser, she describes - and she's seven, mind you. She is seven. She describes this deal, pressure to make a deal. She says how it happened. She wanted this jumbo eraser. Dad says: Okay, but you've got to make a deal.

So what happens there? She describes that in the interview. Then it turns out a receipt pops up that's found in the defendant's car. It's from October 24th, 20XX, from CVS.

And Detective Lopez goes there, gets the surveillance video from that day, and what does it show? It shows the defendant and Mandy and Sandy going into the store, visible on the surveillance video, go into the part of the main part of the store where you can't see because there aren't cameras. And there's plenty of time for exactly what Sandy says happened, corroborating her account.

And then you see them come up to the checkout. The defendant buys that item and a couple others, and they leave, corroborating her account.

Now, of course, Sandy's blood is on the comforter on the bed, just where you would expect it to be if it was going to be anywhere.

You've got possibly her DNA on the defendant's scrotal swab. We'll talk about that. And then, of course, you've got the male DNA consistent with the defendant coming from the inside of her underwear cutting.

Now we're going to talk about the forensic evidence in some detail, in some detail, but what I just said is pretty much what the forensic evidence shows. It moves the needle towards guilt. It's certainly not exculpatory in nature.

Now, of course, some of you definitely could be thinking: Hey, there's a problem here. I think there's a problem. You are asking us to convict the defendant when none of the forensic analyses performed in this case provide smoking gun evidence of his guilt.

And that's exactly right. None of the analyses performed do provide, by themselves, strong evidence of guilt.

And it is also true that occasionally this type of evidence does provide extremely powerful evidence of guilt. And it's also true that this sort of evidence sometimes provides smoking-gun evidence of innocence.

What's important to note here is that none of these tests are evidence of innocence, and that there is a little bit of evidence tending to show guilt, again corroborating Sandy.

The reality is, in many cases you're just not going to find game-changing DNA evidence. And –

MS. PRESTON: Objection; assumes facts not in evidence.

THE COURT: I'll overrule. The jury will know what the evidence is and is not.

Please continue.

MR. BOLT: Thank you, Your Honor.

There's all sorts of complications and limitations of this sort of evidence, particularly in cases like this. I mean, what you have is a situation where all of the relevant people, they all live in the same small apartment and they have lived there for years. You don't know when DNA evidence is deposited. Everybody who is relevant in the case is genetically related. It makes it much harder to use this type of evidence to actually distinguish people. It relies on genetic differences. When people are genetically related it directly cuts down on the significance that you can get out of this evidence.

You don't always need DNA anyway. DNA towels off. It washes off. And if you think about it, it's not surprising, shocking or concerning at all that there isn't smoking-gun evidence of guilt coming from the forensic analyses in this case, and for a host of reasons.

And so the upshot of the forensic testing is that nothing - the absence of a finding is no evidence that nothing happened, and there's nothing here that points towards innocence. Sandy's blood is on the bed. That's for sure. It's just where it should be. You don't know when it was left.

That scrotal swab, that's the one where Dr. Marcus decided to arbitrarily change the analytical threshold –

MS. PRESTON: Objection; assumes facts not in evidence, "arbitrarily."
THE COURT: I'll sustain.
MR. BOLT: Indeed, what - what evidence was there that - that would allow anyone to distinguish why, with all the analyses, all the DNA tests, all the DNA interpretation that were done - was done in this case, that - where the analytical threshold is exactly the same?

Why? Because they are all tests done in the same lab and they are all being performed at that threshold because of a series of validation studies which dictate that that's where you need to set the threshold in order to properly gauge whether you are getting reliable and reproducible results for your DNA analysis and interpretation.

And the undisputed testimony and the evidence in this case is that all of those results and interpretations are appropriate and valid and accurate and reliable, except for this one where Dr. Marcus decides to use a different analytical threshold.

And she's got her explanation, but you also heard that that's just not how it works. You look at the threshold that she uses, and it is so dramatically different there is, I would submit to you, no principled reason why you should accept that.

But even if you did, a lot doesn't ride on it. There's not a whole heck of a lot that rides on it. The defendant, just to give a sense for situations where you don't get foreign DNA, you know, the evidence is that he hadn't showered for some period of time, that he had had sex with his wife within that period of time, and nobody's DNA except his comes off of the penis swabs.

The scrotal swab that we're talking about, the amount of foreign DNA, which is consistent with both Alejandra and with Sandy, it's a small, very, very small amount. And so it provides some degree of corroboration; it's nothing that is a game changer. The important point is that, don't be misled into believing that somehow it's evidence of innocence. It's not. It's just not.

And then there's the male DNA contained within the underwear cuttings, the front half underwear cuttings, consistent with the defendant. Now again, "consistent with" doesn't mean it came from him. Don't know when it was left. Don't know how it got there. But some corroboration. It's certainly no evidence of innocence, none at all.

Now, those are a lot of like broad, affirmative categories, and every single one of them corroborates what a seven-year-old says, every single one of them; not to mention that it lines up with the testimony of others.

Now I want to talk about the testimony of Alejandra. And she was an interesting witness to watch, and a frustrating witness, probably, at times, too. Nothing is made any easier, ever, when you have things running through an interpreter, to watch or to take part in.

But we heard "I don't know" and "I don't remember" so many times it would be very difficult to count. And when you look at the statements that she has made in the past and you compare them to the statements that she testified to, you're going to find some things that are credible, some things that are very credible, and those things are going to match up with other evidence in the case.

There's also going to be some stuff that looks quite incredible. It also makes you wonder. You know, a good example is, Armando is her son. It's hard to imagine that he didn't live in this apartment for some period of time.

I mean, the defendant has him moving out more than two years, like two and a half years before November 1st, 20XX, but Mandy has him living there, I think Sandy had him living there, too, at some point. The defendant has him living there. It's hard to imagine how Alejandra could forget that he lived there for some period of time.

Now what's that all about? It's hard to know. But she says "I don't know" and "I don't remember" so many times that you really need to think about if she does remember, and you need to look to other statements to find out what is corroborated and what somebody is motivated to say, whether somebody has some reason to say one thing rather than another because of what's going on with them.

Because when you compare with what Sandy says, how with Sandy's clarity as far as fundamentally what she says happened, and you look at what Mandy says about those things, it really lines up fairly squarely.

But to Deputy Garcia, to Sergeant Davenport, Alejandra - I mean, she clearly knows that Sandy disclosed sexual abuse by her father, but it's unclear why, if Sandy told her mom exactly what happened and if Mandy ensured that Alejandra understood, it's hard to understand why she seems to soft-pedal it.

It's hard to understand a little bit about why, when Sandy and Mandy both describe this rule, it's hard to understand why Alejandra denies the rule. She never mentions it to Garcia and Sergeant Davenport, or to Sergeant Cardova. She doesn't mention anything like that.

Asked about concerns or suspicions of the defendant, indications that anything like this had ever happened before, Alejandra denies all of that, just denies being suspicious to Cardova and denies those things to Detective Lopez as well.

But the thing was that two days later, on the 3rd, when the detailed interviews are done and all of this information comes out that Mandy had been abused years ago, that that that was why neither child was allowed to be alone with dad, then it really starts, you know, making a lot of sense.

Again, let's just think about for one second what Sandy says about that. Sandy describes how she wanted to go with her sister, probably partly because it was fun, but partly because there's this rule. And she's upset because her dad is saying she has to stay. The defendant, he testifies and states, to one degree or another in interviews, that he's got to call his wife to more or less to check if it's going to be okay that he's got Sandy while Mandy is at this play date.

MS. PRESTON: Objection; facts not in evidence; misstatement.

THE COURT: I'll respectfully overrule. Again, the jury will know what the evidence is and is not. The jury has been instructed that nothing said by counsel is evidence. Please continue.

MR. BOLT: Alejandra, when she testified, says she is aware that the defendant called and more or less checks to see if it's okay that Sandy stays home with him. And check your notes, but that's the testimony that I believe came from that stand. And I know she's made some statements that were inconsistent at times, but then, once again, when she gets home at 5:00 o'clock or however close to 5:00, what does she do? No one is there. So she calls to find out where Sandy is.

And the defendant, when he testified, sounded like he didn't acknowledge that he received such a call. But in the interviews he does acknowledge that he received a call.

So the point is not exactly what this person or that person said at any given time. The point is to notice just how the idea of this rule, in what Sandy says and in what Mandy says, it just fits right onto all these other facts. It really doesn't conflict with anything. It goes with it and it explains things.

It gets interesting when Alejandra testifies that actually, "Yeah, even though I never admitted it to any of the police back then, there was this rule. There was." And she admitted she told her daughters about it, and that she was unclear just how it related to the defendant.

Now why in the world would you have a rule like this unless you thought there was a reason for it? Because, of course, when Alejandra testified she begged off of the things that she had acknowledged to Detective Lopez about her suspicions regarding the defendant, about Mandy having complained about sexual abuse, about personally witnessing troubling behaviors. So she testified, "Yes, there was this rule, but it was just because I grew up with it and so I imposed it," as if somehow that alleviated her from explaining why it existed.

But why it existed? Look at the kids. Look at the kids. Look at what they say. What they say makes sense.

And once again, what do we know? We know that there was this CPS investigation that the parents are soft-pedaling, are minimizing. I mean, there was some stuff going on at that house. There were concerns.

So Detective Lopez gets that. He gets this information from Sandy and Mandy and then he starts putting a degree of pressure on Alejandra to be honest about anything she witnessed. This rule. He wants to know whether she actually confronted the defendant, accused him of sexually molesting Mandy years ago. It turns out she did. It turns out she did.

Now did she come clean? Was she fully truthful? I admit to you that's an open question. But what was very clear and what was very credible was after she was pressured to be truthful and after she disclosed what she did about inappropriate things she saw, suspicions that she had, Mandy having complained of being touched when she was a very young girl, and about confronting the defendant on these issues, what was very credible was her reaction when she expressed her fear that these things could mean that her children would be taken away.

And that was a fear that, when you start thinking about it - I mean, why is mom minimizing during a CPS investigation? Obviously, no one wants to admit these things. Maybe there's some shame. Maybe there's some embarrassment.

We know there's fear. And we know how important and how deeply twisted Alejandra got when her financial support got arrested for raping her daughter. The whole financial thing was very troubling for her, was something that made her upset. And so when you watch that and you look at how that played out, Alejandra is clearly not providing information that she has early on. Later she provides it, but only with some pressure to be honest.

But then her motives demonstrate that what she does disclose as far as her knowledge that the defendant is a risk to molest her children, given all the other evidence, makes her credible when she acknowledges that the rule exists, acknowledges that there was a disclosure from Mandy years ago, and that there was a confrontation with the defendant.

Now when you look at how all of this also lines up with the CPS investigation, it's kind of the same thing: minimize, deny abuse; you are protecting yourself and the defendant more than the girls.

And so you think for a second and step back. What kind of household does sexual abuse like this take place in? You know, what kind of household do children get victimized and are afraid to tell outsiders, instead keeping it inside?

And here's your answer: It's households like this.

You also have additional information which shows just how in love Alejandra is with the defendant even after she knows everything he did.

Now, so let's talk about Mandy. You know about the 911 call. You know about how she discloses what she says, "My parents" "This is what Sandy told me. I knew it was penis/vagina. I knew that she was hurt, that she was bleeding. I knew exactly what she was saying. I made sure my mom understood, and then she confronted him, and she confronted him about those things directly."

That's what Mandy says when the police are there and that is what she testified to. Yes. There are some inconsistencies here and there but that is fundamentally what she testified to.

So the police get there. Mandy is a smart kid already. She's 11. She understands the stakes. And she listened for about a half hour during her mother's interview with Deputy Garcia. And it's a long half hour before Deputy Garcia and Deputy Condor talked to Mandy for just about four minutes, a short little conversation.

But when you listen to that, she's been sitting there for 30, 40 minutes thinking about the past, thinking about what is happening now, and she almost discloses her sexual abuse right there.

I would submit to you that when Deputy Garcia or Deputy Condor says something like, "Anything like this ever happen before," and she says, "not particularly - well, maybe, you know, a long time ago when I was little something happened to me, my dad violated me" that this is a word that she uses in a sexual context. It's almost the same as a Spanish word for a rape. And this is English she's speaking. It's not a normal way to talk about physical abuse.

And we know she suffered physical abuse. Both those kids did. That's why Sandy is reasonably afraid of her father, why the defendant even admitted that from the witness stand. He admitted to physical abuse.

THE COURT: We'll take a recess at this point until 11:05. Please do not discuss this matter amongst yourselves or with anyone else. Please do not form or express any opinions concerning this matter.

I'll look forward to seeing everyone at 11:05. Thank you very much. We're off the record.

(Short recess.)

4

12th Juror – Steve Dietz, engineer in Santa Cruz startup, early-thirties no kids. Father is a lawyer.

I can't believe he's going to fuck this up. It should have been open and shut. Bolt's meandering close is about the worst I've ever heard. Aside from the stuttering and backtracking, it's just horribly organized. He jumps from one point to another, then almost seems to be interrupting himself.

Worse, he's introducing doubt. Yeah, I'm sure he thinks he's countering points that Preston made, but he shouldn't even bring them up. He should be focusing on his strong points, not trying to find excuses for his weak ones. And the DNA threshold thing! Only an idiot would believe that Dr. Marcus chose an unacceptable threshold.

And he kept going on about this doesn't prove him innocent and that doesn't prove him innocent. Doesn't he get it that the judge and Preston have hammered home that the defense doesn't have to prove innocence. Every one of those points is a major hole in his case and he can't seem to stop pointing it out.

It's been two hours of non-stop monotonic monologue. I actually welcome Preston's objections just to give us a break. And he's just getting started. He may end up boring the jury into an innocent verdict.

Don't get me wrong. I still believe that Flores is guilty. I just can't believe this closing. And the worst part is that most of the jurors don't realize that after Preston does her closing, Bolt gets another chance to convince the jury. I'm sure it will be a repeat of what he's just said and what he's going to bore us with for the next couple of hours. I wish I could just step out until Preston's back on. After all, I'll get the rest of Bolt's snooze-fest in his second closing argument. But that's not possible for me.

Anyway, during the break, Matt and I stepped outside and tried to talk about damage control. But one of the problems with this building is that it's all glass. There are a few of the jurors that do laps and they could see us talking outside. I tried to convince Matt that our conversations would appear innocent. Hey, we're the two youngest jurors and have our whole lives to talk about. And after all, most of the jurors talk to each other, just not about the case.

But he was nervous, so we cut it short. We agreed to meet tonight so we could make up for Bolt's deficiencies when we get into the jury room. We'll have a solid concerted attack to convince any doubters that Flores is guilty as sin.

5

THE COURT: Let's go back on the record, please. Mr. Flores is present. Counsel are present. All of our jurors are present. Please continue, Mr. Bolt.

MR. BOLT: Thank you, Your Honor.

So Mandy almost discloses in that little four-minute segment. It's worth listening to, because it's on her mind in those 30 minutes. She is sitting in her room and mom is getting interviewed, and she's just heard the things that her mom was saying as well.

So then it's a trip to the hospital. And Sergeant Davenport interviews Mandy. And again, Mandy is full of facts, accurately describing what she told Deputy Garcia as it relates to her sister.

At the end of that interview she's asked if anything has ever happened to her, and she just lets it go.

But then, what do you know? After the S.A.R.T. exam is complete, Amanda Hernandez hears something that makes her want to just go ask. And so she takes the time to buddy up a little bit, to build a little rapport, bring her some hot chocolate, sit down with her. And she asks, "Anything like this ever happen involving you and your dad?"

And Mandy discloses. She said, "Yeah, it happened to me a long time ago. I don't remember how old I was, but I told my mom."

Certainly it makes sense not to go back and re-interview Alejandra and re-interview Mandy at that point in time. This is already after, like, 11:20pm or so when the S.A.R.T. exam is over. That's when this interaction with Nurse Hernandez takes place.

So then we have the detailed interview with Detective Locke. And you see there a child who is reluctant to disclose, and she obviously is. They kind of go back and forth a little bit. But, ultimately, there's no pressure. There's just an encouragement to be truthful. And ultimately, "Well, I don't remember very much about it." "Well, why don't you just tell me what you do remember," or something very close to what Detective Locke says.

And when she says that, Mandy describes, she discloses an event. It happened a long time ago. She, in her mind, she remembers her mom being pregnant, and she describes getting forced into a situation not entirely unlike what Sandy suffered.

But she describes the defendant touching her, taking off his pants, leaving on his underwear. She describes being penetrated. She describes it being against her will.

And she describes very clearly that she tells her mom. Her mom is aware of it. There's a confrontation that involves threatening to call the police, that involves, according to Mandy's recollection, an admission or an acknowledgment of responsibility. And police do not get called. And that is why the rule is in place.

And, look, nobody is saying there aren't other reasons, too. Both kids relate that their dad has a tendency to misbehave, if you will, when he's been drinking too much. They both relate that. And they both relate that generally, the rule is to protect them from harm coming to them. Mandy is clear that this is when it started for her. Sandy is clear that that rule has been around for as long as she can remember.

Now Mandy testified at the preliminary hearing. And I don't know how clear all of that is in your mind. But comparing how the child sounds when she's talking to Detective Locke, frankly when she's talking to other law enforcement people, about more on the issues involved with Sandy, you look at all of that and compare it to what she looks like on that stand when she is saying nothing happened, and there's a massive demeanor difference. Huge. Huge.

Other things are clear from that preliminary hearing testimony. It's clear that that child feels no need to hide the fact that she feels overwhelmed by pressure. And imagine, imagine, I don't know if you recall the part from the jail calls, where she is on the phone with the defendant and he is like, "Where am I?"

"Jail," Mandy says.

"Yeah, that's right. And I may never get out of here." Sandy is no dummy, ah, or Mandy is no dummy. She knows. Is that designed to put pressure on her? Yes.

Mr. Flores, who in violation of protective orders, contacts everybody, tries to get them to change their story or not show up. Do you think he wants pressure being put on them? Yeah.

Also, you heard in the jail calls stuff about people from the defendant's family, Alejandra wants to know, "Why is your family mad at the girls? What did they do? They didn't do anything." Well, I got an idea. Mr. Flores tells everybody that he didn't do it, except the people who know that he did, and he wants people that he can try and sell that to. That's why. That's why. Mandy knows what this means when she testified at the preliminary hearing. Bless her heart. She still testified, at the same time that she was saying that "Detective Locke coerced me into making these statements against my dad," which is different than her in-court testimony in this trial. But at the preliminary hearing, she still said that she remembered that her dad admitted it when he was confronted about it. Watch it. It's in the tape. She still testified to that.

And what you see when you start comparing the demeanor and you start comparing the quality of the information and the nature of the motives in play, what you start to see is that just because she came to court and said nothing happened, that doesn't mean nothing happened.

And you have all the information in the world in front of you, all the credible evidence that you need to convict Mr. Flores of crimes against Mandy.

Just make a note of it. In her trial testimony Mandy no longer was claiming that Sandi coerced her, ah, that Detective Locke sort of coerced her into saying these things. She basically just said that she made up a lie, with no real justification or explanation.

It's always one of those things. As you can tell from the testimony, from Mr. Flores's testimony, and all of the rest of it, these kids suffered physical abuse. You know, you don't need to make up sexual abuse when you are the victim of abuse. You can just tell the truth about what you're the victim of.

But at trial, what you notice is that, unlike Sandy, who was so nervous and anxious and scared when she hit the stand, and some of those feelings evened out and decreased as her examination went on, with Mandy it was a little different. With Mandy, she seems to get a little bit more agitated and frustrated, not so much at the beginning, but as it wore on. Until at the end, she's complaining about questions being asked a bunch of times, you know, expressing frustration at all of these things.

And my point is not that she shouldn't do that. My point is, think about what she's doing. She came to court and already took all of this stuff back.

If these things happened, which I submit to you the evidence strongly supports that they did, then she came to court to lie. And then after all of these years, she's coming back once again to lie. She can't be happy about that. That's not something that makes her feel good inside. She is horribly conflicted here, obviously.

But at the same time, her testimony is very different than Sandy's testimony, because Sandy stood up for herself. Mandy, she just had to swear to tell the truth in a big building in front of all of these people, judges, lawyers, jurors, people in the gallery, bailiff, clerk, interpreters, court reporters, and lie. No wonder she's frustrated. No wonder she's irritated.

But there was also a massive disconnect, a massive emotional disconnect. You see, you might recall her testimony where she's talking about all the things she feels angry about and frustrated about and upset about and put upon about, and all of the trouble, all the emotions that she's feeling. And there are a lot of them. She didn't want to be here and she didn't like any of this stuff.

And it's understandable why. And I fed her every softball I could to let her express how she felt. She felt terrible for having let her sister be alone with her dad. She felt and expressed tremendous guilt about that.

She expressed a lot of antagonism for having to come all the way back here after all this time. And again, it is a big burden. But no matter how many invitations to tell us all the things that you feel bad about, you know what the one thing that she never, ever, ever expressed feeling bad about, in any way feeling bad, feeling guilt whatever? She never felt anything about having wrongfully accused her father of sexual abuse; never expressed it.

MS. PRESTON: Objection; misstates the facts.

THE COURT: I'm sorry. I missed your –

MS. PRESTON: Misstates the facts.

THE COURT: I'll overrule. Again, the jury will be responsible to evaluate the evidence.

MR. BOLT: It doesn't misstate the facts. She didn't express any kind of guilt whatsoever about it. And I would submit to you that's because she feels none. She feels none.

You know, why would she? She didn't wrong her dad. She just doesn't want to be responsible for what he's going through. Now, here's the thing: The defendant, in his interview with Detective Lopez on the 3rd, he is asked about being accused of having sexually molested Mandy, and he acknowledges that - not that he did molest Mandy, but that Alejandra accused him of it.

And although he couldn't remember the exact time frame, he acknowledged this years ago, and he puts it in the right general period. Detective Lopez asks him about the fact that he was accused by Alejandra for having touched Mandy inappropriately, and the defendant fires back, "I want - I told her we should call the police."

And what does that tell you? That tells you that not only did this accusation happen, but Alejandra threatened to call the police, once again corroborating Mandy in multiple ways that are absolutely critical. Alejandra obviously threatened to call the police. And you bet she had reason, because Mandy disclosed.

And who knows if she was fully forthcoming for her own reasons, but she witnessed things that were disturbing to her. And if the defendant acknowledges that he was accused of sexually molesting Mandy, which he did, then clearly Alejandra accused him of it.

And the thing is that if Alejandra accused him of sexually molesting Mandy, it's clearly because Mandy disclosed abuse to her. And if Mandy disclosed the abuse years ago, then when you watch that video of Mandy being interviewed by Detective Locke, then you will be convinced, when you compare it to the recantation, that she was abused. She was touched sexually by her father. And that's why she feels so guilty for having left her sister alone with her dad because she wanted to go play with her friend by herself. That's why.

So what causes Mandy to recant? Many things. There is so much family pressure. The defendant, "I'm in jail. I may never get out."

So Mandy is sexually molested, too. She's credible. Her disclosure to Detective Locke is credible, and it's corroborated, even if only inadvertently corroborated by the defendant and her mother.

Now I've been talking about a lot about affirmative ways that you know what happened in this case. But to see just how clearly this evidence demonstrates the defendant is guilty of these charges, you've got to fully consider the idea that maybe Sandy lied about everything. Maybe she lied about being raped. It's a total fabrication. Imagine that. The defendant is innocent. He is a victim who has been wrongfully accused, a victim of a false accusation. And you've got to think about that. It's very useful because it forces you to look at the evidence and see what fits. Because, again, this is a case with no middle ground. And appreciate what would have to be true if, indeed, he were innocent, if indeed this was a lie. First off, Mandy has got to be in on it. Sandy obviously would have to be in on it because she's the one who is lying. But Mandy has got to be in on it. Alejandra has got to be in on it. Alejandra has got to be in on it for the same reason that Mandy has got to be in on it, because she comes into the bedroom and finds out about the bleeding genitals. And she confronts the defendant. So she's got to be in on it. The only thing is, none of it looks like they are coconspirators. They are not working together. And so the witnesses just seem to like line up behind what Sandy says. And what the defendant says? It doesn't mesh.

Everybody knows that argument was about Alejandra learning that Sandy had been sexually abused by her dad. That's what they were arguing about. That's what's on the 911 call. That's what makes sense.

So when the defendant says to Roy Cardova, "No, it was nothing like that. We were arguing about jealousy" and then he flees for no reason, it doesn't make sense.

You would think that if this was fabricated, if it were made up, you would think that Mandy would squarely get behind what Sandy had said. But she's not necessarily doing that. You look at her statements to Sergeant Davenport, and Mandy is expressing a degree of confusion. She hears Sandy mention that something happened at the shed. It's unclear exactly what. And Mandy is telling this to Sergeant Davenport at the shed storage unit. Was it the bed or the storage unit?

I submit to you Sandy has always been clear, but Mandy is not. She isn't squarely backing her sister up. Alejandra is not squarely backing her daughter up. She seems to be soft-pedaling everything, saying things that are directly in conflict with what Sandy says, denying the rule, denying she ever had any concerns or suspicions about or knowledge about her husband.

But no matter how you cut it, for the defendant, for this to be a lie, then the defendant has to flee that house, that apartment, for no cognizable reason, because there's just nothing, there's nothing that's going on there that would cause a normal person to leave.

And what he says is that she's fine, she's not injured, when he leaves.

And so what does that mean? That means that if the defendant is innocent, then that injury was caused by something else. So it's either self-inflicted, Sandy either does it to herself, or there's some sort of massively implausible accidental injury that is exceptionally uncommon, as we've discussed, and then they spontaneously use it as part of a way to frame the defendant, a person who nobody wanted gone, not Alejandra and not those children.

They didn't know what can of worms they were opening. Mandy didn't know what can of worms she was opening when she called 911 for help. She just saw a situation getting way too intense. They are arguing about something that is serious. The defendant is blocking Alejandra's way. He is taking her phone when she is trying to call the police. It's getting way out of control.

And it is. So make no mistake, if the defendant is innocent, then she was fine. That means she has to be injured, she has to do this in a self-inflicted way before the police arrive, which is quick, or it has to be like a hidden injury. But one where even when the defendant is there, Mandy is on the phone telling the 911 operator that it's there.

And if the defendant is innocent, then why is he lying about that argument? And the answer is because he's guilty. But we are not playing that game right now.

So the defendant sits down with Roy Cardova, and what does he say? I mean, first off, what do we know? Nobody tells him why he's being picked up when they collect him at 3:00 a.m. from his truck. He doesn't ask.

He tells Sergeant Cardova, "I'm here because of an argument with my wife." And then you just watch how it unfolds, how just an additional piece of information keeps on being dropped out by Sergeant Cardova, which the defendant just keeps on denying. "No, no, it wasn't anything like that. Nothing having to do with a kid, nothing having to do with harming a kid, no, nothing having to do with harming Sandy, no, nothing, nothing, nothing." All the while, all the way up until the defendant finally mentions, "Oh, but I did get this call where I learned that Sandy was bleeding from her genitals."

And then on the same page, finally, Sergeant Cardova breaks out the word, "Yeah, you are accused of rape." And the defendant is not offended.

But let's just back up. So through all of that he is not curious why he is arrested. None of these things - none of the greater specificity are causing him to volunteer information or to say, "Wait, does this have something to do with my daughter and her being in the hospital, bleeding? Does it?"

He is not curious. He's not curious why he is being questioned. He's not curious why he is being arrested. And there is that emotional disconnect in him.

Because it just builds, builds, builds, builds, until you are accused of raping your own seven-year-old daughter. He is not offended at being accused of rape. He is not offended at being accused of child molestation. He's not offended at being accused of raping his own seven-year-old.

And isn't that just a huge problem for the notion that the defendant is innocent? Isn't that just a massive problem? He is way too okay with these questions, with what his family is saying about him.

I mean, if he's innocent, why isn't he reacting within the broad range of how a normal person reacts? Like, for instance, why not be a little upset, like angry? Why not be offended? Why not be concerned for your daughter?

But what is he doing? He is just emotionless. And the thing is, part of that is due to the fact that he is just too okay with these concepts of child molestation and rape, because in his mind they are not all that bad.

He doesn't see it like a normal person sees it. He doesn't react like a normal person reacts. He is okay with it. And just understand that it doesn't matter, from this perspective, whether the defendant learned about being accused of raping Sandy at his apartment, when Alejandra and Sandy and Mandy say it happened and the evidence corroborates that it happened, or if it happened in a phone call that was made between the time that he left and the time that the police arrived, before they were at the hospital. It doesn't matter if he learned it from some phone call later that night placed from the hospital. It doesn't matter.

What is clear is that by the time he is sitting there in front of Sergeant Cardova, he knows that he is being accused. So if he is innocent and wrongfully accused, his behavior is baffling. It doesn't make any sense. It fact, you would think this is how you make yourself look as guilty as possible, by denying you have any idea of what's going on, by just pulling the, "I don't even know" stuff.

He should be angry. He should be disgusted. He should be

worried about Sandy. And he's not. He should be any of those things, and he's none of them.

And how does he find himself talking in this way, that, "I don't remember whether I raped her"?

I mean, he says, "No, I didn't do that," but then it's like, "Well, your daughter says you did. You know, is she lying?" "I can't say that."

Well, "Don't remember"? Innocent people don't say stuff like that.

MS. PRESTON: Objection; facts not in evidence; Fifth Amendment; misstates.

THE COURT: Misstates evidence?

MS. PRESTON: Yes.

THE COURT: All right. I'm going to overrule. Again, the jury will know what the evidence is and is not. Again, the information offered by counsel is not evidence.

Please proceed, Mr. Bolt.

MR. BOLT: Thank you, Your Honor.

Now you may like or you may not like things that the police did. But when you look at that video, this is not an instance where coercive police interview tactics explain the things that come out of his mouth and the way he reacts. It doesn't at all. It's just not coercive.

And any time that, that there's anything more intense going on, those aren't the things that are providing the evidence of guilt. Those aren't the areas where the admissions are occurring.

And the idea that somehow Mr. Flores wasn't understanding English or Spanish at times, doesn't explain the statements he made, doesn't explain the way he acted. None of that does.

If you look at those transcripts, and what you see is when you get to the parts where it shifts to English, sometimes you don't even realize it, because if you are just looking at one side, it's just English. If you look to your left, suddenly, and you realize that there's English there, too. He is saying the same stuff in the same way. He understands it fine. There's a couple of spots where he misunderstands something, and it gets cleared up. Plus, that's a guy who understands English. He said so from the beginning.

You can go on and on with these things. You really can. But let's talk about some of the issues with the defendant's trial testimony, which is his account as to why he is innocent of these charges. Because there's some critical features of that testimony that are just the opposite of the way that credible witnesses testify and it just doesn't match up with the evidence. It doesn't mesh.

Marital problems. He talks to Sergeant Cardova quite a bit about that. He talks all about marital issues. They just don't have any right now. Things are pretty good. That's what you see. That's what he says. And, you know, testifying, "I'm too embarrassed to say that we are near divorce."

I'm sorry, he's not too embarrassed to say they were near divorce at some other time. Why on Earth would he be too embarrassed now?

And, of course, Alejandra, when asked about the same thing, she gives consistent answers, just like he does, like indicating that they aren't having problems right now. They have had problems, but they are not having problems.

Now Detective Lopez goes even further than Sergeant Cardova on these issues. He gets all of the same type of information about how they are not having problems now, but he actually talks to him about October 31st, in the evening, and what took place. And, of course, the defendant tells him that he didn't go to work that day because he was sick. And the defendant has himself going to bed early that night, before anyone else in the household had gone to bed. But the defendant did remember his wife eventually coming to bed where he was sleeping.

Now what was his trial testimony? His trial testimony was that on the 31st, he went to work. He gets into a fight with his wife. He manages to go out with friends and get drunk, and then manages to come back home and, apparently, fight again. Now here is the thing. He doesn't talk about any of that, any of that. And if it were true, he would have; another thing massively inconsistent on those marital problems.

Now on Armando, who is a big old red herring in the case, there's nothing about Armando that had anything to do with these charges, I would submit to you. But they talked to him about Armando, aside from the defendant not liking the guy smoking marijuana in the house, there's not a whole lot that comes out that's negative about him.

The defendant worked with him. He moved out like two and a half years ago, according to the defendant. He wasn't really seeing him around the time. But it wasn't this like huge, ominous thing.

And the drinking, the statement that the defendant is making, managing to pound six or seven beers or whatever it is at the harbor while he is fishing, that's nothing that he told any of the other officers.

And why is he doing that? It's because there is a halfway attempt to kind of sort of try to start to explain why he isn't able to remember things. But none of that is in any way consistent with what is told to the officers and none of it is consistent with what the other witnesses express.

Alejandra has him drinking a beer before the argument, when he bails, when he flees for no reason. Sandy has him drinking a beer. Nobody has him drunk. Nobody has him in any way obviously impaired by alcohol at all. Nobody has him drunk-driving all over town. And so all of that, it's all massive changes in a convenient way, none of which connect with the other evidence that you all have heard.

Now then, it's worth going into the way that these jail calls figure into all of this. Because when you look really closely at the information contained in those seven calls, what you see is that that is a horribly strained, horribly strained account that the defendant testified to.

They are not secretly talking about alcohol. No. No. The strained interpretation, no. When you look at them closely, the first call coming in just after not even 24 hours since he raped his daughter, and it's like a seven- or eight-minute call, something like that, maybe even it's a little shorter, what's he doing?

He calls and wants help getting bail. And the thing is that you listen to Alejandra, she's talking to him, you know? She's talking to him. She's not flipping out, which says something about her. I mean, she's upset, but she's already worried about money.

But the defendant is just expecting that she's going to help. There's no pretending that, you know, what if he is really innocent? Why isn't he asking her, "Hey, what in the heck happened to Sandy? How did she get injured? Is she okay?"

It's none of that. There's not even a fraction of that. Now how can that be? Well, one answer is that he already knows. But he doesn't ask about her. He doesn't mention being framed. And he thinks his wife is responsible for it, everyone. It doesn't come up.

So then they don't talk, even though the defendant is calling constantly, calling Mandy constantly, all in violation of the protective order, which is exactly how you would act if you were totally innocent, in a strange world.

So it's the 30th. And he apologizes. And what does he say exactly? This happens because, as always, Alejandra picks up the phone and he asks, "How are you?"

"Bad."

"How are the kids?"

"Bad."

It's like, "Why don't you pick up my calls?"

"Because don't - please don't call."

That's what always happens. But she goes on "What for? Why? Why did you destroy us? Why? "

The defendant says, "Why?"

"Why did you destroy everything?"

He says, "Let's not talk about any of that, okay. I just want to you tell you I'm very sorry for what happened. The truth is I also - um - I don't know, I don't know - when or to what extent I can do these things. I'm sorry for what happened."

"I don't know when or to what extent I can do these things." That was just the very first of a lot of different things he says. There is no frickin' way he is talking about alcohol. Nope. This looks like it encompasses both Mandy and Sandy. And make no mistake, every single time Alejandra is saying things like, "Why did you do this," she is not talking about, "Why did you have a few beers?"

There is no reason why it would sound like this. You know why it does sound like this? Because Alejandra, when you look closely, doesn't want to get him in any more trouble. But she loves him. She misses him. She is hurting, because she can't believe that he has put her in this position.

And the defendant says, "It's so easy to say, "Why did you destroy us?"

He never says, "What do you mean, destroy us? I didn't do anything. What in the hell is going on? Why am I here?"

I'm sorry. We can have a stipulation that he was advised by a lawyer. You are not hurting your case by saying, "I didn't do anything. What is" –

MS. PRESTON: Objection; Sixth Amendment; Fifth Amendment.

THE COURT: I'll sustain. Move forward, please.

MR. BOLT: But you can go on with these things, and they are a gold mine of a window inside what that relationship really is like.

He is asking for forgiveness constantly. And Alejandra is suffering. And she describes how the children are suffering. And she's talking about things that just absolutely do not square with the idea that, "Oh, I'm just apologizing for everything that has ever happened."

You really need to go back and look at those, but I want to point out a few good ones, like he doesn't care if they give him more charges.

Alejandra, talking about the apartment, "It's scary. So many things happened. The girls are afraid."

She tells him how she's not going to lie. "I love you very much. My pain is stronger."

The defendant: "I can't be alone. That's all I'm saying. You all are the machine that keeps me strong. If it wasn't for you guys I wouldn't be alive. I'm alive for you. You guys are the ones who made me, gave me strength to go through everything I went through. The only thing, I've been blind, I didn't realize is the only thing. It's too late to realize everything now."

On the 8th, the defendant wants to know who drops off the kids, who picked up the kids. Why? Because he wants to dissuade them. He wants to know that stuff. He is asking: "Who picks them up? Who takes them to school? Who picks them up?"

She says, "What the heck do you care if I'm the one who takes them?" "Ms. Carrie picks them up, and she can take them over from you, right?"

"Right."

"What's the problem," she says

"Nothing. Just wanted to know."

The defendant constantly saying he is going to change. This is a concept that comes up a lot: "Then it depends on you. If you want me to stay here all my life, I can stay all my life."

She says, "I'm not saying that. I'm not going to decide. I can't decide about anyone."

He says, "With that, you're going to make a little bit of money back," talking about selling the truck. "In the meantime, it can help you all."

She says, "Well, I know. I know all that. But what about the moral aspect? Because the money - what about that? No one, no one pays for that with money. I'll tell you, no one is going to fix it, the damage."

She is not talking about drinking. She's talking about the damage that he has caused to her children, and a little bit of money isn't going to fix it.

"The way you feel."

"I feel that way, too," he says. Please let me talk to the girls."

"No."

There were a couple of occasions where there is clear pressure being put on the girls, Mandy specifically. On the 9th of January, he wants help. "Help me get out. Help me get out." Alejandra: "I don't have anything to get you out. I can't. Here, everything is within the law. I can't do anything, nothing, because I haven't crossed anyone. The ones who told the truth was your daughters. It wasn't me. I haven't said anything. Justice is what's going to decide here. And I didn't decide this. You should have thought about that a long time ago. I don't know at what point it went through your mind, if you were high or what you were thinking."

He says, "Don't talk about anything that can make it worse for me."

And she is so nonspecific. She loves him. She doesn't want to make it worse for him, but she can't help it. Because you'll see, you know, where she's torn between the way she feels and protecting her girls, and she says it.

THE COURT: Mr. Bolt, it's noon. What's your ETA?

MR. BOLT: I guess probably about 15, 20 minutes.

THE COURT: Any problem with reconvening –

MR. BOLT: No.

THE COURT: - at 1:30?

MR. BOLT: No, that's fine.

THE COURT: Please do not discuss this matter amongst yourselves or with anyone else. Please do not form or express any opinions concerning this matter.

I'll look forward to seeing everyone at 1:30. Thank you. We're off the record at this time.

(Lunch break.)

6

10th Juror – Amy Friar - late 60s - retired CPS social worker.

I'm glad Mr. Bolt brought up the jail calls. It's clear to me that Mr. Flores is guilty. He admitted it. He may have seemed nice on the witness stand, but I think he's just a good actor. He was too calm on the stand and too calm during the interrogations.

It's too bad Mr. Bolt's closing statement is so long, but if you think about it, there's just so much evidence to review. Yes. Much of it was confusing and some of it was contradictory, but as Mr. Bolt says, the fundamental facts are there. Mr. Flores raped poor little Sandy and molested Mandy.

I can't imagine that any of the other jurors think Mr. Flores is innocent. I've seen these immigrant homes where the alcoholic father abuses the family. Too often nothing is done. This time, they got him. I'm just sorry it took three years to bring him to trial. Alejandra and the girls tried to move on and now it's all been brought back to them. Hopefully this part of their suffering will be over soon.

I'm also glad that we're almost done with the trial. Mr. Bolt said he'd need another twenty minutes to finish his closing statement. I hope Ms. Preston's closing statement isn't as long. After all, she only called a few witnesses. It isn't likely she will change my mind.

I'm certainly glad we have people like Mr. Bolt working for us.

7

THE COURT: Let's go back on the record, please, regarding People versus Albert Flores. Mr. Flores is present. Counsel are present. All of our jurors are present. Please continue, Mr. Bolt.
MR. BOLT: Thank you, Your Honor.

So pulling out a couple of other notable admissions in these calls, and I really want to emphasize that it is worth it to look at these things and actually really try and compare it to what the evidence is, and what it really means.

But, for instance, on the first call on January 22nd, on the second page, Alejandra starts in, "You already destroyed me. You destroyed. You already destroyed me. Why are you calling me? I feel worse when I hear you. Do you think it's easy, everything that I'm going through?"

He responds, "Well, I know. That's why I told you last time we have to ask God. I told you we have to ask God for things to be different."

A couple pages later, between page four and pages six, Alejandra says, "But it's not easy for me, I tell you. Everything you did, it's not easy or something. I'm confused. Every day is worse for me. Do you think it's easy, what you did, to have you at my side, the girls' dad? Everything is traumatic for me, I tell you. To me, it's a pain to see you where you are, because no matter what you're my husband. Seeing you there, I'm not going to forgive what you did, either."

He responds, "Don't talk about anything."

And she goes on talking about basically that she can't pretend that this isn't going on when she talks to him.

And then he says,: "What do you want? For me to stay here, then?"

And it's not her job to decide, in her mind.

And he comes back with, "You can call and help me."

And she again, as usual, says, "No, I can't do that. I can't help you."

And then, in that same call, the defendant says, "But I'm telling you, with everything I had, all that I've lost, do you think -"

And Alejandra cuts him off and says, "But who ordered you? Who ordered you to do those things? Who ordered you? That's why I'm saying, in what mind did you do what you did?"

He responds, "Three months, Alejandra, without -"

And she cuts him off again, "What were you thinking, or what?"

She tells him that he failed her.

Near the end of that call, on page 10, the defendant says, "You know that you're my wife, and my daughters, that's all I have."

Alejandra says, "All I'm telling you, I love you and I love you very much."

The defendant says, "Huh?"

She says, "I never am going to stop. I love you. I love you a lot. But I'm also going to protect my daughters."

The calls, when you look at them closely, there is one thing that is upsetting Alejandra every single day, and that is coming to grips with her own feelings for the defendant and coming to grips with what he did. And she confronts him constantly with, "You put yourself there. You destroyed us. Who made you do that?" Constantly. It doesn't even make sense to suggest that he couldn't say, "I didn't do it." He was saying that to everybody else, everybody else.

Now those are a really great lens to help judge the credibility of people. But then, when he comes in here and testifies, it's so different than what he said before and so convenient. And when you view his statements through the lens, if he's innocent, it's just hard to make sense of. If you view it through the lens of he's guilty, because that is what the other evidence in the case shows, what you see is that it now, it makes perfect sense. It makes perfect sense.

All of his omissions, all of his failures to tell the truth, all of the changes between what he says to the detectives and what he says now, all of it explains that he is trying to create a different reality where the people involved had a motive to fabricate. And they don't. They simply don't.

Now, I want to walk you through exactly what the charges are in this case.

So just starting with Count 1, the first - the charge is - Count 1 is sexual intercourse with a child, occurring on November 1st, 20XX.

The first six charges all have to do with Sandy and what happened at the apartment that afternoon, before going with her father, fishing. There are six counts related to that episode: obviously, sexual intercourse with a child, sexual penetration with a child, aggravated sexual assault on a child based upon the forcible rape, rape by force, and two counts of forcible lewd act.

Now I'm going to just go over the elements as I explain how these charges make sense within the context of what you all know the evidence is. And so looking a little bit more closely at the jury instruction for Count 1 and Count 12 as well, this is the instruction that you will have in the jury room. And it says: To prove that the defendant is guilty of this crime, the People must prove that - and I just want to make a point right out of the gate. This is a case with all kinds of information, as you know. There is so much information in this case that it boggles the mind. I mean, it's really difficult to think about it all at the same time, because you have so many different people saying so many different things that are perhaps largely consistent, but there are little differences everywhere.

But what's important is, in understanding the People's burden of proof, is that the burden of proof is the burden to prove the elements of the offenses, not random extraneous information, even if that information pertains to an offense, perhaps.

But, for instance, in this charge the defendant engaged in an act of sexual intercourse with Sandy. Sexual intercourse is defined right down here, and it says: Sexual intercourse means any penetration, no matter how slight, of the vagina or genitalia by the penis. Ejaculation is not required.

So an act of sexual intercourse, what that means is just what this says. It means any penetration, no matter how slight. And that's all that it means. That's the legal definition. That's what the People have to prove in the first element of this charge, nothing more, nothing at all more.

So there's an account, there's descriptions. And you don't have to be convinced beyond a reasonable doubt of every detail provided by a witness. What matters is whether the elements have been proven. And the first element of this charge is simply an act of sexual intercourse.

And then the other elements are simple, as well: When the defendant did so, Sandy was ten years of age or younger. She was seven.

At the time of the act, the defendant was at least 18 years old. He was 30.

So regardless in terms of whether individual detail and specific accounts have been proven, the fact that is the People's burden of proof is an act of sexual intercourse with the ages that are involved here. It is that simple.

And so, obviously, the People submit to you that an act of sexual intercourse occurred on that bed at that apartment that afternoon, and it has been proven.

Now Count 2 relates to the same state of affairs at the apartment. To prove that the defendant engaged in an act of sexual penetration with Sandy, the other two elements are the same.

Now just for you, this is going to come up again so it's worth taking note of it. "Sexual penetration" means penetration, however slight, of the genitalia or anal opening of the other person by any foreign object, substance, instrument or device, or by an unknown object, for the purpose of sexual abuse, arousal or gratification.

If you look a little further down: An unknown object - near the bottom of the screen: An unknown object includes any foreign object, substance, instrument or device or any part of the body, including a penis, if it's not known what object penetrated the opening.

What that essentially means is that if as a group you were to agree that an act of sexual penetration occurred, even if you didn't feel that it had been proven beyond a reasonable doubt that it was a penis, then any object, including a penis, would do. The fact is that the child had been so consistent and the injuries corroborated it, and so I would submit to you that it has been proven beyond a reasonable doubt.

But that is why you are seeing this charged crime. And it does relate to what took place at the apartment, as most clearly described by Sandy during the detailed interview with Detective Locke.

Count 3 is the crime of aggravated sexual assault of a child under 14.

And so the elements here are rape by force or fear on Sandy, and the age requirement. Obviously, the age requirement is not an issue. To find out what is required to prove the forcible rape, you have to refer to a different instruction, and that's the instruction which directly defines rape by force.

And so to prove that the defendant is guilty of rape by force, there are four elements: sexual intercourse, not married, no consent, and then the defendant accomplished intercourse by force, violence, duress, menace or fear of immediate and unlawful bodily injury to Sandy or to someone else.

And if you believe what Sandy said, then you know that the defendant used force and menace and threat of force to get her onto the bed, to remove her clothes, to overcome her resistance, because she didn't consent.

Her actions screamed that. Everything that she did conveyed that to the defendant.

And it's sort of an odd concept to talk about consent when you are talking about a seven-year-old child. But, again, this is Count 3, and it has a different set of elements. Whereas in Count 1 and 2, consent is not an issue, in Count 3 consent is an issue. Count 1 and 2, there is no requirement that the act be accomplished by any kind of force or menace or duress, but that is part of the requirement.

Now here, the evidence supports a rape by force. It supports a rape by menace. It supports a rape by threat of force. It supports a rape by fear of immediate and unlawful bodily injury. Sandy was afraid for all kinds of reasons.

And so that is the specific requirement to prove the aggravated sexual assault. Basically you add the ages to the definition of rape by force, and that's what Count 3 is.

Now Count 4 is the same. It's forcible rape. So it's basically a lesser included offense which is charged as a separate count.

Now what that means for you in terms of analyzing this is if you believe that the evidence has proven rape, then all you are going to do is to find him guilty of that aggravated sexual assault, because the only difference between those two are the age requirements.

And it's hard to imagine how you would come to the conclusion that the age requirements aren't met. So when you see the verdict forms, Counts 3 and Counts 4 will be on the same form.

And now Count 5 and Count 6. These are two counts. Now, again, this is a different crime, and you're going to see this crime in Counts 5, 6, 11 and 13. They have different elements as well.

Now in each of the crimes you've seen so far, it's required a specific act, either a sexual penetration or a sexual intercourse, as legally defined. What you will notice for a lewd or lascivious act is that you have a much more general act, literally any touching of the child if the defendant had the intent of arousing, appealing to or gratifying the lust, passions or sexual desires of himself or the child. That's what a charge like this is going to turn on.

You have received what's called a unanimity instruction which relates to specifically Count 5, Count 6 and then Count 8. But we'll get to that.

Now what that means, you see, when you go through the evidence you'll see there are actually many different touchings upon which a conviction could be based, many different touchings. One, for instance, is a touching by a penis to a genitalia.

But there are many. Even the pulling off of the pants involves a touching, and it's happening at a time where the defendant is harboring the requisite intent.

Just looking through the elements: willfully touched any part of a child's body, on the bare skin or through the clothing. That is so broad. That is so broad.

Using force, violence, duress, menace or fear of immediate and unlawful bodily injury to the child or someone else. Now, you'll notice that the definition of "force" as it relates to a lewd or lascivious act accomplished by force is different than the definition of "force" in the rape or sexual penetration context.

I submit to you that the evidence of force is sufficient here, but it's much more obvious that acts that the defendant committed were accomplished through violence, duress, menace or fear of an immediate and unlawful bodily injury, because those, specifically the unlawful bodily injury, like the child reasonably feared for her safety if she didn't comply; like there was duress because his position as her father and she's a child, and he punishes her and she fears that, and all that is, by itself, sufficient for menace and duress.

And so there's this technical definition, but it doesn't need to be accomplished by all of these. It only needs to be accomplished through one of them. But it's okay if it's a combination.

And then, of course, the defendant committed the act with the intent. Now that's the specific intent, which is different than the other crimes so far. All of those simply require an act that was done on purpose, an intentional act. And this one is different to the extent that it has a specific intent. So the act has to be with the intent of arousing, appealing to, gratifying the lusts, passions or sexual desires of himself or the child.

And the reality is, of course, that the context and the acts themselves speak for themselves as far as what the intent is.

I'm taking the time to explain it because it's important that you understand it. This is a case where if you believe it occurred, then these elements are quite clearly met. If you don't believe it occurred, then they are quite clearly not met. But it's not difficult to fit what the evidence supports here as far as happened into these elements.

But it is worthy of note that there are two counts, and there are many touchings so that can be sufficient.

For instance, when the defendant is forcing her pants off, when he is covering her mouth, when he is touching her in any way during that event, I would submit to you that the evidence supports that he harbored the requisite intent.

So for each of the forcible child molest charges, there is also a lesser included offense. And the lesser included offense is simply what's called a lewd act. And a lewd act is the elements are the exact same, only they don't have to be accomplished through force, threat of force, duress, menace, all that stuff.

Now under the law and under the instructions, you guys are allowed to consider the greater or lesser offenses in evaluating the evidence in whatever order you want. However, can’t vote to convict on the lesser until you've unanimously agreed that the greater crime has not been proven.

Now, again, when you look at Count 3, the aggravated sexual assault with the rape, and then the lesser included is rape, the only difference is the ages. So it's hard to understand how you would ever find him not guilty on the greater and guilty on the lesser. And so, in a similar way here, the lesser being absent the forcible requirement. If you believe it happened, the evidence is very strong on all those features.

And it's interesting to note that the touching, it does not need to be done in a lewd or sexual manner. And that's just to make it clear that there doesn't need to be something inherently sexual about the touching at issue. That's why the stroke of somebody's hair, the touching of their foot, if it's done with the right intent, it violates the statute.

Now that's Count 5 and Count 6.

Now as it relates to Counts 1 through 6, there is a special allegation that you need to consider for each of those offenses. And so the special allegation is that the defendant inflicted bodily harm on Sandy in the commission of the crime.

Now the bodily harm at issue here is the injury to her genitals. And you heard the testimony about that, and there are pictures in evidence for you to look at to whether that injury is a substantial physical injury resulting from the use of force that is more than the force necessary to commit the offense.

And I would submit to you that it's clearly substantial. It was bleeding from the time that it occurred, into the night, and it even bled when it was examined two days later. It hurt.

It was caused by blunt force trauma. And it is a substantial physical injury. And it was the result of the use of force that is more than the force necessary to commit the offense. Because regardless of which count you consider in Counts 1 through 6, you can commit an act of sexual intercourse with only the slightest penetration. And this penetration was not slight. This penetration was forceful, and it was forceful enough to cause this injury. And so that is more force than is necessary to commit the act. It requires less force.

And so if you believe that it occurred, then I would submit to you that the evidence is very, very strong that you should find that that is true.

Now that analysis applies to the first four counts very clearly.

On Five and Six, if the touching that you consider is penis to genitals, then the same analysis applies. If it's a different touching that you are considering, then you have may have a different conclusion. And that's depending on what the touching is.

Now Count 7 is charged as a false imprisonment.

And what this means, the defendant intentionally and unlawfully confined Alejandra Rivera. The defendant's act made Alejandra Rivera stay or go somewhere against her will. This does not require that the person restrained be detained or confined in jail or prison.

Now what are we talking about here? We're talking about what occurred during the argument. Now if you were to just listen to Alejandra's in-court testimony, you might not even know why this was charged, although maybe you would. But if you listen to what is described much more closely in time, this argument gets heated, and at one point the defendant is preventing her from leaving. At another point, when she is trying to call for help, he takes her phone. And that is what this count is referring to.

Count 8 is concealing or destroying evidence. To be guilty of this crime, the People have to prove these two elements: the defendant intentionally and unlawfully destroyed or concealed any object, matter, thing, or record; and two, the defendant acted with the intent to prevent the item from being produced in evidence at any trial, inquiry or investigation authorized by law.

Now the evidence in this case which relates to this count, there are two primary examples. Sandy describes that the defendant gave her or provided her a towel that she wiped herself with after the rape occurred in the apartment. She describes that he took it. And that is one act.

There is a separate act which is what occurred at the storage unit where she was made to change underwear, taking off her bloody underwear, according to Sandy, the defendant put those into a bag, and they were never seen again.

Now if you believe that he did one or the other of those acts, then I submit to you that the evidence would be sufficient to convict him on these. Because if he did either of those things, then he is clearly doing them to conceal or destroy evidence. You could also, if you believe that he had Sandy shower, that also potentially destroyed evidence. And if you believe beyond a reasonable doubt that he did that, like the child says, then that would be sufficient to convict him on that as well, because if he did that he did it with the intent to prevent the item, matter, to be produced in evidence.

Now the next three counts, 9, 10 and 11, they all have to do with Mandy. And these are really similar. They are similar crimes that we're talking about. Count 9 is an aggravated sexual assault. So this is a similar crime to the aggravated sexual assault which was alleged in Count 3, except the difference is that rather than it being focused on an act of sexual intercourse, it's on an act of sexual penetration. Because what Mandy discloses is that the defendant forcibly penetrated her genitals with fingers.

And so, similarly, this refers you to another instruction which defines "sexual penetration." And these elements are going to be very similar to the elements of rape. Element one, an act of sexual penetration. Penetration with fingers is exactly that. That penetration was by using a foreign object. You'll see that a finger is within the definition of a foreign object.

But even if it was something else, if you believe penetration occurred, if you believe that she didn't consent to it, and you believe her description, then clearly that act was accomplished by force.

The only difference between Counts 9 and 10 is that 10 is the lesser included offense. Similarly to Three and Four, those are going to occur on the same verdict form, and you can consider them in any order you want, but you shouldn't convict him of the lesser unless you have unanimously voted not guilty on the greater crime, the greater being aggravated sexual assault.

Now then Count 11. This is Mandy. A lewd act accomplished by force. Similarly, there are a number of different touchings that can satisfy it, but the most obvious is touching her genitals. It doesn't require penetration, but it does require the specific intent which, if you believe it, is easily inferable from the circumstances.

Similarly, you'll see that there is the simple lewd act lesser included offense.

Now Counts 12, 13 and 14, those counts relate to Sandy. They all are alleged to have occurred on or about November 1st, 20XX.

What it relates to is simply the testimony that she gave at the preliminary hearing, where she alleged an additional act of sexual intercourse occurring while she was supposed to be fishing. And obviously the evidence is different, as it relates to those counts, than all the other things she talks about, because, as you well know, that's not something that comes up in the other interviews. And it's worth watching the video of her preliminary hearing testimony and comparing it to all the evidence in the case, because I would submit to you that there is nothing about that, regardless of what you think about that, there's nothing about that which takes away from the credibility of what she had disclosed.

Now as it relates to each of the Counts 1 through 6 and 9 through 14, you must consider the allegation of multiple victims. And this is how that works. If you convict the defendant of committing a crime against Mandy and a crime against Sandy, then this allegation is going to be true for every one of those crimes.

If you commit or convict on a crime against Mandy but not on a crime against Sandy, then it would be not true for each of the crimes.

If you convicted on a count against Sandy and not Mandy, then it would not be true.

So if you convict on a count of both girls, then it's true for every count involving both girls.

And so those are the elements of the offenses. I'm going to turn on the lights here for a moment.

There is a lot of evidence in this case and it's a lot to go over. I do get a chance to respond to the defense. And so if it is as the defense claims, you should ask yourself this: If it is that the defendant is innocent of these charges, if it's true that he is wrongfully accused of these crimes, then why isn't there any corroborating evidence here for this supposed claim of innocence?

MS. PRESTON: Objection, Your Honor; Fifth Amendment; burden shifting.

THE COURT: I'll overrule. Again, the jury has been advised that the sole burden rests with the People and the burden is beyond a reasonable doubt. The defendant does not have to prove anything.

MR. BOLT: Thank you.

THE COURT: Please continue, Mr. Bolt.

MR. BOLT: Thank you.

And again, they just absolutely don't have to prove anything. However, so much of what is proven by the statements that the defendant made, both to law enforcement and in this courtroom, the ones made to his wife on jail calls, and the things that he has done, like trying to get witnesses to change their story or to not show up in court, violating protective orders, fleeing the apartment when it's hard to understand how an innocent person would do that, the misstatements to police - all of these things, they show a consciousness of guilt. And I submit to you that the evidence is very clear, and the affirmative evidence on its own easily supports a conviction. But to ignore all of the ways that the defendant has behaved, all of the things that he has said, the way that he comes in and tries to change facts in order to suit the situation that he's in, all of these things show a consciousness of guilt.

And since this isn't a case with a middle ground - the child is not mistaken when she identifies Astroglide from a lineup, like a photographic lineup, as, "That's the bottle my dad used," she is not mistaken. She is either telling the truth because these things happened, or she is just lying about it.

And if she were lying and if the defendant were innocent, wouldn't you expect that with all the different witnesses and all the different pieces of evidence, that there would be something substantial in addition to the defendant's own conveniently selected words to corroborate the idea that this is all a lie? And wouldn't you think that there would be some way, some plausible way, that they would have of explaining how Sandy could have suffered this horrible injury to her genitals?

MS. PRESTON: Objection; Fifth Amendment; burden shifting.

THE COURT: Well, again, the jury knows where the burden of proof lies and where it does not.

Please continue, Mr. Bolt.

MR. BOLT: Thank you.

And I'm sure Ms. Preston is going to answer that question for you. I'm sure she will.

MS. PRESTON: Same objection ongoing to this line.

THE COURT: So noted. Overruled with the admonition to the jury.

Please continue.

MR. BOLT: Because that's not the truth. The truth is that these girls were sexually abused. The evidence proves that. And when I get a chance to speak again, I'm going to ask you to return verdicts of guilty on these charges.

THE COURT: Thank you. Ms. Preston, do you need a couple minutes to set up?

MS. PRESTON: I do. Thank you, sir.

THE COURT: All right. Let's everybody just stand up and stretch a little bit, if you so desire.

(Pause.)

(Off the record.)

8

Jurors thoughts during the stretch:

1st Juror – Laura Miles - late 60s – writer - no children.

I'm really not sure about this case. For me, in spite of his somewhat confused closing statement, Mr. Bolt makes a strong case. How do you explain the injuries? And those jail calls. I think he may have admitted that he raped Sandy. But then there were all those lies. Yes, this would make a great novel. I'll have to seriously think about writing one once I know the outcome.

2nd Juror – Barbara Hatch - mid-40s - ER nurse married, no kids.

That was a painful closing. Mr. Bolt really needs some help in his presentations. And yes, he did make some good points, but with the lack of DNA evidence and my belief that the injury just doesn't match up with the claims, I strongly believe Mr. Flores has been wrongly accused. Hopefully Ms. Preston will convince the doubters.

3rd Juror – Linda Lancaster - early 40s - personnel manager in a larger corporation – married - no kids.

I don't buy it. DNA evidence was missing and if anything, exculpatory. There were just too many lies from Alejandra, Mandy, and even Sandy. I'm looking forward to Preston's closing after this boring close by Bolt.

4th Juror – Evan Garcia - mid-40s – Hispanic – Silicon Valley Entrepreneur, film fanatic. Unmarried no children.

Boring but strong closing from Bolt. But he just doesn't have the evidence. If it had been me; if I'd committed this crime and I had a truck, I'd have headed for the hills. No way I'd park a few blocks away. Albert has got to be innocent.

5th Juror – Melissa Duplisse , early 70s, retired nurse.

The judge refused to let me go. He was very nice about it and thanked me for my service. And he emphasized service. I admit that I was flattered when he told me that the court needed people like me – average people – to really hear these horrible things. Judges, lawyers, and the authorities get jaded judging these terrible crimes. It must be up to us, the people, to see things clearly. I do. There's no question in my mind that Mr. Flores is guilty. I hate to admit it, but I dozed a few times during Mr. Bolt's closing statement. But what I did hear was clear. Mr. Flores is an evil man who must pay for what he's done to his children.

6th Juror – Andy Harrigan, early 50s, Supervisor at the California EPA, one daughter about to graduate from high school, another daughter away at college.

Could Bolt have done a worse job prosecuting this case? I don't see how it ever made it this far. Poor Albert has spent 3 years in jail. He's lost his job, his new business, his family. His life is ruined. And for what? Because he threatened to leave his wife and take the children?

After that painful closing speech by Bolt, I'm looking forward to what Ms. Preston has to say. I hope she makes a final point with the timeline that doesn't match up. That will convince anyone who still thinks Albert is guilty.

7th Juror – Sue Markovsky - late 40s, unmarried, no children - recent arrival to the area. Political activist.

Well, I didn't think so at first, but poor Albert has been crushed by the system. Accusations from his wife and kids and everyone jumps on board. Just the length of Bolt's argument tells you how much shit they all put together to try to bury Albert. Whatever happened to innocent until proven guilty? I admit, in cases like this, I'll always give the benefit of the doubt to the victims, especially children, but come on. How did this ever make it to trial?

8th Juror – Ben Singleton - mid-30s - state park ranger - 2 kids under 10.

What a snooze-fest. Yeah, I know. Seven weeks of testimony won't get summarized in an hour or two. Then again, going over it again and again smacks of desperation. As the Judge ordered, I'm keeping an open mind until we get to deliberations. And realistically, right now, I can see it both ways. I could make a strong argument for guilty, especially the injury, and I could make a strong argument for not guilty – no DNA and he didn't run. I can't wait to finally hear what the others have to say.

9th Juror – Erica Hesse - early 40s- CEO of a rapidly growing high-tech company. Single no children.

Nearly eight weeks away from my startup for this? I thought trial lawyers were supposed to be strong public speakers, but my nerdiest engineer could have done a better closing. Disorganized, rambling, and a case that fell apart long ago. Too bad the Judge didn't grant the directed verdict of innocent requested by the defense.

10th Juror – Amy Friar - late 60s - retired CPS social worker.

There is no question in my mind that Mr. Flores raped poor little Sandy and molested Mandy.

12th Juror – Steve Dietz - engineer in Santa Cruz startup - early-thirties no kids. Father is a lawyer.

I said it before. Bolt is a fuck-up. The second half of his closing put a couple of jurors to sleep. There's no doubt in my mind that Flores is guilty. But it's clear that several of the other jurors are looking at Bolt skeptically. No, with disdain. This is going to be a tough deliberation. Hopefully Matt and I can take control.

13th Juror – Maria Fugetti, retired physician's assistant, late 60s, 3 grown children.

I may have been confused before, and it's true that I don't understand why so many people lied, but I'm clear that Mr. Flores is guilty. I feel sorry for him, but he is guilty. I'm so glad that Mr. Bolt explained things so slowly. He made everything fit together. I can tell that some of the other jurors are skeptical. So I'm truly glad that I'm just an alternate. I don't want to argue with people. And it looks like I get to go home today. This painful experience is finally at an end and I'll be able to tell Richard, my husband, all about it. I just hope I can stop thinking about it soon. It's been my whole life for almost eight weeks and it seems to have taken over. Yes. I hope I can stop thinking about this case.

14th Juror – Jonathan Comstock - retired early 70s - ex-engineer.

You know where I stand. Ms. Preston kicked Bolt's butt, and we haven't even heard her closing. I wish I could be in on the deliberations. It seems like I've wasted eight weeks of my life. It's taken a lot of time, a lot of agony, and I don't even get to be part of the final decision.

15th Juror (now 11th Juror) – Mathias Wright, Silicon Valley engineer, early-thirties with 2 children under 5.

Bolt is right. How did she get those injuries? The right answer is the simplest. Flores is guilty. Matt and I are going to double-team everyone voting for innocent. This guy is going down!

16th Juror – Mark Mentor, early 60s, retired ex-Silicon Valley startup CEO.

It's almost over. I feel useless. I think I have a lot to contribute to the deliberations but I don't get to. I go home. Three of us go home today. I think the woman is relieved. Jonathon, who I've talked to several times on breaks, feels the way I do. We've just given eight weeks of our lives to this case, stressed out our families, and we don't get to participate in the deliberations. It doesn't seem right. Aren't 15 voices better than 12 in a situation like this?

9

THE COURT: Let's go back on the record.
Ms. Preston, at your convenience, please.
MS. PRESTON: Thank you, Your Honor.

They lied. They lied to get out of a bad situation. They lied to protect each other. They lied to protect themselves. They told small lies. They told big lies; lies so big they couldn't take them back, lies that were convincing. They started to believe them themselves, lies so powerful that they built and they spread and they grew until they consumed the truth.

"The truth will set you free," the sergeant said.

"I didn't do it."

"Tell us the truth now and it will go better for you in court."
"I didn't rape my daughters."

"What rates man from animal is that men admit their mistakes."

"I didn't do it.

"And you will find proof I didn't do it."

Albert Flores told them the truth, but it was too late. By then, only a few hours after this accusation, when all they had to go on was the words of a troubled young girl, and an injury that could have been caused by something else, they had already convicted him. They had already closed the case.

By the time evidence of innocence started pouring in from the Department of Justice, no blood and semen mixed on that comforter, his DNA not on Sandy, where it absolutely would be if this had happened the way that she said it did, and her DNA not on him; by the time Sandy's story started to change in material, incredible ways; by the time Mandy got up on the witness stand and said, "I lied, I lied"; by the time they found out that Alejandra needed immigration help for Armando; by the time their case started to fall apart, it was already too late. Lies had already consumed the truth.

It's hard to call someone a liar. It's especially hard to believe that a child would lie about something like this. And yet we know that children lie about sexual abuse. Children misattribute blame to the wrong person. They are suggestible. They can describe detailed, vivid sex acts that never occurred.

How do you tell the difference? How do you know when a

child has lied? How do you spot the lies?

Lies change as time goes on. They become embellished and edited and revised, gaining more detail, becoming more interesting, because the person who is telling the lie is a storyteller. They are responding to their audience, adopting, editing scenes, changing the details to become more vivid or believable. Lies change. Sex on a bed becomes sex in a shed, or even sex on a beach.

Please don't make the mistake of minimizing what happened. On April 15th, 2014, when Sandy Rivera stood here and she took the oath to tell the truth, she got up on this witness stand, she sat here, and in the very same tone of voice that she had just used to describe her dad raping her on her parents' bed, she described a detailed, vivid account of sex on the beach, sex on the rock, sex on a rock at the Santa Cruz Harbor on a Friday afternoon with people just a stone's throw away.

You watched as she embellished and she edited and she revised her story to fit what her questioner wanted to hear. You could almost see her mind working in that video. She had just been up at the DA's Office watching the videos. We learned that from Bernadette Ramsey.

They were showing her what they wanted her to say, the story that they wanted her to repeat on this witness stand: "We need the story about your dad raping you." And she dutifully got up there and she gave that story in almost of the same words that she had just seen on the video.

But then the prosecutor - not Mr. Bolt, Mr. Hanson - at the preliminary hearing, he starts to ask her about the beach. And poor Sandy is thinking, "They want a story about rape. They want a story about sex. I just gave them the story they just told me to tell. Apparently that isn't enough. So I've got to give them what they want."

And so here, on the fly, question by question, you can practically see the prosecutor trying not to reel, trying to stay cool, trying to think what to ask next that won't make this whole mess worse.

She comes up with this fantastic lie that couldn't possibly be true. The problem when you tell a lie like that is that it changes everything.

Think about your own lives. Think about when someone has told you a lie like that, a big, convincing powerful lie. Can you trust that person's word with the most important decision in your life? Can you trust that person's word with Mr. Flores's life? If Sandy can lie about sex on the beach, she can lie about anything.

How can you spot a lie? Sometimes the liar comes clean. Sometimes the person simply says, "I lied." It requires a lot of courage, but it happens. And it happened here.

We all watched Mandy's interview with Detective Locke. We all watched her detailed, vivid account of sex that occurred supposedly when she was three, three years old, at an age where she wasn't really able to express herself, at an age where memories, if we have them, are incredibly thin. She gave a detailed account of sex.

But we also watched when Mandy, not once but twice, at the preliminary hearing and at this trial, when she took the stand and, even knowing what they wanted her to say, even having just watched her video, even just having been told, "This is what we need," she wasn't willing to do it.

In Mandy's testimony, in Mandy's process, in what we watched Mandy go through, we can understand a little bit about what's motivating Sandy. Once you make this accusation, it's incredibly hard to take it back, incredibly hard. It requires a lot of courage. It requires a lot of resolve. And when you do it, they don't believe you. That's not what they wanted to hear, "I lied." How do you spot a lie? There are glitches in the matrix. Sometimes lies aren't obvious. Sometimes you have to actively search for the truth. And you can find that truth in the inconsistencies, the incongruities, in the irregularities.

When someone is telling you something that they want you to believe, they get louder with lies. You have to look at the edges. You have to look for those things that don't make sense. Because, yes, you could go your whole life believing in that lie, living in that matrix; but if you are paying attention, there will be things that make you look behind the curtain, glimmers of light in the darkness, cracks in the facade, things that just don't make sense.

There are glitches in the matrix here, things that I hope when you heard them and you saw them gave you the sinking feeling that Mr. Flores might be innocent, falsely accused.

Why do the kids have to keep being reminded, if it's true?

Why, when Sandy testified, was she talking about what she

had said, not what had happened?

Why, when Mr. Hanson tried to catch Mandy in something when she said, "Look, you know, I lied," why didn't he then start talking about "what you said, not what actually happened"?

Because the prosecution team picked a story and they tried to fit everything else that's happened in this case inside of it, no matter how tortured that process was going to be. Lies had already consumed the truth. They weren't willing to look at it differently. They weren't willing to see what was right before their eyes, and they had to keep reminding the kids, they had to keep reminding Alejandra, of what that story was.

What is going on with Alejandra? She can't admit to me even the simplest things about, "This is my house. That's the dinner I cooked. That's me on the video screen."

But then there are the bigger, more troubling things. She's not willing to admit anything about her son, Armando, nothing about how close they actually were, the relationship they all had, not even that Armando lived with them.

They may seem like small, peripheral things, but there are glitches in that matrix that make you think: What is she trying to hide? Is something else going on here? Why can't she just tell us the truth? Why is nobody willing to admit this was an unhappy home?

When Alejandra and the girls testified, it was like pulling teeth to get them to admit what CPS already knew. This was not a happy family. This was not a normal domestic home life. There were problems.

What is going on with Armando? Armando is not, as the prosecutor put it, a red herring. Armando is a serious question in this case. Because we know that ten days after the accusation, Alejandra calls the victim's assistance program and asks for help for her son and immigration. And the reason why she can get that help is because now Armando is her sole source of support. The timing is too perfect to be a coincidence.

Even without that timing, the way that Alejandra answered questions about Armando gave us a peek behind the curtain. It was like a hot potato that she just didn't want to get near.

"Armando? I have a son named Armando. I'm not that close to Armando. He's an adult. I don't know where he was living. I don't know - I never have contact with him."

But we know that isn't true because Mandy, in her interview

with Detective Locke, talks about how, the very same day when they didn't show up to their interviews at the Sheriff's Office because they were too sick, they went and they watched Armando's soccer game. Their older brother, right?

Alejandra was very close to Armando. Mandy and Sandy were very close to Armando. And it should give you pause that they were not willing to admit that, because there is nothing wrong with that in and of itself.

What are they trying to hide?

What is going on with Carrie, the lady who picks the kids up from school?

You know, you may have thought nothing until it got so weird. What we know about Carrie is that she stood here in this courtroom and she told the judge, myself and Mr. Bolt that she had picked the kids up from school that day.

What we know about Carrie from Alejandra's interview is that a week before, Sandy had been crying and didn't want to be with her any more, and Alejandra made some statement about how she no longer trusts Carrie.

And what we know about Carrie is that she came with Alejandra those first few days of trial to support her here, but when she was ordered back to testify she got on the stand and changed her tune completely: "I don't know if I did pick up the kids. I hardly ever picked up the kids. I don't know what's going on here. I have nothing to say."

Why? If you have nothing to hide, if there's not more going on here, why don't you just get up there, take the oath and say the same thing that you said before? "Yeah, I took the kids home from school that day. Yeah, Sandy was having some problems with my grandson. So what? It has nothing to do with this."

The fact that it got so strange raises questions that deserve answers.

How do you spot a lie? Lies are inconsistent with the forensic evidence. In this case, the DA's Office and the Sheriff's Office, they had this evidence tested over and over by different analysts in many different ways. They knew it mattered. They knew it mattered because DNA and forensic evidence is the gold standard for proving contact. They knew it mattered because Sandy described violent, bloody, sweat-laden, lubricant-laden sex involving ejaculation.

If it happened, the forensic evidence is going to prove it.

They can't now say that it doesn't matter, that you wouldn't expect forensic evidence in a case like this, because we all know that defies common sense.

DNA is sensitive up to a picogram. One-trillionth of a gram of substance is what they were looking for when they tested that evidence.

One-trillionth of a gram of sperm, one-trillionth of a gram of sweat, one-trillionth of a gram of Mr. Flores's skin cells. If it happened, it would have been there. And the absence of the forensic evidence in this case is a smoking gun. It is a smoking gun of innocence.

The DNA that's not on the comforter is inconsistent with Sandy's lies.

They found blood on the comforter in the exact spot that Sandy was lying when the EMTs and the officers showed up to examine her, to talk to her, in the exact spot where her mom was checking her.

And if you look at the positioning of the blood, in all of the photographs and the exhibits, with the officers circling things, you will see that the position of the blood is nowhere near where Sandy said this rape supposedly happened.

I think it's also really important, another glitch in the matrix, that you are looking at a made bed. You are looking at the top comforter of a neatly made bed.

Why does that matter? It matters because Alejandra testified that it was a busy morning. She never makes the bed in the morning. It was a busy day. She had to get to work. Everything was crazy.

If this rape had happened the way that Sandy said it did, it would have happened on the unmade bed. It would have happened somewhere underneath that comforter, on the sheets, on the blankets, on the mattress, where there was nothing. Sandy was lying on the made bed, waiting for the officers to show up. Even putting all that aside, even putting all of that aside, there is no DNA or sperm from Mr. Flores mixed with Sandy's blood; powerful evidence of innocence, a smoking gun.

Where is the lubricant that had his DNA in it from this messy sex scene?

Where is the sweat she said was pouring from his body?

Where are all of the skin cells that that friction would have left there?

It's not there because it didn't happen. Mr. Flores's DNA or sperm is not in or on Sandy.

Mr. Bolt would have you believe that DNA is so fragile that you can just wash it off with a warm cloth.

You do not leave your common sense at the door when you walk into this courtroom. There is a reason why DNA is the gold standard for physical contact. There is a reason why the sheriffs and the DAs and all these analysts went to so much trouble to try to find it here. There is a reason why you would have expected to find at least a picogram, at least a picogram, of Mr. Flores's DNA on or in Sandy had this happened, because if it happened it would have been there.

Sandy's DNA or blood was not on Mr. Flores, except for that one DNA allele consistent with both Sandy and Alejandra found on the scrotal swab.

You know what? Who cares what Dr. Marcus said? Who cares about thresholds? Who cares about any of it?

Mr. Flores was unwashed. Unwashed. There is no way, without twisting and turning and defying reality, to explain how the kind of sex described by Sandy, this bloody, sweat-laden sex, didn't leave Sandy's DNA and blood all over this man; a smoking gun of innocence.

His DNA or sperm isn't on her underwear, except for a few alleles consistent with transfer in a home environment. In some ways, the underwear evidence is neither here nor there because of how easily DNA transfers; right?

And yet you would expect there to be a lot more if this really happened the way she said it did, if he had really gone and got her new underwear and helped her change it, his DNA, instead of Alejandra's, would have been on the outside of that underwear. It wasn't there because it didn't happen.

The washcloth, evidence that Alejandra and Mr. Flores have sex.

The Astroglide. No fingerprints from this lubricant bottle. And what we know about the DNA is it was a complicated mixture. What we also know about DNA is that liquidity, friction and volume affect the quality of the profile you're going to find.

If this had happened the way that Sandy said it did, with the sweating, with the bleeding, with the ejaculation, and Mr. Flores, after all of this happened, had been - taken that bottle with his hand and crawled up onto that toilet and hid it in the swan, that liquid, high-volume, friction-filled transfer would have been all over it.

DNA transfers so easily that Denise Farrow from the DOJ transferred almost her entire profile onto a control sample while she was taking every precaution in a sterile environment to not transfer a picogram.

This type of sex would have left DNA. It would have left forensic evidence, even with washing. It is the smoking gun of innocence. It is powerful evidence that there is something else going on here and that Albert Flores didn't rape his daughter. "I know I didn't do it, and you're going to find proof I didn't do it."

But by the time that proof came pouring in from the DOJ, the fire was already out of control. The lies had consumed the truth, and they ignored it.

How does this happen? How does this happen?

Why didn't the prosecution team take a fresh look at this case when the best efforts of the Department of Justice couldn't find the forensic evidence they knew should be there if it happened? Why didn't the prosecution team take a second look at this case when Sandy got up here and, on video, in front of a shocked audience, started talk about sex on the beach?

Why didn't the prosecution team take a second look at this case when Mandy said, "I lied," and came up with a very descriptive story of sex that just didn't happen?

Why not?

I think it has something to do with the charge. I remember sitting in this chair seven and a half weeks ago, when all of you were scattered throughout the audience and the charges were read. I heard audible gasps from the People in this room, shock, horror, rage. And that is a natural reaction that these accusations inspire.

Once Sandy made that accusation, it's like a spark in a tinderbox, and all of the professionals, all of the adults rush to protect her, insulating the accusation against attack, nurturing it, nurturing her. That totally makes sense. That just completely makes sense; right?

The problem is the rush to protect can become a rush to judgment. We know that children make these accusations falsely, and we know that sometimes the wrong person is sitting in this chair, an innocent man. But the system is set up to not really take that into account. Once the spark hit the tinderbox, the fire starts to rage, and before long it's out of control.

Let's think about the rush to judgment here and how we saw it in the testimony of certain witnesses. And again, well-meaning people rush to judgment in cases like this. I'm not here to throw stones. I'm not here to attack. I'm simply here to ask you to be careful to not make the same mistake.

Nurse Hernandez, after the exam, she starts to question these children, even though all of her training tells her she's not supposed to do it. She knows she is not a forensic interviewer. She knows it's not being recorded. She sees that injury and she starts to insulate the accusation against attack. She starts looking for evidence against Mr. Flores, something she can go to say to Sergeant Davenport that will help shore up this case.

Unfortunately, what Sandy apparently tells her is something that turns out to not be consistent with anything else. Unfortunately, she goes to Mandy and that turns out to complicate things because Mandy doesn't say the same thing to detectives. But you can see her rush to judgment, wanting to offer the detectives a little bit more.

The interrogating detectives, they were honest with you. "We're looking for a confession. We think he's done it." Less than 24 hours after the accusation, he is being convicted. Case closed. The gavel has fallen. That's it. We're headed here.

Detective Lopez interviewing Alejandra about Mandy, this extremely uncomfortable, high-pressure interview where Alejandra is trying to be cooperative. She's afraid of losing her kids.

He implicitly lets her know that that's a possibility if she doesn't do what they say. And he is trying to feed her bits of the story that Detective Locke had just got from Mandy, a story that Mandy came up with to protect Sandy, a story that Mandy came up with because she was angry at her dad, and everything is starting to spiral out of control in this rush to judgment. The rule.

From day one, it was a tortured effort to corroborate Sandy, tortured. If you look back at the interviews, if you look back at how everyone's statements changed and twisted and moved, nobody ever gets it quite straight, despite being threatened, despite being reminded, because it didn't happen.

Sex on the beach. What is a prosecutor going to do with it?

Mr. Bolt didn't open on that. We heard very little about it here in his closing. And yet it's charged in three extremely serious counts.

Because, man, what do you do? You are going to lose credibility if you argue to 15 smart people like you that it happened. And yet if you admit that it didn't, Sandy's entire story falls apart, because if she can lie about that she can lie about anything.

And I know that none of you are sitting there and thinking that on those rocks on that jetty, with her little puppy in her hand, Mr. Flores raped her on a Friday afternoon at the harbor beach. That didn't happen. And speaking of soft-pedaling, it's been soft-pedaled from here (indicating), because it doesn't make sense.

Nurse Hernandez went through an uncomfortable cross-examination about why she has checked "finger" on the history that she took, because she realizes it's not consistent with the prosecutor's theory of the case. She's met with them. If Sandy said finger, if Alejandra said finger, then, man, that's just one more huge contradiction that we have to deal with at trial. And so we get this just bizarre explanation for why "finger" is checked, because everybody is trying so hard to insulate this accusation against attack, well-meaning people, well-meaning people in their rush to protect Sandy, in a rush to judgment.

This is why we have jurors. This is exactly it. Because the 15 of you are the first people to look at this case critically, doubtfully, skeptically. You are the first people to sit here and not just listen to the accusation and say, "Done. Case closed. Next."

You may have been tempted when you heard the charges, but each of you had enough respect for the system and the process to set aside that initial feeling of horror, to set aside that initial feeling of rage, and to come in here with open and clear minds, presuming Mr. Flores to be innocent.

If you do that, if you go all the way back to November 1st, 20XX, and you look at this case from the perspective of innocence, you look at this case from the perspective that Mr. Flores is innocent and he is falsely accused, and if you expand the timeline, if you look at everybody who Sandy had contact with, if you look at everything that could have happened here, if you really do the hard, careful work to tear this case apart, hour by hour, person by person, question by question, there are reasonable possibilities consistent with innocence that nobody bothered to explore.

Halloween. Nobody bothered to investigate what happened that night, who they were with, where they were, whether the kids were supervised, when, what was going on.

School. Why wasn't that school day torn apart hour by hour with interviews with teachers, interviews with students, trying to understand different places this could have happened, trying to understand different people Sandy was exposed to, different pressures she could have been under in this environment where we know that she is bullied.

Between school and home with Carrie. Why is it that the defense just happens upon Carrie because she is here as a support person, and I'm able to order her back to court, subpoena her back to court?

Why, when Alejandra, Mandy and Sandy all say in their initial interviews that somebody picked them up from school, and Alejandra said she no longer trusted that person, and Sandy had been crying the week before, it had something to do with a grandchild, why didn't the prosecution team, law enforcement, find Carrie and talk to her?

Because of the rush to judgment. The case was already closed.

Home before fishing. What was Sandy watching? What was she doing? Was she on the Internet? What about social media? Nobody asked because the case was closed.

Fishing. A slip or fall while sitting on the rocks. Jagged rocks, consistent with a vertical object injury, never explored, never considered, because the case was already closed.

Home after fishing. Alejandra says that she goes into that room at some point, when she's home there and Mr. Flores is watching TV. Alejandra has this self-reported history of checking Mandy's genitalia; another kind of glitch in the matrix, another thing that just stops you in your tracks and you go, "What? What are you talking about?"

Alejandra freely admits that at some point she put a three-year-old on the bed and started to do an internal examination.

That is not normal behavior. It's a peek behind the curtain that maybe Alejandra has been through something, that maybe Alejandra has done something, that maybe there's more going on here than meets the eye.

None of it was explored because the case was closed. The gavel had dropped. Mr. Flores was convicted in less than 24 hours and they were done.

There is no way, sitting in this chair, falsely accused, that you can answer all of these questions. But there are reasonable possibilities consistent with innocence that you people who came here with open minds - to think about and see.

Someone else could have hurt Sandy, somebody on Halloween, another child, Armando. Something could have happened at school; a bully. God forbid, but it happens, staff.

Curious play with another child. Something could have happened with the carpool lady, Carrie or with her grandchildren.

Again, the most likely scenario? Experimenting, curious play experimenting that Sandy couldn't admit, shameful and embarrassing.

She had to find another explanation.

Alejandra checking Sandy, I hate to think that that's possible, but it was a strange thing for her to say and I have to throw it out there, that that is not normal. And it makes me wonder what's going on there.

Sandy could have hurt herself, at the playground, during or after school, a skateboard, a scooter, fall or curious play. Yes, falls onto this type of object are rare, but they happen. There are reasonable possibilities consistent with innocence.

At the beach, sitting or slipping on sharp rocks.

After school, during the time she was with Carrie or alone in her room, self-exploration, self-curiosity; more likely another child, frankly, but it's possible.

How did the lie start? It is very possible that Sandy came up with it. It's not necessarily true that Alejandra was in on it and Mandy was in on it. They certainly became part of the growing lie as they all tried to protect and help each other and, you know, stay in the good graces of the DA. But that doesn't mean that they all sat there and came up with this. That's just not what it means at all.

Sandy could have come up with the initial accusation alone, or with the perpetrator, who again could have been a child that she was exploring it and curious with. She could have come up with it out of shame, fear or anger.

Maybe she was being abused by someone else. Nobody ever bothered to investigate that.

Alejandra could have come up with it. I think that's a little less likely. She certainly had motives to nurture the accusation once it came out, to insulate it. She could have come up with it, convenience, desperation or fear. I don't know.

Mandy and Sandy could have come up with it in anger for their dad; again less likely, but possible.

They all could have come up with it together; less likely, but possible.

There are reasonable possibilities consistent with innocence that were never explored here. The gavel dropped and that was that.

How do they know about sex? Most likely they had seen it. Most likely they had seen it, exactly like Mandy and Sandy both pretty much described. Most likely they had seen their mom and dad having sex. This is a family that shared a room for years, and the parents had sex when their kids were asleep.

It could have been Armando and his girlfriend; most likely mom and dad had sex. Mom and dad had sex using lubricant. When you are a kid and you see your mom and dad having that kind of sex, it sticks with you.

School. When I asked Mandy how she came up with all those details that she gave Sandi Locke about what she said her dad did when she was three, she was really candid with all of you: "We learned it at school. Kids talk about it. Our teachers talk about it. We're exposed to the Internet, TV, movies, music videos, social media, a school curriculum."

We like to think that our seven-year-old children have never considered the kind of sex that Sandy described, but the reality is, is that kind of sex and even more graphic sex is everywhere. It's everywhere. You would have to live under a rock, and these kids didn't.

Other children. It's possible. The possibility is consistent with innocence.

Once a lie starts, it takes on this life of its own, and it's really hard to get out of it.

Sandy wants to please the adults. She is hiding the real origin of the injury, whatever that is, probably, again, another child, exploratory play or self-exploration; possibly a fall. But more likely, because of the shame that caused her to lie, it was something that she did that she didn't want to admit.

Maybe the truth is embarrassing. Maybe it's scary. Maybe it can harm somebody she loves. They keep reminding her to make sure she gets it right. Maybe she even started to believe it herself. But, you know, given that on the stand she told you, "I don't really remember this at all, just this much, a little bit, I'm just telling you what I saw myself say on the video," I don't know. I think she's telling you what she saw herself say in the video at that point.

Why does Mandy keep lying? She's pressured. She is angry with her dad. She's protecting Sandy. She is protecting her mom. And eventually she admits she is lying, giving us a window into how hard this would have been for Sandy, who is younger, to take this back.

Why does Alejandra keep lying? It's very possible she had nothing to do with the initial lie, and to this day maybe doesn't even know it is a lie. That's possible.

But why does she keep going along with it?

Why does she alter her reality to fit what Detective Lopez wants to hear?

Why does she start trying to protect and insulate people she cares about, like Armando and Carrie?

She does that in part because it solves some problems for her, maybe: unhappy home, custody dispute, divorce, solve some problems for her with her son, Armando. She immediately catches on this as a possible way out for him.

And then it's this carrot and stick approach that the detectives take with her: If you cooperate with us, we'll help you. If you don't cooperate with us, you are failing to protect. And you know what happens when you fail to protect.

Why is lubricant in the swan? I don't know. Talk about a red herring, right? If you really think about it, people use lubricant when they have sex. If you live in a small home with children, you put the lubricant somewhere where the kids aren't going to find it.

We know that Alejandra and Mr. Flores used lubricant, possibly Armando and his girlfriend used lubricant. The fact that they found lubricant in this house, when this is a sexual family, probably with sex that kids have seen involving lubricant, is not that surprising at all.

The only surprising part was the lack of forensic evidence on the lubricant, if you believe what the prosecution wants to tell you.

And then there's the possibility that it was put there by someone between the CSI search and the search warrant to support Sandy's story; frankly a lot less likely. It's lubricant in a house that has people who have sex. It's not that big of a deal. Mr. Flores took the stand to answer your questions, even though he knew he didn't have the answers to most of them; a man with a fifth grade education from El Salvador, a man who had already been interrogated by three different interrogators in two different languages, a man who knew he would be questioned hard, decided that he wanted to tell you the truth.

He knew he didn't have to. He had been advised, "You have the right to remain silent," both when he was arrested and here.

He knew it wouldn't be easy. He knew he couldn't explain everything, that there would be misunderstandings, that he would forget certain details of what he had said back then, and that a very skilled prosecutor with three to four times his education would take a crack at him. But he did it. He got up here. The fear that I have when I say to the 15 of you, "The defense calls Albert Flores to the witness stand," is that you will be expecting more than a man with his education and his experience can possibly deliver, that you will not be able to picture where he has been since 4:15 a.m., that you will not be able to understand the pressure, the anxiety, the horror of the situation that he is in, and that when he sits up there you will be expecting Law and Order, where there is some plot twist, he neatly ties all this together and, as the prosecutor had asked us to do, gives you a plausible story of how this happened that doesn't involve him.

Let me tell you the problem with being innocent, and it's a problem that guilty people don't have. The problem with being innocent is that you didn't have the time, you didn't have the foresight, to come up with an alibi, to come up with a fall guy, to come up with a defense, because you are just going along with your regular day, going through the motions, doing what you do, going to work, whatever, not knowing what you are about to get falsely accused.

Guilty people have thought all this out. Guilty people make great witnesses. They have thought all of this out. They are not just sitting there fumbling around in their own minds, in their own heart, about who could have done this to their child.

They're seizing on any explanation that might support their innocence. They are coming up with it. They are offering it.

Mr. Flores did none of that. Mr. Flores was as confused as you should be after seeing this evidence, still wondering what happened, likely never going to know, because perhaps the only person who knows isn't willing to say.

THE COURT: Ms. Preston, is this a good time to take a break?

MS. PRESTON: Thank you, Judge. It is.

THE COURT: All right. We'll take our midafternoon recess. We'll recess until 3:30.

Please do not discuss this matter amongst yourselves or with anyone else. Please do not form or express any opinions concerning this matter.

I'll see everyone at 3:30. We're off the record at this time. Thank you.

(Short recess.)

8

12th Juror – Steve Dietz - engineer in Santa Cruz startup - early-thirties no kids.

Damn, she's good. She's everything that Bolt isn't. Thoughtful, organized, and a great speaker. No fumbling. No stuttering. No backtracking. Just a straight path that anyone can follow. I could see some of the jurors I was sure were on our side nodding their heads. This is going to be tough!

9

THE COURT: All right. Let's go back on the record, please, regarding People versus Mr. Flores. Mr. Flores is present. Counsel are present. All of our jurors are present. Please continue, Ms. Preston.

MS. PRESTON: Thank you very much, Your Honor.

Mr. Flores took the stand even though he knew he didn't have to. He took the stand to tell you the truth. But it didn't stop there.

When he was arrested, they told him, "You have the right to remain silent." He chose not to. He chose to tell the truth there, too. He chose to subject himself to their questioning, to put himself through what we all watched for nearly ten hours.

What he didn't know when he sat down with the interrogators is that they had already judged him. What he didn't know when he sat down with the interrogators is that he was marching toward a judgment that they had already laid out there for him.

Ten hours, two days, three interrogators, two languages. You watched for his entire first interrogation, as he told them over and over and over, in as many ways this man from El Salvador with a fifth grade education under incredible stress, pressure, confusion and shock could do, "I didn't do it. I didn't rape my daughter. I didn't do it. You are going to find the proof. I didn't do it. I didn't do it. I didn't do it."

And you watched with your own eyes and your own hearts as those interrogators chipped away at the block, using their training, using their experience, using their education, using skills that they had honed to become effective over years and years and years, of breaking people like him down. You watched him crumble.

I'm not sure the interrogation tells you as much about Mr. Flores as it does about our system, as it does about the procedures, march to judgment once they've made up their minds.

In the end, he starts to doubt his own mind. He says that in the interrogation. He starts to doubt his own mind. They have lied to him about everything that matters. They have made him believe that the evidence is irrefutable that his DNA is inside his daughter's vagina, that everybody agrees he did it, that everything is on the table, and the only thing left is for him to explain it. Is he a man or is he an animal? "Don't you love your daughters? Don't you love your family? Don't you love yourself?"

It goes on and on and on and on and on and on and on, and he is exhausted. By that second interrogation you know he's been in jail, you know he's been in that crowded unit on these bunk beds full of other men, broken down and exhausted. Three days of this procedure, three days of this procedure, march to judgment, and they probably could have got him to say anything. If they would have fed him the details of that rape, maybe he would have just fed it right back to them: Okay.

He kept offering, "I'll make it up. Tell me what you want me to say. I'll make it up." He doesn't know that he's being videoed or recorded. That's one of their big secrets, along with all of their lies and their ploys and their ruses.

He is just like, wink, wink, "just let me go. Fine. The court will go easier for me. Everything will go easier for me. The proof is irrefutable. I'm done. I've been convicted. I'll just make it up. Just tell me what to say and I'll make it up."

It tells you a lot more about our system than it does about him.

In the end, he tries to come up with some sort of a compromise that might make this tortured process come to an end, moving from "I didn't do it" to "I don't remember," interspersed with, "I didn't do it" to "I don't remember. My daughter is not a liar. I didn't do it. I don't remember." They exhaust him. They deprive him of hope. They use every trick in the book to break him down emotionally and psychologically, everything they can, everything they can. And he believes them. He believes their lies about the evidence. He believes their lies that, "If you confess, it will go easier for you." He believes their lies, insinuating that maybe he would be home for Christmas if he just said what they wanted to hear.

If he had had that story in his mind because he did it, he would have given it to them. He didn't know what to say because it never happened.

The jail calls. You can make an awful lot of the jail calls, but what I want you to think about is the word "jail." It's not something a lot of us have to deal with in our everyday life, but when you make a call from jail, a jail call, you are calling from jail.

You are calling from that unit, that overcrowded, populated place full of other men.

You are calling on a line that you know is being recorded because the operator tells you that, your attorney tells you that, everybody tells you that. You don't have any privacy. You don't have any rights. You are reaching out to the outside world, walking a tightrope, and one misstep can be the end of you.

This is not some intimate type of call, some glimpse into their relationship, some glimpse into Mr. Flores's and Alejandra's soul. They both know it's being recorded. And it's like a cage match, where he is not sure that he can trust her. He's pretty sure he can't. She knows she is being recorded. She talked with the detective about a pretext call; right? She understands that these calls are going to be listened to and heard, so she's also in a cage match. Whether she is in on this or not, she has to keep perpetuating the story that her family has told.

The difference between him and her in this cage match is that she's got all the weapons and he's got nothing. She's in control. She is his lifeline back to his job, his kids and his freedom. Without his freedom, he has no way to figure this out. If he makes her mad she'll decline his next call. And if she declines that call, he sits there in that jail, in that unit, crowded full of men, desperate.

He's got to get out to understand where things went wrong. He's got to get out to figure out what happened here. He's got to get out. Denying her accusations about anything will make her mad. He knows that from their life experience together, an experience that Alejandra testified about, an experience that he talked about in his interrogation, an experience that he talked about on the stand.

She accuses him of things. She's jealous. She has a hot temper. When she gets mad, things start to happen. He cannot afford to make her mad. In this cage match, he is bending over, pulling the white flag, showing her his empty hands. She is in control. He needs her to post bail. He needs her to get out so that he can figure out what's going on in this match.

Alejandra knows she's being recorded. Don't believe for one minute that this was some intimate situation where she's being real and he's being real and this is authentic. Just like those interrogations with its ruses and its lies, just like that pretext call where they tried to get Alejandra to call and trick him into something, the jail calls are part and parcel of this procedural march to judgment.

Mr. Flores knew that because he had a lawyer. The irony is that had he not been advised pursuant to that stipulation, right, had defense counsel not told him, "Change the subject. Don't admit anything. Don't make Alejandra mad. Don't get controversial. Keep everything mellow" - he may have done exactly what Mr. Bolt said he should have done, but he had been advised that she was a live, ticking bomb, and that he better be careful with it.

Much has and will be made about his asking his sister and his nephew to try to contact the girls so they wouldn't testify against him, so they would tell the truth. But what you are not going to hear a lot about is how he told them to lie. If there had been evidence that he had told them to lie, to lie, you would have heard it.

I don't think it's right that this is inconsistent with innocence. I don't think you have to accept that. It's inconsistent with law-abidingness, to violate a protective order.

But, man, when you are in this situation, where you are sitting here desperate for contact, desperate for solutions, your attorney has been told that they can't contact anybody that matters in the case, everyone is just sitting around on their hands going, "I guess we're going to go to trial."

If the victims didn't want to be contacted, nobody could do it. Alejandra doesn't have to take his calls. Mandy doesn't take his calls. And that's their right. Fine. But imagine the desperation, imagine the panic, imagine in this procedural rush to judgment that you are sitting there, one foot in front of the other, and at the end of that procedure, at the end of that process, the result has already been predetermined. The gavel fell in the first 24 hours. You are convicted. You're done.

Step back from all of that for a minute, from the ruses, the procedures, the interrogation, these staged, recorded calls, all of it. Step back for a minute and use your common sense to think about how Mr. Flores would have acted if he knew he had done this, if he knew he was guilty.

He would have hid the bloody comforter and the lubricant outside the house. They want you to believe that he was so sophisticated that he was able to come up with ways to get rid of washcloths and underwear, and not only able to get rid of this evidence, but able to wipe a picogram, a trillionth of a gram, of forensic evidence off of every surface that mattered, including his own body, despite the fact that everybody agrees he stunk and hadn't washed.

This mastermind, this criminal genius apparently left a huge blood stain on the comforter in the master bed. What? This mastermind, this criminal genius who is able to scrub picograms of DNA off of his daughter, out from the inside of her vagina, off of his scrotum and his penis and his clothes and his underwear, off of every possible thing that mattered, so that he can say to these interrogators, "Look for evidence. Find the truth," knowing it won't be there, this criminal genius left the bloody comforter on the bed and the lubricant in the swan? No.

Alejandra and the girls testified that Mr. Flores just sat there calmly, drinking a beer and watching a baseball game or watching TV, when the girls came in, "Mommy, we need to talk to you." No, no, no. No, no, no. If you have just raped your daughter and done this whole scrub job to clean your entire life of every shred of evidence, when the girls come out and they want to talk to mom, you either stop them from talking to mom, you do some kind of a preemptive strike to explain what's going to happen next, or you get out of there.

Because if you are that smart that you can mastermind all of this, you are not just going to sit there calmly drinking your beer, knowing that your little girl is now going to tell mom you raped her. Why not just keep driving?

I am baffled by the constant use of the word "flight." Let me tell you what flight is, people. Flight is when you flee. Flight is not when you get into your car and you drive across the street to Ben's Market and you go to sleep.

Flight is when the writing is on the wall that you are going down, you are going down hard, and you get in that car and you fill it up with gas and you drive the speed limit all the way to the border. That's flight. And you cross that border into Mexico and you go home to El Salvador. That's flight.

This is not flight. If flight is evidence of guilt, if flight shows that you are conscious of your guilt, the complete lack of flight that occurred here is powerful evidence of innocence.

Why not give the confession they want? We've talked about that. They had convinced him that, "If you just tell us this and that and the other, everything will go better. We already know it all happened. We already have all the evidence." A guilty man at that point would have just said, "Let me tell you. I screwed up. In a moment of drunken, impulsive depravity, I did this to my little girl."

It didn't happen because he didn't do it.

Why beg the detectives to look for evidence? "Look for evidence. Look in my car. Take my computer. Search my body. Search Sandy's body. Give me a lie detector test."

You would have to be a cool, calculated mastermind to pull off that, knowing that you had just had bloody, sweaty, lubricant and ejaculate-laden sex with a kid. Come on. It doesn't take more than a fifth grade education to realize that you are going to be all over her, she is going to be all over you, and the jig is up.

No. They are not going to find anything, because he didn't do it.

I am not going to go through every jury instruction, every count with you. I'm going to focus on two instructions, instructions that will help you as you go back into the jury room and you are trying to reach a consensus.

Because each of you are very different people and each of you will go back there with different ideas of the evidence, different ideas of common sense, what's normal, what's expected, different things that caught your eye in this case, different glitches in the matrix that you saw and noticed, different life viewpoints. I'm going to focus on two, circumstantial evidence and reasonable doubt.

Please take a look at the circumstantial evidence instruction. Figure out the difference between circumstantial and direct evidence and think about how it applies to this case.

In your instruction packet, you will see that you handle circumstantial evidence differently. You handle it with care. You will find that if there is circumstantial evidence, if you can draw two or more reasonable conclusions from that evidence, one points to innocence and one to guilt, you must accept the conclusion that points to innocence.

You are going to want to think about circumstantial evidence when you think about the blood on the comforter, when you think about the lubricant, when you think about Sandy's injury.

Each of these is only circumstantial evidence, which means that if there are reasonable possibilities consistent with innocence, reasonable possibilities of how the lubricant bottle got there, reasonable possibilities of how Sandy was hurt, reasonable possibilities of how the blood got on the bed, such as she was lying there when the EMTs came, you must accept the conclusion that points to innocence. Even if you are having trouble with it, even if you really think that the other conclusion is much more likely, the law tells you what to do.

Reasonable doubt. Proof that leaves you with an abiding conviction that the charge is true. What that means is that the decision that you're making today is not one that you can take back. What that means, it's a decision that you make today that will change someone's life forever. And in 30 years, when you look back on this decision, an abiding conviction is one where you say:

I have no doubt that I did the right thing. I have no doubt that there was no doubt. I am confident that I did the right thing.

Reasonable doubts are just reasonable questions. You are reasonable people. Your every question is reasonable. You asked dozens of reasonable questions in this case. Those were all reasonable doubts, things that were niggling as you, things that just didn't quite fit right, things that you wanted to have answers to before you could make such an important decision in this man's life.

Make no mistake, the burden rests here (indicating Mr. Bolt). It is his job to answer those questions. That burden never shifts to Mr. Flores. You cannot prove your innocence. It is nearly impossible.

If the prosecution didn't answer your reasonable questions, you have reasonable doubts. And you only need one reasonable doubt to leave only one verdict. Once you find that doubt, the verdict is not guilty.

There are different versions of a not guilty verdict. Not guilty does not mean innocent. Not guilty means the prosecution has not met its burden to prove every element of this case beyond a reasonable doubt. It means that they have left unanswered questions, reasonable, unanswered questions that you would expect to have answered if this happened.

Even if the prosecution gets very close to meeting its burden, but doesn't get there, the only verdict left is not guilty.

I need you to understand that in our constitutional system, a system that is enshrined in our Constitution, a system that our founding fathers set in motion to protect every single citizen from the power of the government - which is frankly a David and Goliath type situation for every person who sits in that chair - they gave criminal cases the highest standard that we have: beyond a reasonable doubt.

When you think about how high that is, I want you to think about this chart. If you think Mr. Flores is innocent, that's a not guilty verdict. If you think Mr. Flores is possibly guilty, that's a not guilty verdict. If you think Mr. Flores is likely guilty, that's a not guilty verdict. If you think Mr. Flores is, more likely than not, guilty, that's a not guilty verdict.

If you believe that the government has proven this case with clear and convincing evidence of his guilt - clear and convincing evidence is a standard the government uses to take children away from their parents. If you believe they have met that standard, that is a not guilty verdict. Beyond a reasonable doubt is higher than that.

I'm going to sit down. The prosecutor is going to get back up here. He gets another chance to argue his case, and they usually save the best for last. I'm going to sit down after spending months, years with this case, after looking at this evidence with a fine-toothed comb, critically, skeptically, doubtfully, desperately, and I'm going to pass that torch to you.

This is a scary moment from where I stand, because I know I'm going to be waking up for the next weeks, months, maybe even years, wishing I had said this, wishing I had said that, wishing I had made this point, wishing I had done more. But I pass this torch to you with the faith that you will now look for the doubts the way that I have, and that you will do it with the same methodical, conscientious interest that you scribbled over 80 questions in this case, because you people care and you want to get this right.

As you do it, I'm going to point out some easy tracks that are devastating in a case like this.

Children don't lie. Yes, they do. They lie about this.

If I question this, what will other jurors think of me?

I can't risk a not guilty. What if he did this? You can't do that.

Discounting the complete lack of forensic evidence, letting Mr. Bolt gloss over it and say it's not evidence of anything. There's nothing there, so it's not evidence of anything. What? The absence of evidence is powerful evidence of something, powerful evidence of innocence.

The defense could have answered your questions. No. The burden never shifts here, because we are in a David and Goliath system. The government has the power. We are in a system where you heard Carrie say that she shut my investigator down at the door.

We are in a system where you learned that the defense was told early on: You can't contact any of the people that matter. That is the system we have, and that is why the burden rests here.

Don't get confused and think this is a search for truth. It's not a search for truth. The truth may die with the one or two or three people who know it. This is a search for doubt. It's a search for reasonable doubts. There is not going to be any credit roll, where this whole case gets tied up neatly and handed back to you. All we can hope for is that you follow the rules, apply the burden, and when you find that reasonable doubt you vote not guilty.

Don't believe for one second that beyond a reasonable doubt is not so hard to prove. It is the highest standard that we have. It does matter, and it is very, very hard.

Mr. Flores did not rape his daughters. Sandy's accusation sparked a fire. That fire started to burn. And before long that burning, raging fire had completely consumed the truth.

The 15 of you are here to pore through the ashes of that fire, to look at the evidence critically, doubtfully, skeptically, to give Mr. Flores the benefit of your every reasonable doubt. And if you do that, there's only one fair verdict on this evidence, and more importantly this lack of evidence, and I'm asking you to find Mr. Flores not guilty.

Thank you.

10

9th Juror – Erica Hesse - early 40s- CEO of a rapidly growing high-tech company. Single no children.

Wow! What the hell is Patricia Preston doing here working as a public defender? This woman is brilliant! I work with a lot of attorneys, mostly business-related, but I've sat in on my share of trials, and I've never seen such a talented attorney. I'm sold. Of course I was before even if Bolt did plant a few seeds of doubt. But now, no question. Flores is innocent. I'm sure Preston's closing changed a few minds. I wonder if I could hire her once my company goes public.

11

THE COURT: Thank you, Ms. Preston.
Mr. Bolt?
MR. BOLT: May I proceed, Your Honor?
THE COURT: Yes.
MR. BOLT: So I haven't saved the best for last. I thought that was a pretty great argument, to be honest, and it was interesting to watch as well. It's an excellent argument.

It's a difficult argument to respond to because there is so much contained within that argument that is not contained within the evidence and the very instructions that you are supposed to follow. Those are the ones where the temptation is to speculate or to guess or to be incorrect in thinking that any reasonable question equals a reasonable doubt. That is the real risk.

Now, make no mistake, kids do lie. Adults lie, too. People lie. They make mistakes. They tell the truth. They forget all across the board. But make no mistake, this is a search for the truth. It is your job to weigh and consider all of the evidence in trying to determine where the truth lies -
MS. PRESTON: Objection, Your Honor; misstates the law, search for the truth.
THE COURT: I'll overrule. The jury will know and has been advised as to the instructions. They will follow the law as I instruct. Thank you.
MR. BOLT: But like I said at the very beginning of my argument, there is no middle ground, and that is clear. Because either Sandy is lying or the defendant is guilty; not that she's wrong about something, not that she has forgotten things over time, but she has to be lying.

And so what you are really doing for starters is ask yourself: Is a seven-year-old kid, the kid that you met, is that kid able to orchestrate this type of a dynamic where a remarkably credible disclosure occurs?

Where they have to include people in her lie but they can't at the same time? Because if Sandy is fine when the defendant leaves, well, that happened when Mandy was on the phone, and Mandy was already saying what was going on, what had happened.

If even that is true, then you have already know the defendant has lied about all kinds of stuff. How she could be fine and manage to get hurt in that small window of time? That's just beyond the imagination, absolutely beyond the imagination. Now the standard is beyond a reasonable doubt. But like I was saying, not every reasonable question equals a reasonable doubt, because reasonable doubt relates to the elements of the offenses.

Here's a case where there's lots of reasonable questions. Everybody has got reasonable questions that they could ask based upon the evidence in this case. Absolutely. But the issue is whether, as to the elements and the element alone, whether you have an abiding conviction that the charge is true.

And it's not an absolute certainty, and it is the same standard that's used in all criminal cases, from the most petty to the most serious. And your job is to weigh and consider that evidence and try and determine what the facts are. The facts are the things that really happened. The facts are what's true; to separate the facts from the lies; to find the truth. Yeah, absolutely. Absolutely.

MS. PRESTON: Can I have an ongoing, Your Honor?

THE COURT: So noted.

MR. BOLT: And don't be scared by the circumstantial evidence instruction. Circumstantial evidence is a great thing. But this really is a direct evidence case, where the circumstantial evidence either corroborates or doesn't corroborate. So the circumstantial evidence in the case helps you determine who is telling the truth and who is lying and how to tease that apart.

But the law is very clear that circumstantial evidence is evidence that indirectly proves a fact, like you know that the ground is all wet outside, and that's a piece of circumstantial evidence that perhaps it was recently raining.

Direct evidence is something that directly proves a fact. So if Sandy testifies that, "My dad raped me," that's direct evidence. If you believe her that's direct evidence. Now both are acceptable, according to the law, and neither is entitled to any greater weight. It's that simple.

And when there are two reasonable interpretations of evidence, one of them points to innocence, yes, you must accept it. But the critical word there is "reasonable." So you don't get to speculate on a whole bunch of different things and then act like those are reasonable interpretations of the evidence.

Now what am I talking about? Well, I'm talking about a lot of different things. Let's look at an example. Counsel has argued maybe the injury occurred on Halloween, maybe at school, maybe one of Carrie children did it. Maybe Alejandra did it while checking her. Maybe some random kid experimenting with her. Maybe she did it to herself. Maybe. That's speculating, because there's no evidence of any of that.

There's all kind of evidence from which you should conclude that the child got home and was fine. Mandy left and then the child was with her father. Then when the child was back in the presence of somebody other than her father, the child was hurt. That's what you have a lot of evidence in support of.

Is it possible that Sandy could have had some accident down at wherever she was? Which we're only relying on the defendant, for starters, as to where that was.

Is it possible? Sure it's possible. But guess what. There's no evidence of that. So there's no reasonable interpretation of the evidence where Sandy gets injured down wherever she was with her father by some accident. There's no evidence of that.

And you know what? Of course, Sergeant Cardova asked the defendant all about that. Absolutely not. No falls, no nothing. Well, so did Detective Lopez. Nothing.

And so how is it reasonable to think that Mandy calls the police, and says, "She's bleeding," says, "My mom is confronting my dad about having just sexually abused my sister," only none of that's true? Instead, what's happening is what the defendant says?

And then the police are on the way and he bails? And then either Sandy self-inflicts or somebody else does it to her. Is that reasonable? No. There's no evidence of that at all.

And it would be not just speculating. How is that even interpreting the evidence? That's just rejecting everything and postulating some fact. I mean, something that is theoretically possible but is not within the evidence at all. That's not reasonable. That's not how you are supposed to do your job.

MS. PRESTON: Objection; misinterpretation of the law; misstates Fifth Amendment.

THE COURT: I'll overrule. Again, the jury will follow the instructions as the Court has provided. Please continue.

MR. BOLT: Now that's just one example. There's, frankly, a lot of examples. There's a lot of examples of speculating. Counsel just asserts, just absolutely asserts, that if this happened, of course you would find all kinds of DNA. Of course you would find this. And so if you didn't, it means it's false.

That's not true. There's no evidence of that. And believe me, if they could call some reputable person - their expert certainly didn't testify to any of that.
MS. PRESTON: Objection; misstates facts.
THE COURT: Overruled. The jury will know what the facts are and what they are not.
MR. BOLT: "You would have found evidence - DNA on her. You would have found DNA on the Astroglide. Even if somebody is toweled off, even if they are washed with hot water, you are still going to find it."

That's not the evidence. That's not the evidence. To find a reasonable doubt based on that stuff, that's speculation. That's absolute speculation.

And what all of the analyses that was done in this case, what it shows is that it was a thorough investigation. It shows that people tried to look for evidence.

But, I mean, let's be clear. If you are so crafty, you are so clever, you are so smart and you are so lucky, I guess, that you could make something up like this child made up and just have all of the subsequent investigation corroborate what the child is saying and have this person who you are framing just act as guilty as they possibly can . Yeah, when you run from the police like he did when the police were coming, that's fleeing. That's running away from the police, and that's flight.

But you can't plan for that. Certainly Sandy is not responsible because he acted guilty. That's the defendant acting guilty.

So if you are so smart that you can come up with and stage this type of thing, well, guess what: You are smart enough to put some to put some DNA on a towel. I mean, you live together. It's not that hard, if that's what you were going to do.

But see, that's the problem with all the forensic evidence anyway, is that to push back on some of this stuff, there's blood on the bed. And it's in exactly where you would expect to find it if the child had been naked from at least the waist down and been on that bed in a sexual assault like what's being described here. That's a fact.

Now somehow it has no meaning if it's not mixed with semen? That's not true.

And if there had been semen that was located on the bedspread specifically, you wouldn't know when it was left there. You would have no idea. And that's the thing with the blood.

It's some evidence, but it's not. It's not smoking-gun evidence.

It would be so easy if what you were doing was framing. I got an idea. Like rub your bloody underwear on something that has the defendant's DNA on it, and then, and then you can wear it. That's evidence.

But none of that happened. Why? Because the defendant stole that underwear. He got rid of it.

You do have to use your common sense. You do have to use your common sense. But when you use it and you actually get down to the specifics of the evidence in the case, there isn't any reasonable interpretation of this evidence that points to innocence.

There's lots of questions you can ask, but those questions don't relate to the fundamental core of whether this child was raped. It doesn't relate to the fundamental core of whether Mandy was abused.

You would think that if there was collaboration in attempting to falsely accuse the defendant, you would think that there would be a little bit more cooperation between these people. But there isn't. This is not how a false allegation looks. And the closer you look at it, the clearer that becomes.

That's why I really encourage you, to the extent that you have questions, you know, counsel makes so many comments where I can't disagree with every single factual contention that I disagree with. I can't write that fast and it would take too long.

But what I can tell you are some remarks here and there and responses to the things that she said. And when you are talking about, for instance, Armando, and how it's too convenient that they are getting help from the DA's Office such a short time after this. No, there was a request for help. There wasn't evidence at all that anything was done, nothing at all. There's no carrot and stick.

Her life, Alejandra's life, the lives of these children, except for the fact that they weren't getting abused by their father, but other than that, their life became harder when the defendant was arrested.

And there's no motivation that makes any sense whatsoever that somehow, if you have to stick with a lie? What are they going to do? Move them back from Colorado to Santa Cruz to punish them?

No. What happens with the passage of time is that any

motivation to lie goes away - if there ever was one, which there wasn't here.

Why? Because look at what everybody said at the time. These girls loved their mother and loved their father.

Were they afraid of him? Yeah, absolutely. Totally reasonable to be afraid of him. He threatens to hurt you. He does mean and disgusting things at times. You are not even allowed to be alone with him, and he is your father.

And as far as that being somehow some made up thing or something that was, even worse, made up by somebody involved in the investigation, not at all. Listen to the statement from Sandy, the only statements from Sandy, really, prior to getting interviewed by Sandi - Detective Sandi Locke, it's what she says in the call, which is super short.

And so the first time somebody sits down with her and says, "Let's start at the beginning, tell me about this stuff," she describes it. She describes it. And then her sister describes it as well, and it matches on with the greater factual context. And it explains a lot. It explains why Alejandra - who half the time is behaving in ways that actually help the defendant.

So kids do lie. But look at what Sandy says to Deputy Davenport. Davenport says, "Are you in pain?"

And the child obviously nods, because then he says, "Where?" And then there's - Sandy says, "Like right here."

"On your thighs, where the" -

"Like right here." She is pointing to her genitals.

He says, "Okay. How did you get hurt?"

Then the child says, "Like I" - something unintelligible - "well, I did, but he was squeezing me too much, and then, um - and then it was - keep hurting, and then it started to bleed." "How was he squeezing you?"

"Like with his thing, and then like really hard, like putting it in, and it hurted and it started to bleed - bleed."

"To which thing? Penis?"

"Yeah."

What child could come up with a description like that? What adult? I mean, let's be honest. A kid can't make up this stuff. They can lie, but the way that this is all orchestrated, huh-uh.

And listen to that. She describes it as "squeezing me too much, like with his thing," talking about being penetrated, it's squeezing too much.

Now, that does smack of truth. And the reason why is because this child doesn't fully understand the dynamics of what she's describing. You can see how subjectively to her this idea of squeezing captures how she would feel. But she's not getting squeezed. She is getting stretched. And those are different.

Because she doesn't really have a clean and clear understanding of the physical dynamics to even describe it in ways that are sort of anatomically correct. But she sure does subjectively. In that child's experience did it feel like squeezing? Yeah. That's stretching. And that is a credible way to describe it. And the testimony is filled with stuff like that.

Alejandra, Sandy, Mandy, you can say all kinds of stuff about them. Particularly with respect to Alejandra and Mandy, they are easy to attack because they have said opposite things. They've contradicted themselves.

And Sandy is easy to attack, too, because she has gotten mixed up. She has said things that have been different at times. But you have to look at it all together, and this is remarkably credible.

All of this stuff about Armando, about benefits, their lives weren't better. They didn't do this. There's no evidence, and it doesn't even make sense, that they would do this for benefits from the state. There's no penalty for them to be honest.

Would have been an unmade bed, that kind of thing?

But the blood on the bed, I did want to say, that blood didn't come from when Alejandra checked her. That occurred in the girls' bedroom, where Alejandra checked her. And as it was described, the child was standing up. The child wasn't sitting with a bare bottom on a bed in the girls' room or on the bed in the master bedroom.

Now that evidence still is what it is. It's not smoking-gun evidence of guilt. But what you have to realize is that none of that is smoking-gun evidence of innocence, because you would have heard different evidence if that were the case.

All kinds of just factual statements, how the audience at the preliminary hearing is shocked. Where is that coming from? Where is that in the evidence? There's so many statements that got made like that. It's just stuff that's not in the evidence. Asking you to speculate about what kind of pressures Sandy might be under, teachers, stuff at Halloween, the whole Carrie thing, it's too weird. It's not weird. It has nothing to do with anything, unless it's in the evidence.

And, you know, you know, the credibility of all the witnesses. There's not one instruction for defendants and a different instruction for everyone else. And so, I mean, look at counsel bend over backwards trying to explain how an innocent guy would just at every turn be guilty, at every turn, just no idea why he's there, and not be curious. Be accused of such horrendous stuff and not be phased by it at all.

Like he can stay, "I didn't do it," or "I didn't do," whatever, but that doesn't mean that he is hitting the right emotional pitch, that he's not connecting what an innocent person feels like with what the lie that he is telling is.

And you can see that with Mandy, too. You watch her demeanor when she's recanting versus her demeanor when she is disclosing, how she talks, how she looks, what she is saying. It's not a rush to judgment. It's quite far from that. You know - and you're not going to decide this case regardless of what you may or may not think about the way these interviews with the defendant went. You verdict is not a review of their performance. You are trying to determine what the truth is, what the facts are.

And it sure was repetitive. They did tell him, obviously, that they needed to know why, that they already knew what happened.

And why are they using these techniques on him anyway? The answer to that is because he comes in there and is apparently giving a story that's at absolute odds with all the investigation so far. And a lot of that is pretty solid. And so that interview is repetitive.

It's repetitive because the defendant keeps on saying things, like, "I don't remember" and having no real explanation for why he doesn't remember. He is not too drunk. Nothing happened that means that he shouldn't remember. He should be able to say these things that happened or that didn't happen. I mean, so he is lying to the police and they are responding to try to pressure him to be more truthful.

More stuff that just comes out of nowhere: Doesn't know he is being recorded. Where is that in the evidence?

That the defendant believed all their lies? Where is all that in the evidence?

The "home for Christmas," if he says what they want to hear, they weren't saying that to him at all. And even still, none of that stuff is helpful as far as analyzing the facts.

But I submit to you that an innocent person doesn't have to come in and tell an entirely different account of their reality in order to try and make sense of the evidence. That, you didn't see from any other witness besides the defendant.

More things that aren't facts: At the jail, sure, these calls are recorded. So to that extent there's no privacy. But to the extent that other people are listening to you talk, to the extent that, obviously, these aren't real conversations, that's not true.

And you really ought to look at those things close. It's worth noting. Alejandra, when she is putting her daughters on the phone with the defendant and he is saying things like, "I'm in jail, I may never get out of here," putting pressure on them like that, you know, she is violating the protective order because she's helping him violate it. And that makes her guilty of that offense, too.

And, again, you know, this is how she really felt. I mean, when you look at it, yeah, you know, you get a sense for that. The pretext call that night, she wasn't willing to do that. She didn't want to help the police like that.

And trying to lay a lot of the guilty stuff that the defendant says and does while in custody by chalking it up to legal advice, I'm pretty sure there isn't a lawyer out there that told him he should be violating the protective order. I'm pretty sure they didn't advise him, "If you want to violate the protective order, just make sure that you realize that Alejandra is a ticking time bomb." No. No.

He is doing what he thinks is right. And he may only have a fifth grade education, although that comes straight from him and no other source. He came here when he was 15. So I doubt he graduated fifth grade when he was 15 or 14.

But in any case, you've witnessed him, you've listened to the things he says. He speaks two languages. He did fine with the police in terms of keeping control of himself. He is a smart individual. He testified here. Like trying to pretend that he's stupid. It strains credibility to look at the type of interview that was going on and somehow the defendant is literally thinking even though he is totally innocent, but he is thinking, "Maybe I really did rape my seven-year-old"?

No. No. He should have been panicking if he was innocent in those interviews, because a normal person would.

Obviously, he would have gotten rid of the bloody comforter

and moved it.

Really? He didn't know that he was going to be dealing with the police coming. He thought that it was enough to threaten that he was going to hurt his daughter to keep her quiet.

Who knows how well those types of things had worked in the past?

So -

MS. PRESTON: Objection, Your Honor; Fifth Amendment; unfair argument; no evidence.

THE COURT: I'll sustain. Please continue.

MR. BOLT: This is a household with a long history of being abusive. He testified that - that he gets violent when he is angry. He is not dishing out corporal punishment in a responsible, metered way. And these kids know it.

So reasonable questions don't equal reasonable doubts. Reasonable doubts are based on the evidence and they relate to elements. And when you get down to the hard work, and it is hard work, you can't replay every interview or summarize it sufficiently. This is detailed stuff. Don't take the words of the lawyers as evidence. Get down to the actual evidence and testimony itself.

Because when you do, you will see, if you don't see already, you will see that you do have an abiding conviction of the truth of these charges. They are not all the same. They are not all the same. But both of those kids were abused.

Thank you.

THE COURT: Thank you, Mr. Bolt.

When you go to the jury room, the first thing you should do is choose a foreperson. The foreperson should see to it that your discussions are carried on in an organized way and that everyone has a fair chance to be heard.

It is your duty to talk with one another and to deliberate in the jury room. You should try to agree on a verdict if you can.

Each of you must decide the case for yourself, but only after you have discussed the evidence with the other jurors.

Do not hesitate to change your mind if you become convinced that you are wrong. But do not change your mind just because other jurors disagree with you.

Keep an open mind and openly exchange your thoughts and ideas about the case.

Stating your opinions too strongly at the beginning or

immediately announcing how you plan to vote may interfere with an open discussion.

Please treat one another courteously.

Your role is to be an impartial judge of the facts, not to act as an advocate for one side or the other.

As I told you at the beginning of the trial, do not talk about the case or about any of the people or any subject involved in it with anyone, including, but not limited to, your spouse or other family members, friends, spiritual leaders or advisors, or therapists.

You must discuss the case only in the jury room and only when all jurors are present.

Do not discuss your deliberations with anyone. Do not communicate using social media during your deliberations.

It is very important that you not use the Internet in any way in connection with this case during your deliberations.

During the trial several items were received into evidence as exhibits. You may examine whatever exhibits you think will help you in your deliberations. These exhibits will be sent into the jury room with you when you begin to deliberate.

If you need to communicate with me while you are deliberating, send a note through our bailiff, signed by the foreperson or by more - by one or more members of the jury.

To have a complete record of this trial, it is important that you not communicate with me except by a written note.

If you have questions, I will talk to the attorneys before I answer, so it may take some time. You should continue your deliberations while you wait for my answer. I will answer any questions in writing or orally here in open court.

Do not reveal to me or to anyone how the vote stands on the question of guilt or issues in this case, unless I ask you to do so.

Your verdict on each count and any special finding must be unanimous. This means that to return a verdict, all of you must agree to it.

Do not reach a decision by the flip of a coin or by any other similar act. I'm certain you are not going to do that, but I need to instruct you in that regard.

It's not my role to tell you what your verdict should be.

Do not take anything I said or did during the trial as an indication of what I think about the facts, the witnesses, or what your verdict should be.

You must reach your verdict without any consideration of punishment.

You will be given verdict forms. As soon as all jurors have agreed on a verdict, the foreperson must date and sign the appropriate verdict forms and notify our bailiff.

If you are able to reach a unanimous decision on only one or only some of the charges, fill in those verdict forms only and notify our bailiff. Return any unsigned verdict form.

And lastly, to our alternates, the jury will begin deliberation shortly, but you are still alternate jurors and are bound by my earlier instructions about your conduct.

Do not talk about the case or about any of the people or any subject involved in it with anyone, not even your family or friends, and not even with each other.

Do not have any contact with the deliberating jurors.

Do not decide how you would vote if you were deliberating.

Do not form or express an opinion about the issues of the case unless you are substituted in for one of the deliberating jurors.

So what we will do with our three alternates is once we part company with our jurors today, we will call you folks forward. You will give a phone number where we can contact you. And as I mentioned previously, we will call you one way or another, either to advise you that the jury has reached verdicts and what those verdicts are, or to indicate that, for one reason or another, one of our jurors cannot continue and we will have to select one of you to come back in as an alternate.

Let's swear in our bailiff, please.

(Bailiff sworn.)

THE COURT: What I'll ask, if the 12 of you could follow - Are you going to set up a room for them now and then have them just pick a time that they can return?

THE BAILIFF: The room is ready to go.

THE COURT: The room is ready to go.

I'll tell you what. I think it's worthwhile for you to go back into the room and just agree as to when you are going to coming back tomorrow morning.

Once the case goes to the jury, you folks are in charge with how you wish to deliberate. You can pick whatever time you want tomorrow. I'm be here from 8:15 on. So whatever time works for you is fine with me.

But I'll ask you to accompany our bailiff back into the jury room. Take everything that you have.

The three alternates, I'll ask you folks to come forward and please advise Heidi as to a phone number.

And again, all you will do tonight is just pick a time that you will come back tomorrow.

What you will have tomorrow are all the exhibits, the instructions and the verdict forms. Okay? Thank you very much. We'll remain on the record for a moment outside the presence of our jurors.

(The jury exits the courtroom.)

CHAPTER 6

THE DELIBERATION

"Life moves on, whether we act as cowards or heroes. Life has no other discipline to impose, if we would but realize it, than to accept life unquestioningly. Everything we shut our eyes to, everything we run away from, everything we deny, denigrate or despise, serves to defeat us in the end. What seems nasty, painful, evil, can become a source of beauty, joy and strength, if faced with an open mind. Every moment is a golden one for him who has the vision to recognize it as such."
- Henry Miller

1

3rd Juror – Linda Lancaster, early 40s, personnel manager in a larger corporation, married, no kids.

It was the end of the day when the judge finally completed his jury instructions. He suggested we visit the Jury Room and decide when we wanted to start deliberating. Bill, the bailiff who had seen us through the past seven plus weeks, led us to the room. He opened the door and we filed in.

"Are you kidding?" asked one of the young men, whose name I didn't know.

"Nope," Bill replied. This is your home until you come up with a verdict.

Everyone looked around solemnly.

It was a small room for so many people, maybe fifteen feet by fifteen feet. Most of the space was taken up by a large oval table. There was a white board on one wall with several different colored markers and an empty five gallon water cooler in the corner with a paper cup holder. The cups wouldn't do much good without something to fill them. I assumed it would be filled by the next morning. There was a laptop on the table and an old fashioned standing fan. I guessed there wasn't air conditioning in the room.

"Okay," Bill continued, "As the judge said, for today, you should just agree on when you're going to start tomorrow. Let me know what you decide and I'll be sure to have all the exhibits here for you to examine when you get in. Any questions?"

"Yes! I have one," said Erica, the CEO who was always in a hurry. "Can we get started tonight and work until we're done?"

"No. I'm sorry. For security reasons, you'll only have access between eight am and four-thirty pm. Let me know what you decide and I'll open up the room for you. Anything else?"

Looking around the room for further questions and seeing none, Bill wished us well and left us to ourselves.

"How about 9am?" suggested one of the older women – another whose name I didn't know.

You know, we'd been together for nearly eight weeks and I only knew the names of a few people. I'd spoken to most everyone, if only a few words, and had multiple lengthy conversations with several, but never had gotten their names. I wonder why. Maybe it had something to do with the judge's instruction about not talking about the case. That kind of imposed a distance between all of us. I'm sure we'd get to know each other during the deliberations.

"How about eight am?" countered the ever-eager Erica.

"Or we could compromise on eight-thirty," suggested Andy, one of the quiet but friendly jurors I'd spoken to many times during our frequent waits in the hallway outside the courtroom.

"All for eight-thirty?" I asked.

Everyone raised their hands and that was the plan.

As we exited, I let Bill know we'd be there at eight-thirty the next morning.

I had a very sleepless night. This case has bothered me from the beginning, and from what I could see of the others, I wasn't the only one.

I had breakfast with my husband Nick who looked at me anxiously.

"Almost over," I promised, smiling as best I could, feeling almost hung over after my rough night.

"I certainly hope so," he responded, taking my hand. "Babe, this has been hard on you. I've watched you toss and turn during the night. You've even cried out a few times. I know you need to unload and I hate the fact that you've had to keep this from me. Not so much that I mind the secrecy. It's just that maybe I could help. Maybe I could help you put it in perspective."

"I hate it too, Nick. I wish I could have talked about it. You would have been best, but even talking to the other jurors would have helped. This has been a really rough case. The other two jury trials were so easy in comparison. This one is going to stick with me a long time, whatever the outcome."

"I still can't believe that you are on your third serious jury trial. All these years, and I've never even had to show up at the courthouse. I guess it balances out. Sorry it had to be you again. Hopefully this will be the last time for you. How long do you think this one will go?"

"I'm pretty sure the deliberations will go quickly. I know everyone is anxious to have this over with. In a day or so, I'm going to tell you everything over a bottle of wine – or two!"

He smiled, cleared, then washed the dishes, and held me an extra moment before kissing me goodbye.

I drove into town and parked in the Front Street garage. The weather had finally improved and for once, I wasn't going to show up at the courthouse soaked.

Everyone was there a bit early and each seemed lost in thought. No friendly chats this morning. We all stared impatiently at the courtroom doors.

At eight-thirty, Bill the Bailiff came out and then led us to the Jury Room where we discovered a big pile – actually several big piles – of the evidence. There were all the documents and interview transcripts that we'd seen before, stipulations that we'd heard about but hadn't actually read, and DVDs of interviews and testimonies we'd seen and heard in court. I noticed that the water cooler was still empty and that it was almost unbearably warm in the room.

Once everyone had taken a seat, I decided to take the bull by the horns.

"Hi everyone, I'm Linda, known for the past several weeks as Juror Number 3. I know that after this insanely long trial we're all anxious to get this done as soon as reasonably possible. So rather than waste a good part of the morning electing a foreperson, I thought I'd volunteer. I've done this before in two other trials so I'm pretty familiar with what we need to do, how to fill out the forms. What do you think?"

I looked from person to person around the table and everyone nodded. A few smiled and looked relieved.

"Okay. Let's take a quick vote. All in favor of me as foreperson, raise your hand."

With eleven raised hands, it was a done deal and we were on our way.

"Excellent! Let's get down to business. I suggest we go around the room one-by-one. Each of us can introduce ourselves with our names and what we do or did for a living if it's potentially relevant to the case, and give a summary of what we think about the case. Is the defendant guilty or not guilty and if so, on which of the fourteen counts."

I looked towards the young man to my left and nodded.

"Ah, hi. I'm Matt. I'm a software engineer and I work over the hill which probably have no relevance to the case. I'd like to review the evidence, particularly Sandy's testimony, but I find it hard to believe she lied about something like this, and in such detail, so I'm leaning towards guilty on the first counts. As for the counts regarding Mandy, I don't see a lot of evidence for those, and that count for false imprisonment just pisses me off – he takes the phone from his wife, cancels the call and gives it back to her? That's false imprisonment? What was the prosecutor thinking?"

Matt looked over at the young man sitting next to him.

"Hi, I'm Steve. I'm also an engineer. I work with a startup here in Santa Cruz. Like Matt, that probably doesn't have much to do with the case. But, I'm with Matt all the way. I think he's guilty of raping Sandy. Not Matt, Flores. The false imprisonment is bogus, and since she recanted her original testimony and since she may have been influenced by the SART nurse to make up a story, I agree that he's not guilty for the Mandy charges."

Seeing everyone nod, I decided to jump in.

"Well, since we seem to have the beginning of a consensus here and I see everyone nodding, maybe we can jump ahead a bit before continuing. How many of us think he's innocent of the Mandy charges and of the false imprisonment charges?"

Everyone raised their hands.

"Great! That takes away several of the charges so our work is greatly reduced. I've noted it and during a break, I'll start filling out the form on those charges.

"I know the charges about Sandy are the big ones, but what about the witness tampering, and concealing and destroying evidence charges; the fleeing. Are they worth discussing? Raise your hand if you think he might be guilty of any of these. Nobody?"

Matt jumped in, "Certainly the Sandy charges are important. You could stretch to say the Mandy charges are important even though she recanted, but false imprisonment, tampering, concealing evidence, fleeing? The guy parked two blocks away, for goodness sake! Sorry."

Most everyone nodded.

"So not-guilty on those?

Nods all around.

"Okay. I've noted that. Let's keep going. Now we can focus on the charges related to the two alleged incidents of Mr. Flores raping Sandy. Ah, I'm sorry. I don't know your name," I said, smiling encouragingly at a somewhat timid elderly woman. "

"I'm Laura. I'm a writer and I write mysteries and thrillers. I admit to always looking for less-than-obvious answers to questions. That may be good or bad in a case like this.

"There was a lot of conflicting evidence and I must say I'm a bit confused. I'm hoping we can talk more about this, but I think he's probably guilty."

Laura looked to her left as we continued clockwise around the table.

"Hi, I'm Amy. I'm a retired CPS social worker.

"I think he looks guilty but I'm not really sure."

"I'm Evan. I'm CTO of a software company over the hill. While that has little relevance to the case, I am bilingual in Spanish and the first generation son of Hispanic immigrants.

"I just don't see any evidence that he's guilty. No DNA, lots of lies from the mother and that Carrie woman. I'd say not guilty."

Evan turned to the middle-aged man next to him.

"I'm Ben. I work as a park ranger in Watsonville. That probably won't impact my views on the case. I'm tending towards not-guilty because I basically agree with Even, but I'm not absolutely convinced. I want to hear what everyone else has to say before making up my mind.

Bend turned to the elderly woman next to him.

"Hello. My name is Melissa Duplisse. I'm a retired nurse, and I've seen cases like this before. These immigrants. They just don't have the same values. This man was a drunk. He was abusive to his wife and children. I believe he raped his innocent seven-year-old daughter."

Melissa looked down at the table, avoiding eye contact with the rest of us. The woman next to her was clearly anxious to have her say.

"Wow!. I'm Barbara. I'm an ER nurse. I do have some ideas about the injury that we can discuss later. In the meantime, I'll just say that I don't see any convincing evidence. The lack of DNA and lack of blood on Mr. Flores just doesn't seem possible if he did it. I'd say definitely not guilty."

Andy, who I'd spoken with many times during breaks was next.

"Hi, I'm Andy. I work for the California EPA. Again, probably not relevant to the case. I think I have some ideas that will convince those who think he's guilty, but we can get into that later. For now, I'll just say not guilty."

Sue, the woman from LA who had recently moved to Santa

Cruz was next. She looked confident.

"I'm Sue. I do social work for the county. I used to be a political activist and organizer in Watts in LA.

"This poor guy is a victim of a system that just chews up minorities, especially immigrants. There's so little evidence, I find it hard to believe it went to trial. Not guilty."

Our over-enthusiastic CEO was next.

"I'm Erica. Most of you know who I am. Not guilty."

I was last.

"Okay. I'm on the not guilty side too. Let's see. So far, we have three that believe guilty, two that are leaning that way, one leaning towards not-guilty, and six that seem to be solidly in the not guilty column.

"The way we did this in my previous trials was we made lists on the white board of arguments for guilty and arguments for not guilty. Then we examined the evidence behind each one and tried to figure out if the evidence was strong enough.

"Of course we have to keep in mind that we don't need evidence of not guilty. As the judge says, the prosecution must prove its case beyond a reasonable doubt. But I still think it's useful if there are strong arguments that might prove someone innocent.

"So why don't we start on the guilty side. I'll be scribe. Okay. What do you think?"

Matt kicked it off. "Well, the most important is Sandy's accusation, and with that, the detail in her description of what happened. I can't see a seven-year-old making something like that up – she couldn't have known about lubricant and the thrusting and the ejaculation without having experienced it."

"Well actually she could have," Sue objected strenuously.

"I don't mean to cut you off, Sue, but for now, I just want to get a list. We can discuss the merits of each point, or lack thereof, once the list is complete. Okay?"

"Yeah. I'm sorry. I admit to being a bit worked up about this case."

"I think we all are," I replied to nodding heads around the room. "Okay, what else?"

"The y-str on Sandy's underwear," Matt continued. "I don't buy that it could have been one of the Hispanic technicians that contaminated it. With a 1 in 120 chance, it's got to be Flores."

"The hidden lubricant," proposed Steve.

"The physical injury," said Melissa the retired nurse. "I don't see any other way she could have received that injury."

"Yes. The testimony of the SART nurse and the forensic examiner," chimed in Amy.

"And though I still believe he's not guilty, I have to say that the jail calls really bothered me. In one, he almost admitted he did it and in others, Alejandra really suggests that he did – that she believes it happened," Andy added.

"Anything else?" I asked.

"Well, there are lots of smaller things," Matt began. "There's the blood on the bedspread, the testimony of Mandy and Alejandra backing up the story. The bargain with the video of the visit to the CVS to buy the eraser. There's the interrogation of Flores where he says he can't remember if he did it or not. I guess that one's not so small. There's Alejandra's testimony that he molested Mandy. There's all the drinking."

"Hold on while I make some notes,' I suggested. "Okay. I think a number of these things are worth keeping track of, but I believe they just back up some of the major points. On the other hand, the thing about Mr. Flores saying he didn't remember seems pretty important. I'll put that one up. Does anyone think the others need to be there on their own merit?"

"I think the bargain and the eraser are important," Steve replied.

"Good. Anything else? We can always add more later as we discuss this. No? Then here's our initial list for key arguments for guilty – not necessarily in order of importance:"

Sandy's Detailed Description of the Rape
Y-STR on Sandy's Underwear
The Hidden Lubricant
The Physical Injury
The SART Nurse testimony
The Forensic Detective's testimony
The Jail Calls
The Bargain.
Mr. Flores saying he didn't remember if he did it or not during the interrogation.

"Now, how about our initial list for not guilty?" I asked, drawing a line down the middle of the white board and writing

'Not Guilty' on the right side.

"No DNA evidence!" Barbara announced to nods from all of the other 'not guilty' jurors. "And no blood evidence on Mr. Flores, his unwashed underwear, or the washcloth. And I know I'm not supposed to refute the Guilty list, but the Y-STR thing is just so weak. There was so little, they almost missed it. If Mr. Flores even touched the underwear, it would be there and it appeared to be in a similar quantity to the amount of Alejandra's DNA – So I'm calling this part of my no DNA argument."

"No fingerprints on the lubricant bottle, and why would it be hidden?" proposed Ben.

"The interrogation," suggested Sue. "He was confused at the beginning and never confessed even after almost ten hours of lies, trickery, and pressure from the police. I couldn't have stood up to that. I would have confessed to anything, especially with the false promises they made."

"The rape on the beach was clearly a lie. For me, that calls into question the first rape." Andy stated confidently. "And, I'm not sure why the defense didn't get into this, but the timeline just doesn't fit. I'll show you all why when we discuss this point."

"I have a problem with the number of lies by Alejandra, Carrie, Mandy, and how Alejandra changed her attitude in the jail calls," added Erica.

"Anything else? No? Okay. I'll add one: he didn't run.

"Here's our not guilty list:"

No DNA.
No Blood
No Fingerprints on the Lubricant Bottle
Why was the Lubricant Bottle Hidden?
False accusation of Rape on the Beach
Timeline doesn't work
Lies from Alejandra, Carrie, and Mandy
Attitude Changes by Alejandra in the Jail Calls
He didn't run.

"Before we break, how about another vote?" I suggested. It came out exactly the same: five for guilty, six for not-guilty and Ben abstained

"When we get back, we can start on the lists, or we can review some of the evidence first. Any thoughts?"

Surprisingly, the very quiet Laura spoke up. "As I mentioned, I'm still pretty confused about all of this. For me it comes down to one question. Did Sandy lie? During her testimony she admitted that she didn't actually remember what happened, that she was just saying what she saw in the tapes she reviewed right before her testimony. So I think we need to get back to as close to the incident as possible. I think we should review the forensic interview between her and Sandi the detective, and then we should look at her testimony at the preliminary hearing from three years ago. Maybe we can see if she'd lying."

"That's a good place to start," agreed Matt.

"Is that okay with everyone?" I asked.

Seeing approval, I suggested we reconvene at ten o'clock I also reminded everyone that we weren't supposed to discuss the case outside the presence of everyone else. We all needed to hear everyone's thoughts and their arguments. No outside discussions.

Once in the hall, I did as I always did during our breaks. I called into the office to handle any crises while I walked laps around the rectangular building. I had long ago figured out that it took me two minutes per lap, so seven laps later, I headed back to the jury room.

As people filed in, I found the DVD for Sandy's forensic interview. I turned on the computer, inserted the DVD, and verified that it did, indeed, start to play. I paused it, then turned the screen so that everyone could see and hear. It wasn't easy – we didn't have a big monitor screen so twelve of us pressed together to get the best views we could.

It was time for lunch when the video finished, and though I was dying for company, I left the courthouse on my own, picked up a sandwich and iced tea at Eric's Deli Café, and found a place in the sun to think about the morning. The simple, basic formalization of the case had gotten me thinking in areas I hadn't considered before and the video had some major surprises in it.

2

5th Juror, Melissa Duplisse, early 70s, retired nurse.

It was unbearably hot in the deliberation room when we got back from lunch, and the water cooler was still empty. Were they trying to kill us or just push us towards a quick verdict?

I found the bailiff and asked him to make sure the water cooler was filled. I asked about the air conditioning, but he just nodded knowingly and suggested we use the fan.

Back in the room, people settled into their seats. The bailiff carried in a bottle of water and put it into the cooler. I thanked him and everyone chimed in, a few jeering in good-natured fun.

Linda, the foreperson, called us all to order much like the judge did during the trial. She suggested we watch the preliminary hearing DVD before we opened discussions.

During the trial, we saw the forensic interview very early on. It was weeks later that we saw the video of Sandy's testimony at the preliminary hearing. Watching them one after the other revealed some contradictions. I don't know why I hadn't seen them before. The child lies. And when she lies, she looks at the ceiling and all around. It's a tell. She did this throughout the forensic interview with Sandi the detective. At one point, Sandi the detective asked her if she saw her father's penis when he finished. Sandy nodded. The detective then asked her to describe it. The little girl looked confused. Not upset, just confused. In fact, as I think about it now, she didn't seem upset about any of this. What I would have assumed to be hard for a child of seven to answer, little Sandy responded confidently and lightly with her head bouncing around, like she was telling a story. Anyway, at this point, little Sandy said she had to go to the bathroom. The detective told her it was just outside the door to the right. Again, I'm not sure why I hadn't thought about it before, but while the detective continued writing up her notes, Sandy could have talked to her mother who was waiting outside. Because when she came in and the detective posed the question again, Sandy had a ready answer. The penis was wet and there was a white liquid dripping out of it.

Theoretically, she was referring to semen, and now, it bothered me that no semen was found on the bed or on Mr. Flores or his underwear.

Worse, in the next video, while testifying, we saw the same ceiling-looking, head rolling as she embellished her story. Now there were more details than during the forensic interview, and even worse, she added a new rape that she hadn't talked about before. I didn't remember that she hadn't described it before. This was clearly a child adding to a lie that people might have doubt about to make herself more credible.

I felt like a fool. I'm a nurse for God's sake! I've dealt with children my whole life. How did I miss this? Was I just too ready to believe this man was guilty? If nothing else, I now have some doubt. The injury still bothered me. As the prosecutor asked in his closing statement, how else did she get that injury?

3

3rd Juror – Linda Lancaster, early 40s, personnel manager in a larger corporation, married, no kids. Jury foreperson.

When we got back from lunch, I asked everyone what they thought about the tapes. Surprisingly, Melissa, who seemed to have her mind made up when I asked their thoughts at the beginning, raised some points I hadn't thought of.

While she still wanted an explanation about the injury, she claimed that she could tell when Sandy was lying. We replayed portions of the videos and sure enough, there was a tell. Ben, the ranger asked her if she was a poker player. Melissa just smiled, but I have a feeling she is, and she's probably pretty good at it.

She also pointed out the fact that Sandy stepped out of her first interview and might have talked to her mother to help her answer questions about what her father's penis looked like. A couple of others chimed in that they had noticed the same thing.

It didn't prove innocence, nor did it mean that everything Sandy said was a lie, but it certainly cast some more doubt. I think a few of those on the fence were starting to lean a bit towards not guilty.

Matt, one of the two who seemed most strongly convinced of guilt jumped in, addressing Melissa..

"I've got two young girls, seven and five. Although I see your point, and it may be a 'tell', it could just be that she does this when she talks about something she's uncomfortable with. I know that Zelda, my seven-year-old does that. She looks at the ceiling and around the room whenever she needs to tell us something that she has a hard time saying. I think it's just that she doesn't want to see us judge her and it's easier if she's not looking directly at us. If you think about it, you can probably remember doing the same thing before you learned that it's important to engage with the person you're talking to, especially in difficult situations."

I saw several nodding heads and had to admit that he had a point. Still, there was some inconsistency here.

We replayed parts of both tapes trying to compare when she spoke directly to Detective Locke and when she looked away. It's true that she looked away on all the 'difficult' subjects. But the 'difficult' subjects were about what had happened.

Then again, when questions about her parents' fighting came up, she had no problems looking at Detective Locke. It's a tough call.

I called for what would be another of at least a dozen votes. There was still no change: five for guilty and six for not guilty, and Ben abstaining.

When we'd exhausted that topic I asked the group what item on our guilty list we should discuss next. Steve, the other young man on the panel suggested that since we started with Sandy's videos, we should continue on the first one on the list: Sandy's detailed description of the rape.

"As Matt said this morning, I just can't see how a seven-year-old girl would have that kind of knowledge about sex. I mean lubrication, the thrusting, the apparent orgasm, the semen? It doesn't seem like she could have made all of that up."

"Well what about the fact that the girls slept in their parents room for several years?" asked Amy, the retired child protective services worker. " We know the parents had a very active sex life. I'm sure the children heard most of what went on. I've seen this before in small households, and as Mandy said at one point, with the Internet, TV, and friends in the know, you shouldn't underestimate what kids know today."

Matt responded, "Yeah, they may know a lot. And I admit that with an older sister who already has her period and with the fact that she lives in tight quarters with her parents, and that the girls have unlimited Internet access, Sandy might know more than most. I could see the thrusting, maybe the noises, but lubricant, ejaculation, and semen? Not likely."

Several heads nodded in agreement, even some on the not-guilty side.

"I'd like to jump in here," said Barbara, the ER nurse. "I may be jumping ahead into the physical injury, but since we were discussing thrusting, I think it's important to look at the injury. I'm an ER nurse and I've seen a lot of injuries, including many to the vaginal areas of women and young girls. I've seen rape victims and I've seen child-rape victims. Obviously this is not evidence, and I'm not an official expert, but my personal opinion is that the injury does not match Sandy's description of what happened.

"She said Mr. Flores put her on the bed, pulled down her pants and put his private part in her private part. Then he started thrusting violently, over and over until he made a grunting sound and took his private part out. She saw it and it was dripping with a white fluid.

"Now, think about the injury. There was a small laceration on one of the labia minora. No broken hymen, no semen inside her vagina, no injuries in her vagina.

"The experts said the injuries were consistent with a blunt object, possibly a penis. I agree.

"But they're not consistent with deep thrusting and penetration. I'm sorry to say that I've seen little girls who have been raped, and even women who have been raped, and this minor laceration just doesn't match up.

"And while I'm at it, let me go one step further. If Sandy was raped more than once, at home, then on the beach, then possibly at the storage locker as Mr. Bolt suggested, there'd be much more damage than a little tear of very sensitive tissue."

"Well how do you explain the injury then?" Matt challenged.

Erica, who surprisingly had been silent up until this point, turned towards Matt and even without standing, she seemed to almost loom over him. He recoiled, seemingly intimidated. You could certainly see how Erica become a successful female CEO.

"I think we could spend a lot of time on defense theories of what happened and why. Maybe we need to. On the other hand, officially, we just need to show that there is reasonable doubt.

"Since I'd like to get this deliberation over with so I can get back to work, I'll cut to the chase. After hearing what Barbara said, I went back through my notes and found something I wrote down because it was unusual. Ms. Preston, who's pretty damned formidable during cross-examination, seemed nonchalant in her cross of Officer Davenport, the first officer on the scene. She asked about where Sandy was when he came in.

"Yeah, we all know she was propped up against pillows on the made bed (which was unmade in the morning when they left the apartment) and was in obvious pain with her hand over her groin area. And okay, I've had injuries that got worse after several hours. But why wasn't she in pain before? She, herself, said she played on the beach with the dog. And why was there so much blood on the bedspread, but only in the place she was sitting when the officer came in? As I think about it now, in light of Barbara's thoughts, I have to ask myself if the injury wasn't quite recent – fresh blood on that part of the bedspread, a little girl obviously in pain when she didn't seem to be before and after she'd spent much of the afternoon playing. I can't help thinking the injury had to be more recent. Could it have been the sharp rocks on the jetty? Or could it be something else?"

"Are you suggesting that Alejandra caused the injury just before the police got there?" Steve asked skeptically.

"I'm not saying that's what happened. It just creates doubt for me. Could a mother convince her young daughter to submit to an injury to ensure that her daughters weren't taken away from her? Could she have coached the girls so they could protect themselves from their father? It's possible. For me, it's not far-fetched.

Steve didn't skip a beat. "But as Mr. Bolt said in his closing, all that is just speculation. It's not evidence. It makes more sense that Sandy is telling the truth and if the injury is more recent, maybe it was the rape on the beach or the storage locker."

"About that rape on the beach," Andy interrupted. "It may be hard to believe, but I remember that day. It was the day after Halloween. I took the afternoon off so some friends and I could go sailing. It was Friday and the weather was so amazing.

"Unfortunately, several roads were closed near the harbor and it took us almost an hour to get there from Capitola. This was about the same time that Albert was taking Sandy to the beach. Traffic was horrible. When we finally arrived, it was so late that we decided to just have drinks on the deck at the Crow's Nest, next to the harbor.

"I can tell you, the beach was packed. There were hundreds of people on the beach and on the jetties, even quite a few in the water. With the crowd, there was no way that Albert could have raped Sandy on the beach. Just no way.

"But that's not my main point here. It's the timeline. I'm a bit surprised that Ms. Preston didn't present this, but let me lay it out for you."

Andy made his way to the whiteboard and started writing. When he stepped away, he had a list of times and events:

2:30 girls get home from school.
2:45 Mandy leaves for friend's house
2:46 Albert rapes Sandy
2:50 Sandy cleans up
2:55 Albert, Sandy and the dog leave the apartment

3:05 Albert buys Sandy a slushy at 7-Eleven
3:15 Albert, Sandy, and the dog arrive at the beach
4:30 Alejandra calls Albert
4:57 Albert stops at storage locker
5:07 Albert leaves storage locker
5:30 Albert arrives home with Sandy and the dog

"Okay," said Steve. "I don't see a problem. Except for your rape and clean up time which from Sandy's testimony took much longer, that's how it went down according to the police. I remember that the storage locker had timestamps and I assume those are the actual times. So what does this prove?"

"Look," Andy began. "I live in Capitola which is closer to the harbor than the family's apartment. That 7-Eleven is just up 7th Avenue from the harbor. We have the receipt and surveillance tape from the 7-Eleven and Albert bought the slushy at 3:05. Assuming only 9 minutes for the rape and cleanup, that would mean that Albert made it to the 7-Eleven from their apartment in less than 10 minutes. That's impossible even with no traffic. On a busy Friday afternoon, with traffic and construction, it's inconceivable.

"Assume the rape and clean up took five minutes instead, though as you said, Sandy testified that the rape lasted much longer. Though as I talk about it, I know I couldn't load up my fishing gear and get any of my kids out of the house and into the car in five minutes. Let's discount that and assume he did leave within five minutes. Even fifteen minutes to get to the harbor isn't possible. I'm surprised he made it in twenty. Looking at this, there just wasn't any time for a rape to have taken place. He had to have left the house very soon after Mandy left."

It was just after three o'clock so I suggested we take a thirty minute break. I called the office and put out some fires as I started my laps around the courthouse.

After six or seven laps, I noticed Matt and Steve outside in the park next to the river. They seemed to be having a heated discussion. I'd need to remind them that we're not supposed to discuss the case outside the presence of the others.

When we got back to the jury room, I did remind everyone that we shouldn't talk about the case outside the presence of the others. Steve rolled his eyes while Matt looked incredibly guilty. I decided to move on.

"Okay. I know we haven't gone through the lists we made point-by-point, but we've covered quite a few.

"To help clarify where we should go next, I thought we'd take a vote to see where we are. So, how many for guilty?"

Matt raised his hand and looked pointedly at Steve who ignored him.

"Ah, come on. This is bullshit! Steve, you can't really think this guy is innocent."

Getting no response, Matt shrugged.

Amy raised her hand.

"Not guilty?" I asked.

Nine hands went up and I raised mine.

"Ben," I asked. "What convinced you to vote not-guilty?

'The injury bothered me. Barbara's clarification made that easier. I hate to say it, but Sandy's obvious pain and the blood on the bedspread seem inconsistent with the events. But ultimately, Andy's argument about the timing make sense. There just wasn't time for the rape to have occurred at home. And as for the jetty, we all know what a warm Friday afternoon looks like down there. Sandy lied about that and I have no confidence that any of her testimony was true. I'm now firmly in the not-guilty camp."

"Okay. Ten to two. I don't want us to gang up on Matt and Amy, so what I'd like to suggest is that we go around the room and all of you who have voted not-guilty tell us why, and if you have any doubts about that verdict. That might give Matt and Amy some points to leverage. Does that sound fair?"

With nods and yesses all around, we started with Steve.

"I'm sorry Matt. I really thought this guy was guilty. He might still be, but with what Andy had to say about the weather that day and the timeline, I'm sure that no rape happened on the beach. If that didn't happen, I have a hard time believing anything that Sandy said. I'm beginning to think she was coached. As far as doubts on innocence, well, I guess the jail calls still bother me as does the interrogation where Flores said he might not remember what he did. But as much as I want to see criminals put away forever, I have to admit that I don't think we should convict if there's reasonable doubt. And there are just too many doubts about Flores' guilt for me to want to see him locked up for the rest of his life."

I turned towards Sue and nodded.

"I know. You all think I'm a leftist snowflake and it's

probably true. But I've spent most of my life seeing minorities and innocents chewed up by the system. I've worked to stop that where it made sense, and I've also worked to put some very bad people away to make sure they didn't continue to ruin the lives of those around them.

"As part of all my activism, I've seen a lot of these interrogations. This one was tough. The guy was shackled for hours. Subjected to lies and misdirections over and over again. Berated in Spanish and in English. At the end of ten hours of this, he still says he's innocent. He volunteers for a lie detector test. He tells them something must be wrong if they've found his DNA and his semen. If it had been me, I would have confessed under all that pressure. For Albert, I think that statement that perhaps he forgot what happened was a bit sarcastic, but was also the only way he could make any sense of what the detectives were stating to be outright facts.

"I'm sorry, but I don't have any doubts about his innocence."

Melissa was next.

"Well, as I said before, I think the child lies. As much as I think an abusive alcoholic father should be put away for crimes against his family, with Andy's timeline and Barbara's ideas about the injury not matching up with the violence of the act, I have serious doubts about the rape. I believe that the only things that still bother me a bit are the jail calls and that Mr. Flores wouldn't say that Sandy was lying. I'm quite sure she was lying, but why wouldn't he admit that?"

Evan responded.

"Let me take that one if I may. As you all know I come from a Hispanic background."

"I just want to remind everyone that most Hispanics are devout Catholics, especially immigrants and many of their first generation children. In all of our Hispanic cultures, first and foremost, children are special. Until a certain age, they are innocents. They don't have enough reason to truly judge right from wrong and hence, their misstatements are not lies, they're mistakes for which the children should not be held accountable.

"Officially in the Catholic Church that age is seven. Children under seven cannot sin. In Hispanic cultures, it is a sin to tell a lie. That can be forgiven during confession by a priest. But to call someone liar is basically saying that person is an unredeemable sinner and is damned to hell. I can't see any

Hispanic parent saying that about their children. This is just a cultural difference between US culture and Hispanic cultures.

"I do believe that Albert is not just not guilty, but innocent. After watching the family, I honestly believe he has been framed to protect Alejandra, her son, and her custody of the children.

"As for doubts about innocence, as I said, I really don't have any. But as for something for Matt to argue, I think the jail calls are the strongest evidence for the prosecution. I have an answer for that too, but I suspect someone else will come up with it. I just wanted to make my one point strongly: don't think that it's unusual that Albert refused to call his daughter a liar."

Laura picked up from there.

"As most of you know, I'm a writer. I love to make things up and to create fantastic scenarios that trick my readers. This case has been a great story. A boy in the fifth grade drops out of school in El Salvador to work in the fields so he can help support his family. After several years of back breaking labor he gets a chance to come to the US. His uncle sponsors him and he starts working at a landscaping company in a small northern California town. Within a year, a family friend comes to the US and seduces the teenage boy. She's seventeen years older. They marry. They have two kids. The boy becomes a man and starts to advance in his career, being promoted and now heading a team. He's handsome and virile in his late twenties but his wife is in her forties. She's going downhill physically and gets jealous. Add in her son from another marriage who comes to live with them and who has questionable immigration status. He's just a year younger that our hero so we can create some conflict there. Perhaps his use of drugs in front of the kids and a drug arrest? Who will the jealous wife choose? Our hero starts drinking to escape the non-stop abuse of his much older wife. During a particularly nasty fight, he threatens to divorce her and take the children. What will happen next? How will the wife save her son from deportation? How will she keep custody of her children? How can she punish her husband and bring him back into line?

"I think we know.

"For me, this explains the jail calls. I believe that Albert was so discouraged after months in jail, that he thought Alejandra would forgive him if he promised to get back into line. If he apologized for threatening her. If things could go back to the way they were. That's what I heard in those calls.

"But then again, I'm a writer. I do make things up. Still as the over-used cliché goes, life is stranger than fiction."

There was a knock at the door and Bill, the Bailiff came in.

"Sorry guys, it's four-thirty. You need to stop for the day. Can you wrap it up in five minutes?

I told him we could and then suggested to the group that we start at eight-thirty the next morning. It had been a long day. Before leaving, though, I asked for one more vote. Amy had changed sides saying that her concerns about the jail calls and Albert being unwilling to call Sandy a liar had been answered. The vote was eleven to one. Matt was the last holdout.

"Before we go," Matt began. "I just want you to know that I hear what you're saying. I see the logic and I admit I have some doubts about Flores' guilt. They may be what you'd technically call "reasonable doubts". But I'm struggling. I still can't believe that little seven-year-old Sandy would lie about something like this. I can't believe that she could have the details of such an unnatural act.

"I'll do my best to think through it. I'll pray on it. I'll let you know my decision in the morning."

He didn't look at the group. He looked defeated, almost on the verge of tears. Steve put his hand on Matt's shoulder, but Matt just shrugged it off as he raced out of the room. I thanked everyone as they made their way out, and turned off the lights and closed the door as I left.

4

15th Juror – Mathias Wright, Silicon Valley engineer, early-thirties with 2 children under 5.

I can't believe they're all against me. Even Steve! We've gotten to be pretty good friends during this trial, having lunch together most days.

Yes. I know we're not supposed to discuss the case, but Steve didn't think that was such a big deal. His father is a well-known prosecutor and if any non-lawyer knows the laws and the court system, it's Steve.

Like me, he's believes in the law. He also believes that courts are too lenient letting criminals literally get away with murder, and in this case, worse. I think what Flores did to little Sandy is worse than murder. How could a father do that to an innocent child. He truly does deserve to burn in hell and to suffer in prison the way he made his daughter suffer.

Steve also thinks that immigrants are a problem. Our ultra-liberal system spends so much time defending their rights that honest people suffer, even little children.

We argued outside during the break. After that ER nurse talked about the injury not being severe enough, Steve was having serious doubts. I think it was something that bothered him all along though he didn't realize it.

He was with me. So were many of the other jurors. We saw Flores as an alcoholic abusive father and husband who had molested his older daughter and raped the youngest.

Okay. I admit that there's no evidence that Mandy was molested. She said she lied and I believe her. I think Ms. Preston made a good point about children being easily influenced by people in positions of authority and in wanting to support her sister, in want to make sure her sister was believed, she let herself be led into saying her father had molested her when she was two or three years old.

I've seen the memories of my two girls and it's obvious she couldn't have remembered something from when she was that little. But you can't blame her for trying to give her sister courage or for wanting to escape from her alcoholic abusive father.

I left the jury room severely depressed. Even seeing my girls and dinner ready on the table didn't cheer me up. I did my best.

After dinner, Joan bathed the girls and I read them a story to help them sleep. Then I told Joan what had happened. She was shocked.

"What are you going to do?" she asked.

"I really don't know. There is no way these people are going to change their minds. I'm at a loss. This man raped his little girl. He can't go free. What should I do?"

"Let's pray on it."

And we did. We prayed. I asked God to show me the way, to make sure justice was done.

We went to bed, and in the morning, God had answered me.

I made my way to the court house and smiled at everyone as I entered the jury room.

Linda started us off.

"Let's start with a vote," she suggested. "Guilty?"

I raised my hand.

"Not guilty?"

All of the others raised their hands.

"Okay," she started. "Shall we continue going around the room?"

"No," I interrupted. "Look. I'm not going to change my vote no matter what. I've thought about it and prayed on it and I know that Flores is guilty and it would be a crime on my part if I voted against my conscience."

"No one is asking you to vote against your conscience," Linda responded. "So what do you want to do, Matt?

"I think we should go back to the judge and tell him we're stuck. He can decide what's next. We're already agreed that Flores is not guilty on counts seven through 14. We can tell him that."

"Before we do that, is there anyone who might change their vote?" she asked.

She looked around the room and one-by-one, everyone said no.

Linda called in the bailiff who asked us to wait a few minutes.

Fifteen minutes later, he came back and led us into the courtroom where we were seated in the jury box.

5

From the court transcript:

THE COURT: All right. Let's go on the record regarding People versus Mr. Flores. Mr. Flores is present. Counsel are present. All of our jurors are present.
And who is our foreperson?
JUROR NUMBER THREE: Me.
THE COURT: All right. [Name redacted]; correct?
JUROR NUMBER THREE: Yes.
THE COURT: Thank you very much for serving in that capacity. Good morning to all of you folks. It is my understanding some verdicts have been reached; is that correct?
JUROR NUMBER THREE: Correct.
THE COURT: Without telling me what the verdict is can you advise me as to which counts verdicts have been reached upon, please.
JUROR NUMBER THREE: Yes. Counts 7, 8, 9, 10, 11, 12, 13, and 14..
THE COURT: All right. And as to the remaining counts where verdicts have not been reached, can you advise me as to how many votes you've had amongst the jury?
JUROR NUMBER THREE: A dozen or more.

3

THE COURT: Without telling me how it falls one side or the other guilty or not guilty can you tell me how those votes fall in terms of the number of folks on one side versus the other?
JUROR NUMBER THREE: Eleven to one.
THE COURT: Eleven to one?
JUROR NUMBER THREE: Yes.
THE COURT: And is it 11 to one on each of those remaining counts?
JUROR NUMBER THREE: Correct.
THE COURT: All right. I appreciate your information in that regard. If you'll indulge me just

for a moment. I'm going to ask counsel to please approach.

(Discussion off the record.)

THE COURT: I appreciate everyone's indulgence and I appreciate the efforts that you folks are going through. I'm going to provide you with an additional instruction at this point and I'm going to ask you to continue to deliberate. I'm going to give instruction 3551.

Sometimes juries that have had difficulty reaching a verdict are able to resume deliberations and successfully reach a verdict on one or more counts. Please consider the following suggestions.

Do not hesitate to reexamine your own views.

4

Fair and effective jury deliberations require a frank and forthright exchange of views. Each of you must decide the case for yourself and form your own individual opinion after you have fully and completely considered all of the evidence with your fellow jurors. It is your duty as jurors to deliberate with the goal of reaching a verdict if you can do so without surrendering your individual judgment.

Do not change your position just because it differs from that of other jurors or just because you or others want to reach a verdict. Both the People and the defendant are entitled to the individual judgment of each juror. It is up to you to decide how to conduct your deliberations. You may want to consider new approaches in order to get a fresh perspective.

Let me know whether I can do anything to help you further such as give additional instructions or clarify instructions that I've already given you. Please continue your deliberations at this time. If you wish to communicate with me further, please do so in writing.

And I'll tell you what. I'll get a copy of this instruction and provide it to you folks. Again, I appreciate your efforts. I'm going to ask you to continue your deliberations at this point.

If we could have these folks return and we'll get

265 a copy of that instruction for them.

6

8th Juror – Ben Singleton - mid-30s - state park ranger - 2 kids under 10.

I can't believe it! Here we are, almost eight weeks into this trial and we can't come to a verdict one way or the other.

That guy Matt. I don't know what his problem is. He just won't change his vote.

The judge sent us back into the courtroom. Linda read the new instructions, but I think it was just to kill time. We all knew that none of us were going to change our votes, so we just had to take some time for show.

After she finished, we continued around the room with arguments for our positions. I pointed out that there were lies from the beginning and that without the DNA, with the injury not fitting Sandy's description of what happened, Andy's timeline, and now the explanations for the jail calls and the interrogation, I was more convinced than ever that it wasn't just a question of reasonable doubt anymore. The poor guy had spent three years in jail, lost his job, his family, and his reputation all on a false charge from a paranoid wife.

Barbara, Andy, and Erica agreed with me. Only Amy and Melissa said that they had reasonable doubt but weren't fully convinced of Albert's innocence. But as timid as they seemed, they were clear that their doubts weren't going to go away. They were firm in their beliefs that Albert should be found not-guilty.

We voted. Eleven to one.

We asked Matt to defend his position. He kept coming back to the injury and asked how it could have occurred other than a rape.

Several of us reminded him that the defense didn't have to prove innocence or provide a theory of how the injury occurred. There was reasonable doubt that a rape had occurred. How was it possible there was no DNA evidence?

But Matt held firm. He argued that Barbara's conclusions weren't evidence, Andy's statements about the crowds on the beach weren't evidence, nor was Andy's timeline. No witnesses brought any of that up during the trial.

I guess he had a point, particularly with Barbara's conclusions. And I suppose with Andy's recollections of that Friday afternoon.

But I remember that Friday too. Classic Santa Cruz Indian Summer. The evidence was that they went to the beach, to the jetty next to the harbor entrance. Everyone knows what that's like on a sunny, warm Friday. And the timeline really was evidence. It was up to us to interpret it and to me and the rest, the conclusion was inescapable. While we didn't have evidence of how long it took to get to the harbor that day, there just wasn't time for the rape at home to have occurred.

Everyone tried to reason with him. We thought his friend Steve would have some success, but Matt wouldn't even listen to Steve.

At one point, in the face of unassailable logic, Matt finally admitted there was reasonable doubt. He is an engineer, after all. The arguments were there. But ultimately, for Matt, he wanted innocence proven. He said he believed that with this kind of crime we have to believe the victims first, then prove innocence.

Surprisingly, a number of the women seemed to agree with him. And I guess I can see the point. Still, we were bound by the law and bound by the instructions that the judge had given us.

It was not up to the defense to prove innocence. It was up to the prosecution to prove guilt beyond a reasonable doubt.

Matt just didn't agree with that.

We took countless votes for form and then called Bill, the Bailiff into the jury room.

Half an hour later, Bill led us back into the courtroom. Looking at everyone, I saw defeat on their faces. We'd spent all this time, had gone through all the agony that this case brought to each of us, and for what?

CHAPTER 7

THE VERDICT

"Just because you think it doesn't make it true."
- Unknown

1 From the court transcript:

THE COURT: All right. Let's go on the record, please, regarding People versus Mr. Flores. Mr. Flores
9

is present. Counsel are present. All of our of jurors are present.
[Name redacted] is our foreperson. And you have the verdict forms at this point?
THE FOREPERSON: I do, Your Honor.
THE COURT: Could you give those to our bailiff, please.
It is my understanding that there is a distinct difference of opinion as to the remaining counts where verdicts were not found. Is that correct?
THE FOREPERSON: Correct.
THE COURT: And there have been more than a dozen votes taken?
THE FOREPERSON: Correct.
THE COURT: And it's 11-1?
THE FOREPERSON: Correct.
THE COURT: And it's 11-1 in which direction?
THE FOREPERSON: Not guilty.
THE COURT: All right.
And the position of the foreperson is that there's really nothing else that could convince, in terms of additional instructions or additional information provided by the Court that would make a difference in this case; is that correct?
THE FOREPERSON: Right.
THE COURT: All right. Thank you very much.
10

I'll accept your representation in that regard.
All right. I have unfilled-out verdicts regarding Counts 1, 2, 3 and 4, 5, and 6.
In light of my discussions with counsel and in light of the information I have received from our

foreperson, I will declare a mistrial regarding those counts.

As to Count 7, we, the jury in the above-entitled case, find the defendant, Albert Daniel Flores, not guilty of misdemeanor false imprisonment as charged in Count 7.

As to Count 8, we, the jury in the above-entitled case, find the defendant, Albert Daniel Flores, not guilty of misdemeanor destroying/concealing evidence as charged in Count 8.

We, the jury in the above-entitled case, find the defendant, Albert Daniel Flores, not guilty of aggravated sexual assault upon a child under 14 years as charged in Count 9.

Having found the defendant not guilty of aggravated sexual assault upon a child under 14 years, we, the jury in the above-entitled case, find the defendant not guilty of the lesser included offense of sexual penetration by force as charged in Count 10.

As to Count 11, we, the jury in the above-entitled case, find the defendant, Albert Daniel

11

Flores, not guilty of lewd act upon a child under 14 years by force or fear as charged in Count 11.

Having found the defendant not guilty of lewd act upon a child under 14 years by force or fear, we, the jury in the above-entitled case, find the defendant not guilty of the lesser included offense of lewd act upon child under 14 years.

We, the jury in the above-entitled case, find the defendant, Albert Daniel Flores, not guilty of sexual intercourse with a child under ten years, as charged in Count 12.

Having found the defendant - excuse me. That's dated and signed by our foreperson.

Moving to Count 13. We, the jury in the above-entitled case, find the defendant, Albert Daniel Flores, not guilty of lewd act upon a child under 14 years by force or fear as charged in Count 13.

Having found the defendant not guilty of lewd act

upon a child under 14 years by force or fear, we, the jury in the above-entitled case, find the defendant not guilty of the lesser included offense of lewd act upon a child under 14 years. We, the jury in the above-entitled case, find the defendant, Albert Daniel Flores, not guilty of aggravated sexual assault upon a child under 14 years, as charged in Count 14.

12

Having found the defendant not guilty of aggravated sexual assault upon a child under 14 years, we, the jury in the above-entitled case, find the defendant not guilty of the lesser included offense of rape by force.

Each of the verdicts that I've read in the record have been dated and signed by our foreperson.

Do the People wish the jury polled?

MR. BOLT: No.

THE COURT: Do you wish the jury polled?

MS. PRESTON: No, thank you, Your Honor.

THE COURT: We will record those verdicts.

Again, I'll declare a mistrial as to the remaining counts.

Thank you. Thank you. Thank you for your service in this matter. This was a long trial. This was a case involving highly sensitive issues. This was a case that you were required to pay particular attention to, and you did that. You were a very engaged, attention-paying jury in this matter.

I can represent to you that I have never had a trial that has had the number of questions that our jurors asked in this case, which was great. It showed you were paying attention. It showed that you were engaged. It showed that you were taking the case seriously.

13

I thank you for that. Mr. Flores thanks you for that. The attorneys thank you for that.

All of the different stops and starts in this trial, you folks were understanding. You were patient. You were cordial. I sincerely appreciate that. There were situations that were beyond the control of anyone in this courtroom as to how this case moved forward, situations involving the availability of witnesses, availability of jurors, availability of attorneys, all of which impacted what happened here. All of you were punctual, rolled with those issues and handled it in a very professional way.

Do not feel that you failed in some way in not reaching verdicts on those counts. Your decisions in this process make a great deal of difference in how this case proceeds.

It's extremely important to Mr. Flores, to his family, to the attorneys, to law enforcement, to any of the individuals that were witnesses in this case. So your efforts are extremely important.

You should be extremely proud of what you did over the past seven weeks or so. It was an honor for me to work with all of you. I must admit that, selfishly speaking, I'm going to miss seeing your faces here every morning. And I'm sorry that we will be parting company

14

in about 20 seconds.

But, indeed, I've enjoyed working with you. It's been an honor working with you. I hope that sometime when I see you out, downtown somewhere, that I will be able to come up and shake your hand and thank you for your efforts personally.

All of the admonitions, in about 15 seconds, are going to be removed. You will be able to discuss this case with anyone you wish, or not discuss the case with anyone; whatever you feel is appropriate.

I can't order you in this regard, but I would respectfully suggest, if you do decide to discuss the case, please don't mention the names of the girls involved. It's a small community. People can start putting things together. Again, I can't order you in that regard, but I would respectfully request that you not mention their names if you discuss it with anyone.

This case took longer than we thought. Let's be honest. There were a series of consistent and inconsistent statements within the testimony and the prior statements offered by many of the witnesses. That necessitated playing quite a few recordings. It took time, and I appreciate your patience in that regard.

Your sacrifice has been extreme in this matter. The community owes you a debt of gratitude for what all of you have done, and I thank you personally for that.

15

And again, if I see you downtown I'll walk up and thank you personally, shake your hand and offer my appreciation for what you folks have done over the past month and a half.

Again, all of the admonitions are off at this point. I'm going to excuse you folks.

I know when I tried cases I was interested in receiving information from the jurors as to what they felt was significant, what they felt was insignificant. You are under no duty to talk to anyone about the case. You are under no duty to talk to the attorneys about the case.

But they may be interested in talking to you about this situation. If you are willing and interested in speaking with them, I will be working with Mr. Flores and the attorneys for about five more minutes. If you want to wait outside and talk with them, I'm sure they would be happy to speak with you. No duty, though. If you want to walk out to your cars and move on with your lives, that's absolutely fine.

So again, thank you very much. It was an honor for me to work with all of you folks. You are excused at this time. Thank you.

(The jury exits the courtroom.)

THE COURT: All right. Let's remain on the record regarding People versus Mr. Flores. Mr. Flores is

16

present. Counsel are present. Our jurors have been

excused.

Again, I'll declare a mistrial as to those counts where verdicts were not reached.

And we will direct our clerk to contact the alternates regarding the verdicts, and advise them that the admonitions are off as to those jurors.

Mr. Bolt, how would you like to proceed at this time?

MR. BOLT: At the Court's preference, we can set it for trial or we can set it for a date to set trial.

THE COURT: I would just as soon have the matter on for setting of a jury trial. Does that much work for you, Ms. Preston?

MS. PRESTON: It does. Thank you.

THE COURT: All right. I'm going to keep bail at the same amount at this point.

Counsel reserve the right to further discuss the issue of bail at the next hearing.

CHAPTER 8

EPILOGUE
AFTER THE TRIAL

"That's life. That's what all the people say, flying high in April, shot down in May."
- Frank Sinatra

1

3rd Juror – Linda Lancaster, early 40s, personnel manager in a larger corporation, married, no kids, foreperson for the jury.

It's been a week since the trial ended. I'm depressed. I never thought it would turn out this way. All these weeks; all the sleepless nights; the time away from work; and for what? No verdict. It's like we didn't accomplish anything. Worse, there's a very good chance that Albert. Flores will remain in jail until the State decides to retry him. His life has been ruined. He was framed for a rape he didn't commit, has spent over three years in jail, lost his family, his job, and his new business, and even if he were to get out, even if the State decided not to retry the case, his credibility is shot.

A lot of people complain about immigrants and how they game the system. But here's a guy who comes to this country and works his butt off to succeed. He learns English, gets a good job, raises a family, and starts his own business.

Okay. He's not perfect. He drank too much and was verbally abusive to his wife and kids and physically abusive to his wife, though that seems to have gone both ways. Then again, he married someone twice his age when he was still a kid. She was clearly jealous as she aged and he came into his prime, and she ruled the roost. It had to be hard to be dominated by someone like her – someone who'd do anything to have her way, even frame her husband and send him to jail for the rest of his life on a false charge. I honestly suspect that she's the one that caused Sandy's injury.

That poor guy.

Yeah. I just can't seem to let it go. You know, after our deliberations, several of us exchanged contact info. We said we'd get together. But that hasn't happened and after several emails and calls, I'm pretty sure it will never happen. I wonder how the others are doing and whether this case still haunts them like it does me.

I did meet with Patricia Preston. We spent a couple of hours going through the deliberations and then through the case itself. She told me a lot about what went on behind the scenes between her, Mr. Bolt, and the judge. She wanted to know what she could have done better, if there was anything she could have done to make a stronger case that might have convinced Matt not to hang the jury. I told her she did an amazing job.

She's depressed too. It's not just losing. As she explained to me, she loses a lot of cases. She's a public defender, and much of the time, her clients are guilty. This time though, she was convinced that Mr. Flores was innocent. She too, believes that Alejandra framed him. She's pretty sure that either Alejandra capitalized on an injury Sandy got from the playing on the rocks at the beach, or from Carrie's grandson who might have molested her. She thinks is possible that Alejandra, herself, caused the injury.

Patricia's mother is a social worker who has seen cases where Hispanic mothers hurt their children, then blamed the injuries on their husbands to get custody and to facilitate a divorce.

In this case, Patricia suspects that Alejandra wanted to protect her son Armando from being deported by taking Albert out of the picture. Albert threw Armando out of the house when he found him using drugs in front of the girls. He threatened to have him deported. When Alejandra defended Armando, and went behind Albert's back, bringing him into the home when Albert was working, Albert threated Alejandra with divorce and with taking custody of the kids. That's what Patricia believes triggered the whole thing. I think she's right and it appears most of the jurors suspected something similar. Why else would Alejandra lie so much?

Sorry, as you can see, I really can't let this go.

I asked Patricia what would happen to Albert now. She said that with a hung jury, the State has the option to retry the case. She was a bit worried that because we found Albert not-guilty on the charges concerning Mandy, that all of the evidence about Mandy and her lies, would be excluded in a new trial. And yeah, I can kind of see how Mandy ended up casting a lot of doubt on the whole case.

Patricia suggested that if I wanted to help with a different outcome, that I either talk to or write to the District Attorney explaining what happened in the deliberations and why they should not retry this case.

I wrote a very long letter and got a call from the Deputy District Attorney. They invited me for an hour-long meeting and I did my best to convince them. I'm not sure how I did though. The last time I looked at the Court website, Albert was still in custody and the charges about Sandy were still outstanding.

God, I feel awful. What else could I have done to help Albert? I did my best as did ten other jurors. But the bottom line is that our best just wasn't good enough. If he gets tried again and is found guilty, this will haunt me for the rest of my life.

2

6th Juror – Andy Harrigan, early 50s, Supervisor at the California EPA, one daughter about to graduate from high school, another daughter away at college

I can't let it go. That poor guy. His life is ruined. Those kids. They're permanently damaged. This lie will follow them for the rest of their lives. And I didn't do enough. I couldn't convince Matt. I'm not sure why. He's conservative, but he doesn't seem unreasonable.

After the trial, some buddies and I went down to the Channel Islands for some fishing, diving, and surfing. The weather was glorious and a nice change from the rain that has been drowning Santa Cruz. I really thought a week in a completely different environment would help clear out my mind. But no. I'm still having nightmares. I see Albert being gang-raped in prison. Except sometimes it's me. I dream about Amy betraying me, saying I molested our daughters. She'd never do that but I dream it anyway. And during those beautiful days surrounded by crystal-clear waters and so much sea life during our dives, I just couldn't appreciate it. I woke the guys sharing a cabin with me and everyone else with my screams more than once. Even after several beers, I just couldn't let it go.

I had promised myself that when we got back, I'd meet with Patricia Preston. But I couldn't bring myself to do it.

Just before the trip, I did have lunch with Mark Mentor, the alternate that I struck up a friendship with during the trial. Before deliberations began, I promised him I'd fill him in on what happened in the jury room. We also talked about getting together after the trial. We're both empty nesters and our wives did meet once when we bumped into each other during a lunch break. We're both surfers and ocean fanatics, and while he's a few years older, it really doesn't show. We connected well during the trial.

The lunch was okay. I tried to keep to the facts about the deliberations. Mark asked a lot of questions and was shocked at what happened. He wanted to go back through the case, and I tried. I really did. But I burst into tears more than once, so he diplomatically changed the subject and I told him about the great Channel Islands trip I was leaving for the next day. He knew two of the guys I was going with.

When I got back, he called to tell me that he was going to have lunch with Patricia Preston and asked if I wanted to join them. I choked up at the thought and wished him the best. I just couldn't do it.

I also know that we'll never get together as friends. He's such a nice guy. His wife seemed nice too and we all have a lot in common. But he reminds me of the case. And my mind starts squirrel-caging. When anything or anyone reminds me of the case, I lose it.

No. It's too bad, but I don't want to see Mark again.

Amy suggested I get some counseling. She really hoped that I would get a lot better after the trial was over. It was a rough two months. Our normally perfect relationship became strained. I was short-tempered. I yelled at her more than once for no reason at all. At least I'm not doing that anymore.

But I am depressed. It's really not over for me and may never be. Amy sees that and it scares her. Maybe I scare her.

I've started seeing a therapist. Her name is Lara. I met her surfing a few years ago. We used to talk whenever I saw her in the surf. Just casual stuff. We've never gotten together socially.

She was reluctant to take me on as a patient, since she knew me outside of therapy. But I convinced her it was her or no one. And no one wasn't a good idea.

When she heard my story during our first session, I could see her concern. This is the first time she's had to work with a former jury member. She suggested that the court should offer counseling to jury members who go through cases like this. She confirmed what I've thought from the beginning. While a jury of your peers is the law and makes a lot of sense, most of us are just not prepared to see this kind of stuff for real. And God, was it real.

Lara says I'm suffering from PTSD. She's given me some anti-anxiety meds which do calm me down in my worst moments and they do help me sleep. Sometimes I don't have nightmares.

And we've talked a lot. But I don't feel like I'm getting anywhere.

We did talk about me going to the District Attorney to try to convince him to let Albert go. She suggested I might get some closure that way. If I succeed, it's over. If I don't, at least I'll know I did everything I could.

But I can't.

I want to forget about the case and all that Albert and that poor family have gone through. I re-live Albert's ten hour interrogation. I hear the jail calls. I see the photos of Sandy's injury. I see the bubbly Mandy telling her lies. I see Sandy making up one lie after another to seem more believable. I see that icy Detective Locke, so intent on putting Albert away that she probably planted evidence and influenced both Sandy and Mandy to lie or at least exaggerate. It doesn't stop.

I don't want to see anyone or do anything that reminds me of the case. I just can't do it.

I don't think the therapy is working. I don't feel better after our sessions. Talking about my feelings doesn't help.

In fact, I think I'm just spiraling downwards.

I love my job, but I just can't concentrate anymore. I've been taking a lot of sick leave. This after eight weeks on the jury and a week in the Channel Islands. I could lose my job.

Amy and I haven't had sex in over a month. We used to have a pretty active sex life for a long-time married couple. But I just can't get interested. I feel like I'm too wrapped up in myself and the biggest failure of my life.

Amy is suffering. I'm just making her life miserable at a time when we should be enjoying our freedom. I've talked to the girls, who may be coming home after their semesters end, but I just picture Sandy and Mandy at their age. I get distracted and confused. I'm not sure I want to see them again. I know I don't want them to see me like this.

I'll continue with the therapy, but I don't know. I don't see a way out of this.

3

16th Juror – Mark Mentor, early 60s, retired ex-Silicon Valley startup CEO.

After all his fumbling through the trial, Mr. Bolt gave a strong closing statement. I was a bit surprised that the prosecution got to have the last word. I would think it would be the defense.

But his statement was strong. It almost got me thinking the defense needed to prove Albert's innocence. After all, if he didn't rape his daughter, how do you explain the injuries she had?

The judge read the jury instructions and then we, the alternates were excused. We were required to be within thirty minutes of the courthouse until the verdict came in. We had to keep our cell phones active.

I stepped out of the courtroom into one of the first sunny days of our drought-busting winter. On the one hand, I felt like a great burden had been lifted. The air was crisp and clean, and my bike ride home along the ocean on West Cliff Drive felt somewhat cleansing.

On the other hand, I felt cheated. I'd just given almost eight weeks of my life to this case and I wasn't going to have the chance to contribute to the deliberations. At least Andy would be getting together with me to give me the gory details.

I really like Andy. We seemed to forge a great connection during breaks in the trial. We didn't go so far as to have lunch together or to get together socially during the trial – it would have been too tempting to discuss the case – but we did plan to get together after it was all over, not just for the deliberation recap, but also socially, and to surf and mountain bike together.

I didn't know how long the deliberations would take. I was convinced not only that Albert was legally not-guilty – that there was reasonable doubt – but that Albert was framed. He was an innocent, hardworking guy who'd just been chewed up by the system. Sure, he was no saint. He drank too much and was abusive to his family, but then again, he had a wife who wore the pants in the family and who was extremely jealous and demanding. It's not an excuse, but it doesn't make him a rapist either. I was pretty sure most of the other jurors felt the same way, but you never know.

Two days later when Heidi, the court clerk, called me to let me know the verdict, she apologized that she couldn't give me notice that the verdict was coming in so I could be there to hear it. Apparently, she can usually do that.

But in this case, the jury announced to the judge that they were hung, that the vote was 11-1. After sending them back in to deliberate with additional instructions and a more detailed clarification of 'beyond a reasonable doubt', they continued, but apparently one juror said there was no way he could vote to acquit on the charges about Sandy (they all found Albert not-guilty on the other charges). The judge declared a mistrial and according to Heidi, the jury basically ran out of the courthouse. Apparently, several were in tears.

A few stayed to talk with Ms. Preston and with Mr. Bolt, most were relieved that the trial was finally over – at least for them.

I almost freaked out when Heidi told me all of this. I could barely keep my calm. I'm glad we were talking on the phone. Sensing my distress, Heidi suggested that I talk to Ms. Preston, that Ms. Preston wanted to talk with the jurors about the case. I got her contact information and called her the next day.

We met for lunch at a downtown restaurant where I'd reserved a table in the back, far from the lunch crowd. I know the owner and told him that this was going to be a sensitive conversation about the jury trial I'd been part of, and that the topic might offend some of his other patrons. He actually closed off our section so we could have some privacy.

Lunch went on for three hours. And Patricia (Ms. Preston) picked up the tab. If it's possible, she's even more devastated with the verdict than I am. She honestly believes that Albert is innocent and has been framed.

I got a lot of information about what went on behind closed doors between the judge and the attorneys. The most interesting for me was about Carrie.

You may remember that in her closing argument, Ms. Preston talked about how Carrie refused to talk with her or her investigator and about how Carrie changed her story about picking the girls up on the day of the trial, then not picking them up. From always picking them up to hardly ever picking them up. I'm still not sure why she lied.

But more revealing was that Ms. Preston didn't even know about Carrie until well into the trial. She had asked Albert about the woman who gave the kids rides home, but he didn't know her last name or address and Alejandra wouldn't give any information about her.

Then, one day Albert looked around the courtroom and told Patricia that Carrie was in the back of the room.

After mentioning this to the judge, Bill the Bailiff asked Carrie to come into the courtroom and she had an on-the-record, out-of-the-presence-of-the-jury discussion with the judge and the attorneys. She said she was there to support her friend Alejandra. Mr. Bolt argued that she shouldn't be called as a witness, that this was just a defense red-herring.

But the judge decided to have Carrie testify and told her she couldn't come to court except for her testimony.

Apparently, because Alejandra wasn't allowed to hear the testimony from other witnesses, she had asked Carrie to come to court to listen and report on what was said.

But even after being ordered to testify, Carrie refused to be interviewed or deposed.

I remember her testimony because it was one more thing that disturbed me. She was actually an out-of-order defense witness. Clearly Mr. Bolt didn't want her there. But it didn't matter. Other than confusing us, her testimony really didn't work for Patricia or for Mr. Bolt. She basically said she didn't remember anything. I came away thinking she must have been hiding something.

Alejandra, and both girls said that Carrie gave the girls a ride home from school, but Carrie didn't remember. They also said that there were some problems with Carrie's grandson who was a bit older than Sandy, but Carrie didn't know anything about it. But for me, it was just one more example of seeing someone lying to protect themselves and who doesn't care what happens to other people. This trial really shook up my faith in humanity's desire for truthfulness.

Also interesting was the testimony from Nurse Hernandez. Patricia asked me if I remembered how they started their testimony, then sent us out of the courtroom, then sent us home for the afternoon. I did.

If you remember, Nurse Hernandez was the one who got Mandy to say that she was molested as a young child. Apparently she wrote this up in a report which was sent to the DA's office and to Bob Aragon, the head of the SART team. Unfortunately, that report has vanished. Or, more likely, there was never a report at all and Nurse Hernandez was just trying to justify what she had done and her current testimony.

Mr. Bolt wanted her testimony to continue. Patricia wanted to exclude the part about Mandy's claims. Then apparently, when the court wouldn't exclude, Mr. Bolt wanted to prevent Patricia from questioning Nurse Hernandez about the report, and Patricia wanted to try to impeach her credibility. The judge felt that was more than fair game – that Nurse Hernandez's testimony needed to be scrutinized and that this could put the whole question of charges about Mandy into question. He definitely split the baby on that one and most of us found Nurse Hernandez's testimony doubtful. For me, that was another nail in the coffin of people telling the truth and doing the right thing.

Once we finished discussing all the things that Patricia could have done better (there weren't many), all the evidence, and what I saw as weaknesses in the prosecution's case, we spend quite a bit of time exchanging theories of how poor little Sandy got her injury.

Sure, it could have been the rocks on the jetty where she was playing while Albert fished. It could have been Carrie's grandson (and that's why Sandy didn't want to ride with Carrie anymore). It could have been someone else. But when I talked about the fact that Officer Davenport described Sandy as 'in pain' when he first found her on the bed, and that the only bloodstains found on the bedspread were in the spot that Sandy was sitting when he got there, and that Sandy didn't appear to have been in pain earlier, I suggested the possibility that it was Alejandra – that she had injured Sandy to create a story that would ensure that she wouldn't lose her kids to Albert and that she and her son Armando wouldn't be deported. That would explain the pain, the bed being made, Sandy's positioning on the bed and the fact that the only blood found on the bed was in that spot – perhaps where Alejandra had injured Sandy.

Sure, as Mr. Bolt said in his powerful second closing argument, it's speculation. It's not evidence. But during the lunch with Patricia, it wasn't about evidence. There was enough reasonable doubt based on the timing of events, on the lies by Alejandra, Mandy, Sandy, Carrie, Nurse Hernandez, and possibly Detective Locke, and on the lack of DNA evidence. No, this was about trying to figure out what actually happened here.

The reality is that we'll never know.

At one point Patricia asked me what I thought about the Astroglide bottle.

I told her that I found this one of the weirdest pieces of evidence offered.

First, we knew that Albert and Alejandra had a very active sex life and that they kept towels and other things in their bedside table to clean up after sex. Why wouldn't the lubricant be there? Was it even conceivable that Albert would have bought lubricant specifically to help him rape his daughter? Also, why was it in such an obscure place in the bathroom? And, since the police searched for evidence that first evening, why didn't they find it? Why did Sandi Locke get a search warrant when she had permission from Alejandra to search the house. Was is just coincidence that Sandi Locke found the lubricant and did the 'lineup' with Sandy?

Patricia reluctantly admitted that she thought that Detective Locke planted the evidence and led Sandy to the identification in the 'lineup'. I say reluctantly because Patricia has great respect for the police and in particular for these sexual assault teams. She couldn't imagine doing their jobs.

But, she does believe in police overreach. As she put it in her closing, there is too often a 'rush to judgement'.

However, she didn't want to go down this route. Again, I get the impression that because of her respect for the police, and the fact that this was speculation too, she didn't want to create more of a complicated mess than we already had.

When we'd exhausted the case, I learned a lot about Patricia herself. She came from a fairly privileged family, but with a social-worker mother, she learned early on that the 'haves' had an obligation to help the less fortunate. As a child, she also got to see injustice first-hand as her mother often came home angry at how her mostly immigrant clients had been chewed up by the system. For Patricia, being a public defender was a life-long dream.

I've known a lot of attorneys over the years (including some very famous ones) and I've seen a number of court cases, but as I told Patricia, she is the most gifted lawyer I've ever seen.

She brushed off the compliment by saying that her belief in her client's innocence made her look good. Yeah, right.

At the end of our lunch, I told Patricia that I was going to talk to the DA. She encouraged me. She hoped that I, along with other jurors, would convince the DA to set Albert free and to drop the remaining charges.

A week later, I spent about an hour with the DA and the Deputy DA. I started out by telling them that I thought Mr. Bolt had a particularly strong closing argument. Then, in a much more structured discussion than I had with Patricia, we went through the strong and weak points of the prosecution's case. Ultimately, I told them that I thought the case should never have gone to trial, let alone be retried. All of the principals in the prosecution's case had been caught in lies. The timing of events didn't work out. There was no DNA evidence when there should have been. Several of the charges seemed to be overreach which hurt the credibility of the other charges – it made the prosecution seem desperate. I think I made a strong case, but I really don't know.

Before I left, I asked if they were planning to retry the case. They responded that they had ordered the transcripts (which would take two to three months to get!!??), and that they would review them in light of our discussions as well as what they had heard from other jurors, particularly from the foreperson who had sent them a detailed argument against retrying the case. They asked me to encourage other jurors to come to talk with them, but I let them know that I suspected that was unlikely. The trial was emotionally demanding for all of us and I thought most everyone just wanted to get past it.

So here it is, six months after the verdict. At least I've been able to talk about the case, though I suspect that family and friends are ready for me to be done with it. The nightmares are rare, but I still find myself thinking about poor Albert.

As of today, he's still in custody. From my online checks, the charges are still outstanding. No trial date has been set, so I suspect the DA still hasn't made a decision. I sure hope they let it go.

Also, I did talk to the DA, to Patricia, and to Judge Campbell about the impact of a case like this on the jurors. I told them about my experience – the nightmares, the relationship impact, the depression, the obsession. And I told them about the impact on others. Surprisingly, they'd never thought about this aspect of our court system.

In spite of all we see on television, video games, social media, and films, most of us are innocent and naïve in the ways of the world, particularly things we don't actually live every day. We hear about immigrants but we don't live with them. We hear about rape, but most of us don't experience it first-hand. We hear about violence and see media representations of it, but we don't experience its impact on people close to us.

Going through a jury trial like this one is a traumatic experience.

All of these legal professionals talked about counseling for the victims and counseling for the accused. They discussed how cases affected the attorneys and the judges. But they had never thought about the juries. I told them that in cases like this one, and in cases where average people are forced to see sides of humanity that they've never seen before, the state should offer counselling to the jury members. Or perhaps the jury members should have some sort of group therapy so that they can unload all their feelings outside of the negotiations in the jury room.

I don't know if this will ever happen, but since the trial, I've talked to others who have been on murder trials and rape trials. They too, came out damaged. We could really use some help.

Unfortunately, for some of us, it's too late.

I'm sorry to say that a month ago, Andy Harrigan committed suicide. He was driving down Highway 1 after a surf session up north of Santa Cruz and he turned right, taking him and his pickup over a two hundred foot cliff onto the rocks below. At the inquest, the CHP officer testified that there was no braking, no skidding.

Andy knew exactly what he was doing.

ABOUT THE AUTHOR

Writer, extreme sports enthusiast, serial entrepreneur, technologist.

Born into a military family, Steve traveled extensively throughout the US and overseas, attending fifteen schools before graduating from High School. After studying mathematics, computer science, comparative literature and French at the University of California, Steve began his career with IBM as a software engineer. He later founded three successful high-tech startups.

A former competition hang glider pilot, Steve continues to surf, ski, kayak whitewater, and dance Salsa with his wife Karen whenever possible.

Steve divides his time between Santa Cruz, California and the Basque Region of France.

For more about Steve, his sports, and his other novels, please visit http://www.stevejackowski.com.

www.ingramcontent.com/pod-product-compliance
Lightning Source LLC
Chambersburg PA
CBHW061949170626
46813CB00006B/2593

* 9 7 8 0 9 8 9 9 7 2 9 6 3 *